I didn't think it'd feel like this. In all the times I let myself go down this path, indulge in this daydream, I thought there'd be waves of panic, a crushing weight on my chest, shackles chained to my ankles from being connected to someone. From being on the receiving end of someone's love. There's too much responsibility, too much faith lying in your actions, too much possibility of heartache.

I didn't want *any* of it.

And then Cade came, sweeping his way into my life, imposing and relentless and persistent, and I'm not the same.

# CAGED IN
## Winter

### BRIGHTON WALSH

BERKLEY BOOKS, NEW YORK

THE BERKLEY PUBLISHING GROUP
Published by the Penguin Group
Penguin Group (USA) LLC
375 Hudson Street, New York, New York 10014

USA • Canada • UK • Ireland • Australia • New Zealand • India • South Africa • China

penguin.com

A Penguin Random House Company

This book is an original publication of The Berkley Publishing Group.

Library of Congress Cataloging-in-Publication Data

Walsh, Brighton.
Caged in Winter / Brighton Walsh.—Berkley trade paperback edition.
pages cm
ISBN 978-0-425-27648-8 (paperback)
1. Love stories.   I. Title.
PS3623.A4454C34 2014
813'.6—dc23
2014025372

PUBLISHING HISTORY
Berkley trade paperback edition / November 2014

PRINTED IN THE UNITED STATES OF AMERICA

10   9   8   7   6   5   4   3   2   1

Cover photo by Maksim/Shutterstock.
Cover design by Rita Frangie.
Interior text design by Kristin del Rosario.

*For Christina,*
*because two little words from you sparked this entire thing.*

# ACKNOWLEDGMENTS

They say it takes a village to raise a child. A book-baby totally counts. Thank you to the following glorious people for being my village:

To my agent, Mandy Hubbard, for reading and loving Cade and Winter as much as I do. For being the perfect mix of professionalism, knowledge, and *Saved by the Bell* gifs. Thank you a million times for taking the stress out of the business side of writing. You are a life and sanity saver.

To the entire team at The Berkley Publishing Group, especially my editor, Leis Pederson, for molding this into the best book it could be. Thank you for making my first foray into traditional publishing utterly painless.

To Christina, for the possibly—*probably*—thousands of texts exchanged when I'd hit a bump or stumble from my outline and need a push in the right direction. I don't know how I got lucky enough to have you be my Plot Whisperer, but I'm keeping you.

To Jeanette Grey for sticking by my side through everything I've ever written and holding my hand every step of the way. I'm running out of ways to say thank you (have I said that before?). My words never feel like they're ready for the world until I've had your input.

Here's to another six (yes, it's really been six!) years. Can't wait to go to Paris as bawdy old ladies and eat Nutella by the Seine.

To Jaime, Caren, Tonya, and Avery for reading, offering your thoughtful critique, and generally being amazing (and pretty) cheerleaders every step of the way. I love you guys like whoa.

To Chef Amy for all your helpful insight and careful advice on the culinary portions of this book, for taking endless pictures of your workstation, the kitchens, and the restaurant and letting me borrow them as inspiration for Cade's work spaces, for always being there with amazing ideas for recipes *and* giving step by step instructions on how to make them. And, finally, for reading this over in its entirety to make sure this book about a chef actually sounded like a book about a chef. I seriously couldn't have done this without your help and guidance.

And last but not least, to the three guys who make my world go 'round: My husband for understanding why I became a hermit the entire month I wrote this and for doing everything in your power so that I got uninterrupted time to write. Thank you for supporting me in my dream. And to the little guys who call me Mom, because you're the most amazing, sweet, compassionate, sensitive, and fun-loving boys I've ever known. Because you're as excited as anyone I've told about my book being in real live bookstores. And because you said, "Mommy, can you mention us in your next book?" And, really, how could I say no to that? I love you, I love you, I love you.

# ONE

*winter*

Seventy-six days.

The number repeats as a mantra in my mind, echoing like a drumbeat with every hurried step I take.

Seventy. Six.

Seventy. Six.

Stale air and dim lighting greet me as I tear down the hallway of my apartment building, jamming my key into the lock of my door and rushing inside. If I don't get my ass in gear, I'm going to be late. If I'm late, I could get fired.

I *can't* get fired.

I toss my bag on the floor, already stripping off my sweater and searching for the minuscule articles of clothing my employer considers a uniform. I find them piled in the corner of my tiny studio apartment. Like tossing them to the side and burying them among a hundred other things would somehow make them disappear. I hate this nightly routine. I hate walking out knowing what awaits me. Knowing what kind of front I'll be putting on. Knowing it's my only choice.

Still, it beats living on the streets, and I'm about fifty bucks from having my ass kicked to the curb.

As fast as I arrived, I'm out of there, grabbing a banana on the way. It's not much as far as dinners go, but it's all I've got. I inhale it as I head across campus, a hoodie and a pair of yoga pants thankfully covering the parts of me I don't want to show every horny college guy I pass. Not that being in the pub is any better. But at least there it's expected, and I feel somewhat protected while surrounded by other people. They can look their fill, but don't touch.

Usually.

When I'm working, I paint a lifeless smile on my face. Laugh. Flirt. Engage. It took me a day to figure out that smiling got me bigger tips. Took me a week to figure out that flirting got me even more.

My head's down as I book it two blocks from the outskirts of the opposite side of campus. Having to stay behind at my last class, I missed the bus I usually take to get to work, but I don't mind walking. It's warming up, the first traces of spring in every newly budded tree, in every sprouted flower. New beginnings, some would say. The season of love and light. The opposite of winter, when everything is harsh.

Dark. Cold. Hollow.

Fitting, really, my mother would name me that.

It's like she already hated me, even then.


I'M ONLY TWO minutes late, but to Randy, my boss, two minutes might as well be twenty. I keep my head down as I blow into the pub, trying not to draw attention to myself. I head into the back, clocking in and peeling off my armor before stuffing my hoodie and pants into my locker. I tug on the hem of my barely there shorts and crop top. Like all that adjusting will magically add three inches of material.

I pause just inside the door of the break room. Walking out is always the hardest step. Coming into the pub, with my regular clothes on, my face down, is nothing. I'm still me. I'm still invisible.

It's hard to be invisible while wearing nothing but this. Hot pink top smaller than some sports bras I've seen. Black boy shorts that cover less of my skin than some of my underwear.

I can hear the raucous laughs of the patrons already. Tuesday nights aren't usually too bad. We have a few regulars, and sometimes people celebrating birthdays, but I generally don't have to worry too much about guys getting handsy with me, or hanging around and waiting for me after closing to see if my flirting actually meant something. Those nights are the worst.

Knowing I can't put it off any longer, I push through the door.

"Hey, sugar," Annette says as she mixes up a drink behind the bar. In her late forties, she's the floor manager-slash-bartender and the only one of us lucky enough to wear jeans and a T-shirt with the pub's logo on it. What I wouldn't give for that much coverage. "Randy's in the office. He didn't notice. You're fine."

I breathe for what feels like the first time since I left class. "Thanks."

She nods and tells me what tables I've got, and I go to work. Shoulders rolled back. Shell in place. Smile plastered on.

Seventy-six days to freedom.

*cade*

This is the reason I wanted to become a chef. This feeling right here. The rush of adrenaline, the high that comes from a well-done dinner service. The sense of accomplishment when someone compliments your dish. That's me on a plate, every time, and there's nothing in the world that feels better than when someone loves what I've created for them.

The energy in the kitchen is buzzing, everyone pumped up after a great night, and I'm one of them, knowing we kicked ass tonight. I concentrate on cleaning up my station at the end of my bistro class, listening to my classmates bustle around me, excitement in the tone of their voices.

"Hey, Cade," Chef Foster says when he stops in front of my station. "Come see me before you leave."

"Sure thing." I wipe down the stainless steel table and then pack up my knives. Once they're secure in my bag, I head to where I see Chef Foster just as he finishes with another student.

He glances at me, then tips his head to the back corner of the kitchen, the only place that'll allow us a modicum of privacy. Once we're there, he slaps a hand on my shoulder. "Excellent work tonight, Cade."

"Thank you, Chef."

"I really mean it. I always knew you had talent, even when you were little, but what you've developed into is more than I could've hoped for."

I stand a little taller at his words, pride swelling in me. Chef Foster—Mark when we're not in school—is an amazing teacher and someone I'm lucky enough to call my mentor. Hearing that from him feels like winning the lottery. "That means a lot."

"Well, you know I don't bullshit." A grin lifts the side of my mouth as I nod, and he continues, "You know these last couple months are crucial for your future prospects. Do you know yet what you'd like to do after you graduate?"

I swallow, a million thoughts bombarding me. Tessa and Haley and working in a kitchen in New York or L.A. and studying in Italy . . . My responsibilities battling with my dreams. Though it's not really a battle at all, because there's no competition. "Well, my long-term goal will be to open my own restaurant. Before that, I'd just be happy to work my way up to executive chef somewhere."

"Are you looking at strictly Italian cuisine?" he asks, referring to my specialty.

"No, but all the better if that was where I ended up."

"Have you started looking?"

"Not yet. Should I be?"

"Probably not, but I'd start mid-May. And, of course, you know you'd increase your chances if you were open to different locations."

"You mean—"

"Outside the state."

I stare at him, unsure of what to say to that. In the past year, he's been hinting at me broadening my horizons for where I'd look, but it's never been anything quite so blunt. If anyone knows how difficult that would be for me, it's him. He's been a family friend for as long as I can remember, and he witnessed firsthand the devastation that rocked my family. Leaving now . . . leaving Tessa and Haley? That's not an option.

"You know I can't do that."

He stares at me for a moment, his jaw ticking. Knowing him as long as I have, I have no doubt he has something he wants to say. Rather than doing so, he eventually gives a short nod, blowing out a breath. "Well, let me know when you need some recommendation letters. I'd be happy to send them."

"Thanks, Chef."

"I'll see you tomorrow. Keep up the good work."

I nod, shouldering my bag and heading out of the kitchen after offering good-byes to a few friends. I'm not even halfway to the parking lot before my phone buzzes with a text message.

*Come out 2nite*

I roll my eyes and quickly type out a response to my best friend before pocketing my phone. I haven't taken five steps when my phone rings.

Knowing it's him, I answer, "Yeah."

"Why do you have to be such a pussy all the time?" Jason asks.

I laugh, shaking my head as I walk toward the street. "If that's you trying to talk me into going, it's not working."

Someone shouts in the background and Jason yells back before talking into the phone again. "Well, what the fuck else am I supposed to do? You haven't been out in *months*."

"You're an asshole. We just hung out when Adam was home a couple weeks ago."

"Hanging out on your couch playing *Call of Duty* does not constitute going out, dumbass."

"Yeah, well, I've been doing this thing called going to classes and studying and working. Not all of us have parents willing to foot the bill through four changes in majors and the extended college plan."

"Hey, I'll graduate one of these years."

I snort. "Maybe."

"And if you're trying to sound like less of a pussy, you need to work on your tactics."

I chuckle, knowing exactly what he's doing. Goading me used

to be effective, back when we were fifteen, sixteen. Seven years later, not so much. "Still not working."

He groans. "Come on, man. It's Sean's birthday. Everyone is out. I'll even buy you a round."

Heaving a sigh, I drop my head back as my shoulders slump. After four hours on my feet in the kitchen, I just want to relax. I feel like I haven't showered in a week. I feel like I haven't slept in even longer. Even still, he's right—I could use a night out.

"Yeah, all right. Gimme an hour. Where are we meeting, Shooters?"

"Not sure. Sean wants to barhop. Give me a call when you head out. I'll let you know where we are."

"'Kay. Later."

I hang up, pocketing my phone as soon as I reach my motorcycle. It's still a bit cold for it to be an enjoyable ride, but Tessa needed the car, so I didn't have much of a choice. I straddle my bike and button up my coat before I rev the engine to life. The loud roar echoes around me as I peel out of the space and rumble down the street.

Riding is my escape—the one thing I take for myself. I forget about my responsibilities—classes and bills and the people who depend on me. My mom always hated this thing, hated it the first day I brought it home, but I think she'd understand my love for it now.

When I ride it, it's my peace.

I STILL FORGET, sometimes. Even after four years. When I walk through the front door, sometimes I expect to hear her in the kitchen, the smells of her cooking greeting me. The sound of her laughter filling my ears. The sense of security and ease I always had before everything changed.

Tonight the house is empty, not even the sounds of Tessa or Haley echoing down the hallway. I check my watch, then shoot Tess a quick text, making sure everything is okay. They probably went somewhere after Haley's ballet practice, but there's still lingering doubt that gnaws at my gut. After living through the kind of tragedies I have, it's hard to turn it off—that constant worry that's always there, lurking under the surface.

As I wait for her text, I jump in the shower, then throw on whatever clean clothes I can find scattered around my room. I'm ready to go sooner than I expected, and I grab my keys and coat on my way out the door, checking my phone for a reply. Finding one there, my worries fade, and I reply, letting Tess know I'll be gone till later tonight.

Before starting up my bike, I call Jason to find out where they are. He's already well on his way to being shit-faced, and I'm not sure this was such a good idea. I love him like a brother, but I can't help that bit of jealousy I get as an outsider looking in at his life. Wondering what it'd be like to be a normal, carefree twenty-three-year-old guy. Where the only thing I had to worry about was where I was going drinking that weekend and who I was going to fuck. Instead I'm worried about keeping my scholarships and paying bills, all the while attending school full-time and holding down a part-time job.

Still, even if I had a choice, I wouldn't have it any other way. I love Tessa and Haley more than anything.

By the time I get to The Brewery, I know the guys have already hit several bars before this one. I spot them in the back by the pool tables. They're loud and obnoxious, roaring over the only other group taking up space inside.

I head over, seeing Jason at the pool table, curled over the bent form of his latest conquest, no doubt "improving" her shooting skills. He notices me, tips his chin, and grins before returning his attention to the girl he's probably hoping to get in the pants of tonight.

I flag the waitress, ordering a beer, and get pulled into a conversation between Sean and Dave about last night's game.

After a while, a hard slap lands on my shoulder. "Hey, pussy."

I look over my shoulder and straighten to my full height. Jason is tall, but I'm taller, and I stare down at him. "You really want to start this? I kicked your ass in third grade. I can do it again."

A laugh rumbles out of him. "Yeah, only because you sucker punched me." He shakes his head, landing another blow on my shoulder. "I can see you're still pissy as hell. We need to get you laid." Before I can retort, he continues, "You get a beer already? What'd ya think of Mandi?"

With a furrowed brow, I ask, "Who?"

"Our waitress. The food here sucks, but the uniforms definitely make up for it."

I stare at him for a minute, before shaking my head. "You're such a jackass. I don't understand how you even get girls to sleep with you."

"Charisma, my friend. *Charisma*. And speaking of getting girls to sleep with me, where's Tess?" He waggles his eyebrows, and I shove him so hard he stumbles back, laughing.

"Fuck off."

Holding his hands up in surrender, he says, "I'm just playing." He's been *just playing* regarding Tess for as long as I can remember. The first time he said something like that, I ended up with swollen knuckles and he had a black eye. He tips his beer in my direction. "Drink up. You need to relax."

A-fucking-men.

*winter*

Sometimes I daydream. Think about what it will be like after I've graduated. Once I have a steady job. A *real* job. Something that doesn't require ninety percent of my skin showing. I picture myself in Maine or South Carolina or Texas. New York, maybe. I've become so good at this, I can almost smell the scents of my nonexistent apartment in some far-off city, can name the colors of paint on the walls, can count the number of dirty dishes in the sink.

When I'm working, it's my escape. When I have to smile and bend over to pick up a customer's napkin or get him something from the kitchen for the fourth time so he can watch my ass as I walk away . . . it's what I think about to get through the hours, the minutes. It helps to remind myself why I'm here. What I'm working for. Why I put up with jackasses who smell of whiskey and cigarettes and cheap cologne. Who smell exactly like my childhood.

"Sweetheart. Hey, sweetheart!"

I'm so wrapped up in my fantasy, it takes me a moment to realize a guy from table seven is talking to me. I hate this part of the night. Those thirty minutes before last call, when everyone is drunk on alcohol and the prospect of getting lucky. The men get rowdy and restless . . . never a good combination.

"What can I get you?"

He crooks his finger at me, beckoning me closer. Internally, I roll my eyes, but my face holds the mask I've perfected in the time I've worked here, and I lean forward until his whiskey breath whispers across my cheek.

"You can get me your number."

This isn't the first time I've been propositioned, and it's definitely the tamer kind I've heard. By now, I have a system in place.

In the time it takes me to imagine what I'd do if this asshole told me that outside these four walls, I keep my eyes down and allow a hint of a smile to curve my lips, shuttering my real thoughts from him. When it seems like I've had long enough to actually contemplate his words, I offer him a regretful look, the corners of my mouth turned down. "I'd love to, but we're not allowed to give our numbers to the customers."

"Just pretend you're not working, then."

I'm standing close enough for his arm to snake around my back, his hand settling on my waist. After thirteen months of working here, I've gotten pretty good at reading people. I know from fairly early on which guys are going to hassle me, which ones are harmless flirts, which ones will get handsy by the end of the night. I called this guy as the latter when he was two beers in . . . six drinks ago. It makes my skin crawl, but I've had a long time to practice this façade. I could win a freaking Oscar for the performances I put on here.

I lean into him slightly—just enough to make him think I'd actually be interested . . . if only we met at a different time, in a different place—and point to the back corner where a mirrored window reflects back at us. "I'd love to, but my boss is watching. I can't afford to get fired." The latter, at least, is true.

Sometimes they're satisfied when I feed them the whole "my boss is watching" line. Sometimes all I need to do is flirt a little bit, bat my eyelashes, flash a smile, bite my bottom lip. Sometimes that's not enough, and I need to lean into them, touch their forearm or their shoulder. Those nights aren't so bad. I still feel dirty after I leave, and I take a shower as soon as I get home, attempting to wash the disgust off me. And then I mark off the days on my calendar and remind myself this isn't for nothing. I'm paving my path the best way I can. The only way I can on my own.

But sometimes none of those work. And this is one of those times. Even though I was expecting it, it's still jarring when his hand slides from my waist until he's got a handful of my ass. If I felt threatened, I'd whip out one of the half-dozen self-defense moves I know, call for Randy, hope he actually did something, and walk away. In all the time I've worked here, I've only had to do that once, though. And even then, it wasn't Randy who came to help, but Annette. Usually, like now, these guys are harmless. Disgusting, perverted pigs, but harmless. Sure, he smells like cheap cologne and alcohol and he's got something stuck in his teeth, but he's too wasted to prove to be a real threat to me.

I do a quick scan of the table, noticing the three other guys packing up their shit, divvying up the check, paying no attention to the dickbag with his hand on my ass. They've been here taking up one of my tables for three hours. Three hours of lewd remarks they think I can't hear. Three hours of leers and whispers about my ass or my boobs. And now it's down to five minutes . . . ten, tops. That's all the longer I need to make it, and hopefully the show I gave them will be enough to warrant a tip large enough to justify feeling dirty. Sometimes I wonder if I wouldn't be better off heading to Roxy's, the strip club down the street, and just getting it over with. At least there, there are no pretenses. Take your clothes off, rake in your tips, go home. And there'd be no touching. I'm not the thinnest or the most voluptuous girl, but that doesn't seem to matter to the guys. If my mother taught me anything in the seven years I was with her, it's to use your body to your advantage if you can.

Before I can smile or bite my lip or laugh, lean in and rest my fingers on his chest and tell him how much I wish I could bend the rules, he yelps and his hand is gone from my ass. I whirl around to a brick wall of gray cotton, and look up, up, up until

I get to the clenched jaw of some guy I've never met. His dark hair is buzzed short, the bulk of his body nearly obscene, the forearms peeking out of his sleeves covered in ink, but that's all I notice before I'm focusing on the fact that he's got Handsy Asshole's arm bent and twisted up and against his back, and he's whispering something in his ear. Something too low for me to hear.

And while I don't have my customer's hands on me or his breath in my face or his eyes fucking my body, I can't focus on what relief I feel because all I can think is that this guy—this asshole who got a little handsy—was how I was going to buy groceries.

And any chance I had of getting a tip probably vanished the second this giant of a man swept his way into something that's none of his business in the first place.

## cade

I spotted her somewhere between discussing the shot made in the final three seconds to win last night's game and the latest version of *Halo*. It would make me sound like more of a guy if I said I was drawn to her because of her tits in that nonexistent shirt or her ass hanging out of those shorts that might as well be panties— which, yeah, I noticed both. But the truth is, her eyes were what drew me in.

They look . . . lifeless.

Sure, she's got the smile plastered on. She's got the glances down—the slight lift at the corner of her mouth, the lip bite—but she's got this air of disdain surrounding her. She's not like the other waitresses—the ones you can tell love working here. They flirt and laugh and touch. It's obvious they thrive on the attention they get in a place like this.

Not her.

She hates it here.

Someone who isn't really looking, who isn't really paying attention to her, might not notice, but I do. Her dead eyes give her away.

I can't blame her. Working here, surrounded by half-drunk men when you're wearing less than some people wear on the beach, has to be tough. The thought of Tessa or Haley ever having to do this makes me sick, and I have to remind myself I'd never let it happen. That's why we're so careful with our money, why we scrimp and save even though we don't have to. Why I work part-time even though the house is paid off, even though my mom made certain we were taken care of. Just in case. If our past has taught us one thing, it's that anything can happen.

All night, I've sat quietly, watching a group of four guys a few tables over getting progressively louder and more aggressive. I've gotten bits and pieces of their conversation—when she's been near, and when she's been out of earshot—and it's done nothing but ignite my temper. I'm waiting for one of them—probably the douche with the fedora—to grab her and pull her into his lap or spill his drink all over her shirt and mop it up with his napkins for an excuse to feel her up. I'm sort of hoping he does, just so I have a reason to confront the shithead.

Jason is bitching about some basketball player and everyone around me is groaning, but all I can see is the table three over from ours. The girl with the dead eyes comes back, and my skin boils as I watch Fedora Asshole beckon her forward and whisper in her ear. She shakes her head, points toward the back corner, and offers him a sad smile, though I can tell it's insincere. She's not sorry about whatever she just turned him down for. And based on the conversation I've caught bits and pieces of, it wasn't anything tame. He probably asked her to suck him off in the bathroom.

And then clumsy as all shit, this drunk ass slides his hand down until it rests on her ass. She stiffens subtly, and I'm out of my chair before I can blink, my legs eating up the space between us until I'm right next to him.

I don't think as I grab his hand, twisting it up and behind his back, pressing until I hear him groan. The image of Tessa or Haley in a place like this with a slimy jackass groping them hits me once again, and I push against this asshole harder, feeling a sick sense of satisfaction wash over me as his pained protests meet my ears.

I lean in, my voice quiet and controlled as I say, "If a girl says no, you listen, fucker."

# TWO

*winter*

The whole thing takes maybe two minutes—from the second the sleazy guy puts his arm around me until he's practically falling out of his chair to leave. Two minutes. After three hours of waiting on them. Of smiles and flirtation and not slapping them across the face when they placed their orders straight to my nipples.

All that effort . . . gone. Erased. In two fucking minutes.

My customer scrambles out of his chair, his friends following behind, eyes wide as they toss money onto the table and walk out. Before they're even out the door, I'm counting it and checking it against the total of their bill, praying that even with this behemoth next to me, obviously threatening them, they managed to leave me a little something. Hell, I'd take five bucks at this point. Five bucks could buy me breakfast, lunch, *and* dinner.

When I've triple-checked my math, I hang my head, my eyes closing, shoulders slumping. I take three deep breaths, hoping for a calm I know won't come.

Seventeen cents. They left me seventeen cents.

I try not to panic, reminding myself I've gotten through worse than this. I've gone longer without any money on hand. Rent's due tomorrow, and with my other tables, I'd made enough to cover it—just barely—but these guys were my meal ticket.

I'm off tomorrow and don't have another shift until the following night, which means I'm going to have to last two days on whatever I can scrounge up in my kitchenette. Which isn't much. I'll have to ask Randy if I can pick up an extra shift tomorrow, even though he gets off on saying no, like he knows when I need it and refuses to help.

"Hey, are you okay?" A large hand settles over the expanse of my shoulder, pulling me out of my thoughts.

And all at once, my day catches up with me. The classes that are kicking my ass and running late tonight and having wasted three hours for a measly seventeen fucking cents, and I snap.

I whirl around, jabbing my finger into his too-large chest as I glare at him. "Who the fuck do you think you are?"

## cade

Her sharp words and the fire in her eyes surprise me. I thought she'd be grateful, maybe offer a thank-you, but if the set of her jaw and the flattened line of her lips—*Jesus*, those lips—are any indication, she isn't just mad. She's livid.

Did I read it all wrong? *Was* she interested in that slimy asshole? Did I welcome his hands on her? But I know I saw her spine stiffen when he grabbed her ass. I saw her inch away from him. I *know* I did.

I open my mouth a couple times to say something, but

nothing comes out. Which is probably good, because it seems she has a lot to say.

"I asked who you thought you were, dickhead." She pokes her finger into my chest again, and even though the top of her head doesn't even come up to my shoulder and she can't weigh more than a buck ten, she exudes a don't-fuck-with-me vibe like some of the biggest linebackers I ever encountered when I was still playing football. "You always go into people's places of employment, shove your way in with your too-big shoulders and your giant arms, and manhandle whatever issues you see until you're satisfied?"

Her voice gets louder with every word that comes out of her mouth until I feel nearly every pair of eyes in the pub looking at us. I still can't find any words, dumbfounded by a reaction completely opposite of what I expected. And struck mute by the sight of her. She looks like an avenging angel, with her long, dark hair, the flush of her cheeks, the fire in her eyes, and the rage rolling off her.

If I thought she was hot with her mask in place, it has nothing on this pure, concentrated version of her.

She's fucking gorgeous.

"Oh, *now* you don't have anything to say." She throws her hands up and walks a tight circle before she faces me again, pointing an accusatory finger at me. "Do you think I work here for fun? Do you think I like having my ass grabbed or my tits 'accidentally' grazed by these drunk, perverted assholes?" Before I can answer, she snaps, "No! I work here for the fucking money, and now I'm out—" She snatches the bill off the table, and her lips move almost indecipherably before she glares at me again, spitting, "Thirty-eight dollars, thanks to you."

"I'm sor—"

She holds up her hand, stopping me before I can finish. "I don't want your goddamn sorries. Go hop on your horse, Prince Charming, and save some other girl. I don't need your help."

She spins, her short legs chomping up the floor space between me and the back of the restaurant, and then she's gone, disappearing behind a swinging door.

I stand there for a couple minutes, vaguely aware of the rumbling laughs coming from my group of friends. Before I can think too much about it, I grab a couple twenties out of my wallet and toss them on the table. They were supposed to be for yellowfin tuna to make seared ahi tuna steaks, but I'll have to make them next week. It's practice anyway, not for a grade, and it's clear this girl needs the money more than I do.

"Bet that didn't go how you expected," Jason yells, and the rest of the guys crack up.

I flip him off, glancing to where she disappeared into the back, remembering the heat in her eyes and her rigid stance, and Christ, everything about this girl is getting under my skin. "Not exactly," I mumble to myself.

# THREE

*winter*

The campus is always busiest this time of the day, with so many classes just starting. I generally avoid it like the plague, getting to the Arts Building earlier, but I was running behind, having spent too much of my morning thinking about the events of the night before. I can't believe the balls on that guy. First, he jumps in without prompting, attempting to rescue me—*me*! I snort, shaking my head as I dodge a group of students on the sidewalk. I can't remember the last time I needed rescuing. When you grow up alone, passed around from foster home to foster home, you learn really damn quick to get self-sufficient.

And then after he "rescues" me, after I tell him to fuck off, he has the balls to toss money on the table for me?

There isn't a doubt in my mind it was him, either. Who else would it have been? The rest of the girls, while they watched the entire sordid affair, wouldn't have given up forty bucks of their own tips just because I got screwed out of mine.

And those dickbags who bailed didn't come back in. The one who had his hand on my ass looked like he was about to piss his pants as he scrambled out of his seat. No way was he setting foot inside again, especially so soon after he made his escape.

That pretty much seals the deal that Prince Charming swooped in, trying to save me again. Apparently he didn't hear any of the words of venom I spewed at him. He was probably looking down my shirt while I was losing my shit, too engrossed in my boobs to pay attention to anything I said.

The anger fuels me all the way through my walk across campus, daydreaming what I'd do, what I'd say, if I saw him again. I don't know if I ever will, but the cash he left is stuffed in my pocket. Just in case. Just in case I get the chance to slap it against his chest and give him a piece of my mind—*again*—since he was obviously too thickheaded to hear me the first time.

Until I do, though, it burns a hole in my pocket, thoughts of what I could buy flitting through my head. And it isn't even anything fun. Instead of thinking about buying a new pair of shoes or books or name-brand shampoo, I'm thinking about groceries. Bread, meat, maybe even those soft, frosted cookies I love but only let myself indulge in if I've got more than a hundred-dollar cushion for my bills. Even still, I refuse to spend it.

I've gotten by on my own for fifteen years. I certainly don't need anyone's help now.

*cade*

"Cade. Cade!"

I snap my head up and glance toward Tessa. "What?"

"Haley's been talking to you for five minutes. What's your deal?"

"Sorry." I shake my head and turn my attention to my niece. "What's up, short stuff?"

"Wanna play dolls?" Her big brown eyes—the only thing she got from her deadbeat father—implore me, and like always, I can't say no.

"Sure. Go get 'em ready. I'll be right in." Before I've even finished talking, she climbs down from the chair, her stumpy legs pounding the carpet as she runs as fast as she can down the hall.

"Seriously. What's with you?" Tessa asks.

I toss the game controller next to me on the couch, letting my head fall back as I close my eyes. "How do you know anything's with me?"

"Well, for one thing you've died five times in the last ten minutes on that stupid game. For another thing, you've been quiet all afternoon."

"Maybe I just don't want to talk to you."

She laughs and swats me against the back of my head. "Please. You *live* to talk to me."

Thankfully, she doesn't prod any more and walks down the hallway toward her bedroom, leaving me alone with my thoughts.

The thoughts that have done nothing all day but revolve around the firecracker at The Brewery. I can't remember the last time I've let a girl get to me like she has. If I'm interested, I get the girl's number, go out a few times, sleep with her if it goes that way, but that's it. I'm definitely not one to sit around and fucking *pine*, constantly thinking about someone.

Even so, I can't get her out of my head. She held so much confidence, so much poise in her small frame, even when she was telling me exactly where I could shove my chivalry. The details of our encounter kept me up last night, and have kept me company all morning. The fire in her words, backed with heaps of pride. Watching her dead eyes spark with life.

I mentally flip through my schedule for the next few days. I don't have much leeway, but it doesn't matter.

I'll be back in that pub before the end of the week.


*winter*

I rank talking to my boss lower than cleaning the toilet bowl. With my toothbrush. He's an asshole, and it's like he takes this perverse pleasure in seeing me—seeing any of us, really—struggle and ask him for his help. Part of me thinks that's why he hired me in the first place. So he could keep me under his thumb, knowing the job he could take away at any moment is the only thing keeping a roof over my head. Keeping me fed.

I'd rather swallow a handful of razorblades than ask him for anything, but I don't have a choice. When I talked to him last night, I had to clench my hands behind my back, gnawing on the inside of my cheek as I asked if I could pick up an extra shift. By some miracle, he agreed, and even though it's only three hours, it's something, and I'll be able to make back what I lost in tips last night. At the expense of time allotted for schoolwork, but when making the choice between an A or a B in the class or eating, sometimes a girl's gotta do what a girl's gotta do.

The professor dismisses my last class for the day, and I grab my laptop, stuffing it in my bag as I glance at the clock while the rest of the students shuffle out. I have forty-five minutes to get home and change before I need to head to the bus stop. I usually stay behind in this class, working on coding and designs and geting a head start on next week's classes, but I can't today.

So wrapped up in getting out of here, I nearly rush right past the couple standing at the bottom of the steps outside. A guy is leaning against the railing talking to a girl I recognize from my class. His face is familiar, and it only takes me a moment to realize where I've seen him before. He was the loudmouth from last night at the pub—the one who's friends with Prince Charming. I stuff my hand in my pocket, clenching my fist around the money there. And before I know what I'm doing, my legs have carried me forward until I'm standing directly in front of him.

"Excuse me." I butt in mid-conversation, and I can't even dig up an apology, too fueled by righteous indignation. I slide in between the two of them, and the girl gives me a narrow-eyed glare, the guy looking at me quizzically.

"Uh, yeah, hi?"

"You were at The Brewery last night, right? With some friends?"

"Yeah," he drags out the word, his eyes flicking to the girl he was talking to before returning his gaze to me.

"You friends with the jackass who left me this?" I hold the bills between two fingers, waving them in front of his face.

"Umm . . ." He scratches his head, looking at me quizzically. "You're—wait. You're the pissed-off waitress?" His eyes travel the length of me from head to toe, and I don't blame him for not recognizing me. My hair's not down like I wear it at work, instead pulled back into a messy ponytail, and I've got on a pair of jeans and a sweatshirt. The fact that he doesn't recognize me without all my skin showing tells me loud and clear exactly what parts of me he was focusing on.

"That's me." I slap the money to his chest, a thousand retorts running through my mind. A thousand things I'd say to that guy if he were here in front of me. But he's not, and his friend wasn't the jackass who cost me three hours of work, so in the end, I sigh and settle on, "Give this to your friend. And tell him I don't need his goddamn money."

I wait until he reaches up and takes the bills, nodding slightly, before I spin around and leave.

I weave my way through the sea of bodies, zigzagging around the slow walkers and the meanderers and the talkers, adrenaline driving my path.

My pride has always been my downfall, and it's bitten me in the ass more than once. For as long as I can remember, it's the one thing I don't bend on. I do everything on my own. I *want* to do everything on my own. If I count on no one but myself, I'm not going to get let down. The minute I start relying on others is the minute I'm undoubtedly disappointed. The minute everything I've built comes crashing down around me.

And even though this isn't new to me, I still wonder if what I did was stupid. I think of all I could've bought with that. Milk and cereal and a whole fucking case of ramen, but even with these thoughts running through my mind, I don't care.

I straighten my shoulders as I march home, confident in my decision.

I don't take handouts.

## cade

"Good work tonight, Cade," Chef Foster says, patting me on the back. "I loved the addition of the Sriracha sauce. Bold choice."

"Thanks." I smile, offering him a nod. "I forced Tessa to be my guinea pig at home. Took me a few tries before I got the right balance."

"Well, you hit it out of the park. Everyone loved it. Nice job."

I can't keep my grin from spreading. If there's one thing I love to hear, it's that people enjoy the food I make. In the kitchen, there's no better compliment; nothing makes me feel higher than that. And hearing it from him, from someone who's known me most of my life and whose professional attributes I strive to emulate, is the highlight of my week.

I clean up my station before slipping my knives into their carrying case and tucking it all away in my bag. Shouldering it, I wave to a few people, then head out the door and into the cool night.

It's late—just after ten—so it surprises me when a voice cuts through the dark. "Cade."

My head snaps to the right, and I spot Jason sitting on the steps just outside the building. He stands as I descend the stairs two at a time until I'm in front of him.

I jerk my chin toward him. "Hey. What're you doing here?"

"I talked to Tess earlier. She told me where you were." He leans against the cement pillar at the base of the stairs and reaches into his pocket, pulling something out. "I have a message for you from an admirer."

Raising both eyebrows, I rock back on my heels. "Admirer?"

He laughs outright. "Okay, not really. She's *definitely* not a fan of yours." He holds up some cash and slaps it in my hand. "The girl from The Brewery. She found me this afternoon after class. Did you know she goes to school here?"

I shake my head at him, my eyebrows drawn together.

"Yeah, well, she told me to tell you to fuck off."

My mouth drops open and my eyes widen as I stare at him. The asshole's smirking. "Seriously?"

He laughs, hitting me on the shoulder. "Basically. I think her exact words were she doesn't need your goddamn money. But damn, it's a good thing she found me and not you. I think she would've killed you with just the fire coming out of her eyes. Either that or had an introduction of her foot to your junk." He shakes his head, smiling. "She does *not* like you."

"Yeah, I'm getting that." I stare at the cash in my hand, my brow furrowing. After the tirade she went on about the money she lost thanks to me, I'm genuinely perplexed as to why she would go out of her way to give this back. When she was calculating how much those assholes left her, I could've sworn I heard her mumble something about buying groceries. She obviously needed the cash. Why didn't she take it?

But if anyone can understand exactly why she didn't, it's me. I *know* why she didn't. It's the same reason I've worked so hard, scrimping and saving since Mom died so we'd never be in that position. I don't want to take anyone's help. I can do this on my own.

It seems the two of us have something in common.

He starts walking, and I follow, heading to the parking lot. I clear my throat. "She say if she's working tonight?"

A choked laugh comes from him, and he stares at me, his eyes wide. "Are you serious?" He shakes his head, focusing on the sidewalk in front of us. "Dude, just drop it. She doesn't want the fucking money. Let it go."

I know he's right. I *should* let it go. I should forget about her and her dead eyes sparked to life and the passion I saw boiling under her skin. Should forget about her touching me, forget about the fact that it was done in pure, undiluted anger.

But I can't get her out of my head, and whether she knows it or not, she's just given me the perfect excuse to see her again.

# FOUR

*winter*

Classes are killing me this week. I lost out on a solid four hours of study time since I had to pick up that shift, and I'm suffering for it. My entire schedule is out of whack now, and I've had to shuffle everything around so I still have time to get in what I need. Working full-time and going to school full-time is more demanding than I ever thought it would be. But I'm in the home stretch now. Fantasies of moving away from here, going to New York or Miami or Chicago, flood my mind. Seventy-four more days, and I'll be free.

I grab the handle and pull open the door of The Brewery, the smell of grease and beer nearly choking me. I walk in, keeping my head down until I'm out front again, stripped of my armor and ready for my shift.

Once I've gotten my tables settled and am at the bar, getting drink orders, Annette says, "Someone was in here looking for you earlier."

"Who?"

She shrugs her shoulders as she mixes a drink for me. "Guy, about your age. Really tall. Big and kinda tough looking—tattoos on his arms and a barbell through his eyebrow, I think."

I furrow my brow. I don't know anyone who remotely matches that description. "Did he leave a name?"

"Nope, said he'd stop back."

I try not to think about it as I work, pasting on my smile and flirting, putting more into the act than I normally do. Fridays are always busy, and I'm more grateful for that than ever, desperately needing the money to make up for what I lost earlier in the week. I let myself be distracted by the monotony of my job, the customers who come and go, the drink orders and the innocent flirtatious smiles and the not-so-innocent passes.

Ten tables and two hours later, Annette waves me over to the bar. "Your guy came back." She nods toward the back corner, and I turn to see where she's gesturing to. It's dark in the pub, so it takes me a minute of looking before I recognize the hulking shadow of a guy leaning over the pool table as Prince Charming from the other night.

Heat infuses my cheeks, my hands clenching at my sides. I should've realized from her description it was him, but I never thought he'd come back here. I'm not sure if he's got a death wish or if he's just fucking with me, and I hate that he came to the one place I feel off my game. If he approached me on campus, ran into me on the street, I wouldn't even think twice before I gave him a piece of my mind. But being here is different. For one thing, while this isn't the classiest place of employment, it's *my* place of employment, and— especially after the other night when I lost my cool—I cannot do anything more to jeopardize that. For another, it's hard to be taken seriously, to demand respect when my bits are barely covered.

Turning away, I go about the rest of the night as if I never saw him. While I'm waiting on my tables, I fantasize about what it'd be like to stomp over and spew the retorts I've had days to perfect. I imagine the look on his face, what he might say back . . .

By the time last call comes around, a hundred different imaginary arguments have sprouted up in my mind. I glance around, a part of me hoping he's still here so I can use one or two on him. I come up empty, though, the pub nearly bare, save for a couple groups loitering at the tall tables and an older guy at the bar, finishing up his drink.

I tell myself the disappointment I feel is strictly because I've had three days to think about what I was going to say to him, and all night to roll the retorts over in my mind. There's no telling what his friend actually said to him. For all I know, he told him to come back because I said I wanted his number.

Blowing a strand of hair out of my eye, I go about my nightly duties, finishing up quickly. It's pitch-black by the time we head out, the only illumination in the parking lot coming from the tiny sliver of moon. I wish Randy would put up some floodlights, but the bastard's too cheap.

"Sure I can't drive you to the bus stop?" Annette asks.

I smile, shaking my head. It's the same thing she's asked every night since my first night here. And just like that first time, I tell her the same thing as always. "S'okay. It's only a block away."

"All right. I'll see you tomorrow, Winter."

"Night," I say and wave, turning and heading in the direction of the bus stop. This part of town is brimming with college students, many still wandering around even this time of night, so I usually feel pretty safe making the short trek to the stop.

Just as I round the corner of the building, a tall form steps out from the shadows. I startle, one hand going to my throat where a scream is lodged, the other clutching my bag and the pepper spray I keep there. As I fumble with the flap, the guy steps toward me again, his face close enough to make out, and my fear quickly dissipates, immediately replaced by irritation.

*cade*

"Sorry. Didn't mean to scare you."

The look she shoots me is made of pure disdain. "Then maybe you shouldn't lurk around in parking lots at fucking midnight. Are you a jackass *and* a stalker?"

I hold up my hands before stuffing them in the pockets of my jeans. "I'm usually neither. You just bring out the best in me, I guess." I offer her a smile, hoping to coax one from her, or at the very least, soften her up a bit.

It does neither.

She stares at me for a minute before shaking her head and looking toward the ground. She's changed into a sweatshirt and fitted pants, her long, dark hair pulled away from her face, and even though she's ninety percent more covered than she was the last time I saw her, she's still beautiful. When she looks back up at me, her eyes spark with the fire I saw that first night. "I'm not sure how else I can say this so you get it, but here goes. I don't want or need your help. Got it? Stay away from here or I'll tell Annette to add you to the Wall of Assholes."

I raise my eyebrows. "Wall of Assholes?"

"Yeah. Assholes who aren't welcome back."

"You actually have one of those? Did you put those guys from the other night on there?"

She throws her hands in the air. "They didn't do anything!"

My mouth drops open, and I stare at her, shocked silent. When I find my voice, my words come out sharper than I intend. "He grabbed your ass!"

Turning, she walks away from me, shaking her head as she goes. She mumbles just loud enough for me to hear, "Believe me, that's not the worst thing they do."

I catch up to her quickly. "Then why do you work here?"

"God, you're like a flea that just won't go away." She gives a quick glance in both directions before she hops off the curb and walks across the street. There are a few students roaming, but it's a Friday night. How secluded is it on a Tuesday? The idea of her out here, walking by herself, bothers me more than it should. "Are you intentionally being this obtuse? Why do people usually work? So I can pay for things."

"I get that. But why *there*?"

She glances at me out of the corner of her eye before moving her attention once again in front of her. There's a weighted silence between us, almost as if she's deciding how much to reveal to me. Finally she says, "Because a partial scholarship only goes so far, and this pays the best for what's available with my schedule. Unless I go down to Roxy's."

My jaw locks, hands clenched at the idea of her working at a fucking strip club. If I thought a guy grabbing her ass got me pissed, it has nothing on someone staring at her while she struts naked on a stage.

Not seeing my reaction, or ignoring it entirely, she continues, "I'm not quite that desperate yet."

Thank fuck for that.

"What about your parents? Why don't they help you?"

"I have a better question: Why are you still here?"

"I know we got off on the wrong foot, but I'm not such a

jackass that I'd knowingly let you walk to the bus stop by yourself after midnight. You do this every night?"

"Careful, stalker, you're starting to sound creepy."

I chuckle, shaking my head. "Seriously, though. I can . . . I could come by tomorrow and give you a ride home, if you want."

She stops suddenly and stares at me, her mouth parted. "Are you seriously hitting on me right now?"

I grimace, running my hand over my hair. None of this is coming out how I wanted it to. "No . . . Yes. Maybe."

She huffs out a laugh. "Okay, now I *know* you're just being obtuse. What part of my fuck-off body language isn't coming across? It's obviously something I need to work on." She turns and continues walking, speeding up slightly.

I take a deep breath, hands shoved in my pockets as I follow her, because sometime over the last few days, I've apparently turned into a masochist. "Look, I wanted to say I was sorry. I just . . . I read your signals wrong, I guess. I thought I saw you stiffen when he grabbed you, and I can't . . . I'm not the kind of guy who can sit back and watch something like that happen, okay? I couldn't do *nothing*."

She doesn't say anything, and we've arrived at the bus stop already. We're the only ones there, and the bus is nowhere in sight. I know I've got a couple more minutes, and I intend to use every one until this crazy, beautiful girl accepts my apology.

She leans against the metal pole of the bus stop sign, her arms crossed as she considers me. "You're really sorry?" At my nod, she continues, "And you won't do it again?"

I force myself to shake my head, even though I'm not sure it's a promise I can actually keep.

"Fine. Apology accepted." She turns her back on me, facing the street, clearly done with our conversation. With me.

Jesus, this girl is making me work for it. I step off the curb and move to stand in front of her. "I'm Cade, by the way."

She doesn't even look at me, her head turned to the side, eyes focused somewhere over my shoulder.

"I didn't catch your name . . ."

"That's because I didn't give it."

I blow out a breath. "No, I mean before . . . the other day. Your name tag? I didn't see what it said."

"Probably because you were too busy throwing your Neanderthal bullshit around and scaring off my customers."

"I said I was sorry. Let me make it up to you."

She raises an eyebrow. "Oh, yeah? How do you plan on doing that?"

"I, ah, I could make you dinner . . ."

Her abrupt laugh surprises me, throaty and deep. From the look in her eyes, the sound is more disbelief than anything. "You're hitting on me again."

I chuckle, rubbing at the back of my head as I stare down at the ground. "Yeah, I guess I am." The rumble of the bus grows louder as it rolls down the street toward us. "So what do you say?"

She looks at me, stares straight into my eyes until the bus stops in front of us, its doors sliding open. Only then does she look away, climbing the first step, and I almost think she's going to leave without even answering. But before the doors close, she looks at me over her shoulder. "Same thing I said before. Go find someone else, Prince Charming."

And then she climbs the rest of the steps, the bus hisses and pulls away, and she's gone.

And I still don't know her name.

# FIVE

*cade*

"Where are you going?"

I freeze, my hand on the handle to the back door. The whole house is dark and silent, but with the hours Tessa keeps, I'm amazed it's taken me this long to get caught sneaking out. And how fucking pathetic am I that I'm sneaking out? I'm twenty-three years old, for fuck's sake.

I don't know why I haven't told Tess any of this, why she doesn't know about the girl from the pub. The girl with the fire in her eyes. The girl whose name I still don't know. I'm embarrassed at the improbability of it. That, somehow, after four years of rock-solid routines, I've let a girl I've known less than a week throw a wrench in it.

But there is something about *this* girl. Her ballsy, fuck everything attitude. Her vulnerability clashing with the pride she has. The secrets she keeps hidden in her eyes. Even after only a week, I want to uncover them all.

Clearing my throat, I turn around and face my sister. "I just have to give someone a ride."

She rolls her eyes, crossing her arms against her chest. "Jason get stranded at some girl's house again? Serves him right. If he'd finally stop doing the fuck and duck and grow up already, he wouldn't have to worry about shit like this." She doesn't wait for my answer, and I don't correct her. After making a quick stop in the kitchen and grabbing some of the crostini I made earlier, she holds one up at me as she walks past. "Be home before curfew."

I snort and turn to leave, slipping into the car this time, hoping maybe it's my motorcycle that's been giving the girl at the pub pause. Except I know it's not. She's been nothing but fire and hostility since last week, but like a masochist, I keep going back. Every night, I'm there for more. There is something about her that keeps pulling me back. The looks she lets slip past her armor, the tiny flashes of the real her. *That's* why I keep going back, hoping for another glimpse.

My days are all packed, and the evenings I don't have my bistro class for credit, I'm at the restaurant serving, bringing in a paycheck, however meager it is. I've figured out a way I can juggle everything, giving me an hour gap of time from midnight to one when I can be by her, but I'm not sure how much longer I'll be able to keep this up. It's easy now, with the spring quarter having just started, but when we get further into the year, closer to graduation and the mounting projects expected of us, I'm not sure I'll be able to continue.

The thing that keeps me going back, that forces me to stand against that back wall night after night, is the thought that hopefully, by then, I'll at least have her name.

*winter*

"You certainly are persistent, I'll give you that."

Before the words have even left my lips, he pushes away from the wall he's been standing against every night for the last week. "Don't pretend like you don't enjoy me walking with you," he says as he falls into step next to me.

My rebuttal dies on my lips, because the truth is, he's absolutely right. He's worked his way into my life with this weird, unconventional routine, and I'd like to say it pisses me off. That I'm affronted he follows me the block and a half to the bus stop, that he offers me a ride every single night, and every single night I refuse, but . . . I've sort of grown used to it. To him.

Every night when I'm working, it's the same. I spend my entire shift thinking about whether or not he's going to be there waiting, then I hate myself a little for even contemplating it. Make a silent promise that I won't let him walk with me, that I'll tell him to stop, that I don't want him there. And then I see him waiting for me—for *me*—and all my objections fall by the wayside.

I've had guys interested . . . in my body and the kind of physical connection I can offer them, but I've never had someone so interested in *me*, even when I'm completely covered up in sweatshirts and jeans, my hair pulled back, makeup wiped from my face. Just me. The feeling is addictive, this sense of being wanted. I know it could be the chase for him—it probably is—but I can't turn off the part of me that craves this attention. After a lifetime of rejection, I soak up every bit of it he tosses my way.

"Besides," he says, interrupting my thoughts, "one of these nights, you'll say yes." His tone is so confident, so sure, and this is all part of the volley that happens between us every night.

I play my part, responding, "Don't count on it."

"Well, if nothing else, maybe you'll at least tell me your name."

I shake my head, looking at the ground before up at him. "I don't know why you don't just go into The Brewery and ask. Or come in early enough to catch a glimpse of my name tag instead of lurking out here in the shadows like a creep."

"Where's the fun in that? Plus, when you finally tell me, I'll know I've cracked your shell just a little."

The smile he shoots me is crooked and imperfect and a little bit harsh and so *him*, it's unnerving. Though I don't want to, I've had days to memorize every inch of him through the light of the moon and the sporadic flood of streetlights, and I have. So much so that I can see the sharp curve of his jaw, the shadow of his close-cropped hair, the arch of his lips even when I close my eyes at night.

He's tall. Ridiculously so—nearly a foot taller than I am. And he's built like a football player or a heavyweight boxer—broad shoulders, huge, defined arms, and this . . . *presence*. His hair is shaved close to his head, close but long enough that if I ran my hand over it, I'm sure it'd have that soft tickling resistance like the rough side of velvet. His eyes are gray or green or hazel—I'm not sure because it's dark every time I've been close enough to see—and so expressive, I feel like I could get lost in them sometimes.

When we pass under a light, the barbell through his eyebrow glints at me, and when he wears certain shirts, I can see black ink peeking out of his collar or the cuffs of his hoodie. I wonder how much of him is covered in tattoos. If he has full sleeves on both arms, or just one, or if they're random designs—some here, some there—if he has any marking on his back or legs, on his chest, and I hate myself for letting something so innocuous consume my thoughts. For imagining what he must look like under the layers he gets to wear.

I tell myself it's only because of the injustice of it all—that he's seen so much of me I want to level the playing field. I hate feeling so naked around him, even when I'm not.

"Maybe tonight will be my lucky night. Maybe I'll blow your mind with something completely random, and you'll think, 'Yeah, I need to go out with that guy.'"

I laugh. "Oh, we've upgraded from an I'm sorry dinner to a date, huh? Then the answer is definitely no."

"Why?"

"I don't do dates."

"I'll wear you down soon enough."

"So, what, you're just going to keep walking with me until I say yes? Some might say that's harassment, you know."

Looking to me, he raises an eyebrow. "Good thing none of those people are around."

The bus stop is just ahead, and it seems like it comes upon us faster every night. When I walked this same block and a half by myself, I could get here in less than five minutes. Since he's started walking with me, it's stretched to ten . . . fifteen minutes, our feet nearly dragging along the pavement.

When we come upon it, we each take up our standard positions. Me up on the curb, leaning against the metal sign post, him standing in front of me on the street. It brings him closer to eye level, though even with this difference, he's still taller than me. The streetlight pours over us harshly, highlighting the angles of his face, accentuating the hollows of his cheeks, the cut of his jaw. He looks ridiculously intimidating, and if I was walking by myself and saw him standing here for the first time, I'm not sure I wouldn't turn around and run in the other direction. The inconsistencies between his tough, brash exterior and his insouciant personality are staggering. And intriguing.

"So what do you say?"

"What do I say about what?"

"Are you going to let me make you dinner?"

I laugh, looking down the street to where I hear the rumble of the bus coming up the hill. "No." I say it automatically, before anything else can come out instead. Because I know if I look into his eyes, if I take even thirty seconds to really look, I'll see the sincerity there, and I'll say yes.

"I knew you were gonna say that."

"Did you? You're a smart one."

He smiles and leans toward me, hands stuffed in the pockets of his jeans as he props one foot up on the curb. "I don't know about that. Coming here every night, expecting a different outcome each time, makes me seem a little dense, I think."

I hum, trying to act unaffected by his nearness. "Yeah, that does seem a little dumb."

"It's a wonder my self-esteem is still intact after all this, really. You should probably tell me your name to help lessen the sting . . ."

I shake my head, sending the smile that curves my lips straight to the pavement so he can't steal it away. Before I can say anything, the bus squeals to a stop in front of us. Cade backs up as I move around him and grip the railing inside the bus. With one foot on the step, I turn. He's watching me, hands in his back pockets, the same hopeful look on his face he's worn every day for the past week, and before I can stop myself, I say, "It's Winter."

I don't stare at him long enough to see his response, but I hear it. His rich voice repeating my name, but still I don't turn around. The doors close behind me with a hiss, and I take my seat. As we pull away, I chance a glance out the window and find him standing there, the smile on his lips cutting straight through me.

And I know I won't say no the next time he asks me.

# SIX

*cade*

"Uncle Cade, will you watch me at dance class tonight?"

Haley's standing in front of me, looking like a bright pink piece of bubble gum with her stretchy tank thing and her skirt and her tights. How am I supposed to say no to her? She's only three. She has no idea I've been a dumb shit all week and I'm paying for it now.

All because I had to see her. *Winter.*

A brief smile sweeps over my mouth as I remember the expression on her face as she watched me through the grimy bus windows after she told me her name. She looked nervous. Nervous and, if I wasn't mistaken, a little excited.

Which is a pretty fucking apt description of what I'm feeling.

Every night when I left the house at midnight, cutting right into the small amount of study time I have, I thought I was okay. I thought I had enough time to get everything done, that taking that hour every night wouldn't affect my classes or my schedule or my life. I didn't think about the domino effect it could have, just that I wanted to see her. I wanted those fifteen minutes of talking.

And it's not like we were talking about monumental things. Our conversations were always about absolutely nothing. Hell, I don't even know something as basic as her major. Don't know if she has siblings or where she lives or what she does in her free time. Every second of the time we spent together was like a volleyball match—hitting the ball over to her just to see if she'd sail it over the net to me or spike it down in front of my face. At first, it was more of the latter. By the third night, I could tell I was wearing her down. She didn't know I saw her look for me as soon as she walked out the door of The Brewery. The first night she did that, I knew. I was in. Her walls were crumbling. Slowly, but crumbling nonetheless. I was patient. I could wait.

It was only a matter of time before she told me her name. And hopefully not long before she said yes.

And as of last night, I had one of the two.

Getting the other is going to be a problem. Yeah, I know her name, but I want more. I want to take her on a date—to apologize again, but it's more than that. Because I want to get to know this girl.

I'm combing over my schedule, trying to figure out when I can sneak in more study time so I can meet her there again tonight. No matter how I shuffle things, though, I'm still an hour short. I have three entrées I need to test before next week's classes, a handful of recipes to write out and memorize, and a ten-page paper focusing on the development and modernization of Cajun and Creole cooking that I haven't even started yet. And I can't push any of it back, procrastinate it to a later date, because I have four shifts serving at the restaurant in the upcoming week. I'm already barely getting by on four hours of sleep—five if I'm lucky. There's no fucking way I can budge there. With my luck, I'll slice my finger open the next time I have to julienne something. I've already messed up twice in class, and my instructors weren't happy.

And now my sister and my niece need me. And above all else, they're my reason for . . . everything.

I grab Haley by the waist, toss her into the air, and let the sounds of her squeals wash over me. When she's settled in my lap, I say, "Of course, short stuff. You know I love watching you."

Tessa calls from down the hall. "We leave in twenty, so do whatever you have to do."

What I have to do.

And that's the bottom line. I'd like to do what I *want* to do. I have been. Winter made me forget about the responsibilities in my life, about the things I *have* to take care of, being the only one around to do so. As much as I'd like to, I can't go see her tonight. Can't walk her to the bus stop, which means she'll be walking there alone.

The thought sends my teeth clenching, my fists curling, but there's no way around it.

This is a good reminder for me. Even if Winter and I start something, I can't let her make me forget where my responsibilities lie.

I won't.

*winter*

I don't know how long to wait. We never said anything. There were never any rules to this, but even still. I came to expect him.

In the week we've been doing this dance, I came to expect seeing his hulking frame against the building, his loping gate by my side as he walked me to where I needed to be.

And now where he usually stands, there's nothing but a few cigarette butts and some trash.

Annette's car rumbles up in front of me, the muffler on the El Camino shot, and she rolls down her window. "Your guy couldn't come tonight?"

I don't want to tell her I'm not sure. That he never said, *we* never said, and now I have this uncertainty in my stomach I'm not used to and isn't welcome. And I definitely don't want to tell her he isn't mine. Instead, I say, "Nope."

"Hop in, I'll give you a ride."

I shake my head, my legs already moving. "That's okay. It's a nice night. I'll see you tomorrow." I wave as I step around the car, hurrying before she can say anything more.

The truth is, I want to be alone. I'm not sure I can handle letting someone in to help when the person I actually let see a blink of the real me let me down. Exactly like I knew he would. It's too much, too much, too much for one night.

I stuff my hands in my pockets and keep my head down as I hustle to the stop. It's my own fault—these stupid expectations I set without even realizing it. My rule in life has always been don't count on people—don't have expectations because then you're never let down. Never disappointed.

And by the hollow feeling in my stomach, it's clear I had them for Cade whether I was aware of it or not.

It's a good reminder. A timely reminder. I have sixty-six days left, and getting mixed up with a boy like Cade is the last thing I need.

Last night after telling him my name, I went home high on

nerves and anxiety. I fell asleep to the image of him under the streetlight. Dreamt about what it'd be like to have him for mine. To open up to him like I've never done with anyone else. When I woke up in the middle of the night, panting and sweating, that should've been enough warning. I'm not meant to form lasting relationships. To forge friendships based on respect and trust.

I'm meant to get through life on my own.

I'm meant to be alone.

# SEVEN

*cade*

I walk into The Brewery four hours earlier than normal. It's stupid, really. It's not like she'll be able to leave with me or to hang out while she's working. I don't know why I do it. Why I don't just wait until midnight, propped against the brick wall like always, but I want to see her. After two days of not being able to come by, suddenly it's like I can't wait any longer. I want to see the flush on her cheeks and the fire in her gray-green eyes and her hair a crazy, riotous mess piled on top of her head. I want to get lost in her husky laugh and see those bee-stung lips form my name.

There are a handful of tables occupied, a few scattered people at the bar, and a couple waitresses milling about, but not the one I want. I spot the older lady behind the bar whom I've seen walk out with Winter before, and I head that way.

"What can I get'cha, honey?"

"Nothing to drink, thanks. I'm actually looking for Winter. Is she in back?"

She stares at me for a moment, and I instinctively stand a little taller, though I don't know if that helps my cause. Most of the time when people see me, they've already formed an opinion of me based strictly on my size or the metal through my eyebrow or the tattoos running down my arms. They don't take a moment to talk to me, to find out what kind of person I am before I'm stamped as a bad seed. As someone who likes getting rowdy, who causes trouble.

With the exception of some stupid-ass instances when I was a teenager, I've never been that kind of guy.

Instead of answering my question, she says, "You're the one that's been walking with her . . . keeping an eye out for her after work."

It's not a question, but I answer anyway. "Yes, ma'am."

She lifts her eyebrows at my formality. "That's good. What you're doing, I mean." She looks away from me and continues wiping down the bar top. "Winter, she's . . . tough. She's been working here for over a year, and she's never so much as let me give her a ride to that bus stop. She doesn't take a lot from other people . . . doesn't ask for anything if she can help it."

I nod, soaking up any bit of information she can give me. While I'd love to get all of this from Winter, she isn't exactly forthcoming.

"I don't know much about her—none of us do. But she shows up on time, she does her job, and doesn't cause trouble. She's a good girl, but she'd spit nails if she ever heard me say that."

I smile, already picturing the indignation erupting on her face.

"I don't know what you two have going on—like I said, she doesn't tell me anything—but I just needed you to know. Be careful with her. In all the time she's worked here, you're the first person who's ever come in here looking for her. I don't think she's got anybody watching out for her." She tips her chin up and stares straight into my eyes. "Well, I am."

My mood suddenly somber, I nod, my eyes serious as I meet her gaze, understanding the warning she's giving me.

She studies me for another moment before she nods and turns away, grabbing a couple beers for the waitress who's waiting at the end of the bar. "Anyway, she's not working tonight." She looks at me over her shoulder, her eyebrows raised. "She was the last two, though."

I rub my hand over my face and into my hair, blowing out a breath. "Yeah, I couldn't make it."

"Maybe next time you can't make it, you call her, huh?"

My arms fall to my side. "That's the thing . . . I don't actually have her number. Or her last name." She shakes her head and looks at me like I'm a fucking idiot, and I can't even fault her for it. "I don't suppose you'd be willing to give me either, would you?"

"How do you think Winter'd take that?"

Even though I don't like her answer, she does have a point. "Yeah, you're right." I nod and push away from the bar, my hands in my pockets. "Okay. Is she working tomorrow night?"

"Better come by and see for yourself." She returns her attention to the register, her back to me, and I take that as my cue to leave.

Once I'm rumbling down the street on my bike, I replay the conversation we had. I knew from the beginning that Winter kept her cards close to her chest, worked hard to keep people out. I'd wondered if it was just me, though. If she was that way because of how we met. But after talking to the lady from the pub, it's clear that's just how she is. Winter's a closed book. A journal with a thousand entries, shut tight and padlocked.

And I can't wait to crack open her pages.

*winter*

When I was thirteen, I thought I caught a lucky break. I was living with the same family for a year—nearly twice as long as any other place I'd been since going into the system. They were nice. Normal. The woman was a receptionist at a dental office, her husband a manager at a department store. There wasn't any alcohol. No drunken nightly fights. No doors slamming, no screaming or swearing. There weren't six other kids vying for attention or food. No bugs in my room, crawling in my bed, dirt in the bathtub, or mold in the corners. There were always clean clothes in my drawers and lunches in my backpack.

For the first two months, I was constantly on edge, waiting for the other shoe to drop. Kids like me—nearly grown kids with sullen dispositions—didn't get placed with families like that. They wanted the babies or toddlers or pretty little girls with pigtails and ruffle socks. They didn't want hormonal thirteen-year-olds who hated the world.

I thought they were crazy for taking me in. For keeping me. But the days ticked into weeks and the weeks ticked into months, and when the year anniversary of being placed there came and went, I knew it was different. I got comfortable in the routine. I let my guard down, just a little. I started to care about them.

I found out the reason they took in a foster child was because they couldn't have any of their own. It was that night, when I was sitting at the top of the stairs listening to a conversation they were having in the living room, that I thought . . . I thought everything was going to be different.

Through overheard, whispered words, I learned they wanted to look into having me placed with them permanently.

*Permanently.*

I'd never had permanence my whole life. Even when I was with my mother, everything was fleeting, people and places and apartments mere flashes in the memories of my childhood. Nothing stuck. Everything was disposable. Even people. Even me.

But this . . . this was different. It was something to be put in the foster home as a place keeper. Almost like rent-a-kid. It was another thing altogether to want to get rid of the yellow tape and *keep* me. I was scared and uncertain and nervous. But above all, I was hopeful.

Hopeful.

A month later, I was back in a temporary group home, and the couple I'd strung my dreams on were happily expecting their first baby after eight years of nothing but futile attempts.

I was a mountain of emotions then, bubbling with teenage angst and topped with the uncertainty of what my place with them was going to be. But in the end, it was the hope that killed me. That glimmer of possibility that maybe my life would turn out different than I thought it would. That the path my mother had set me on when I was seven could have a different ending. That I'd taken a detour, and I might end up someplace so much better, so much brighter than I'd originally thought.

And just like that, that glimmer of light was extinguished, brushed away, and swept under the rug. Like I hadn't heard those words. Like I hadn't been hanging everything I had on the possibility of something more with someone else. With a family.

Realizing you're the only one you can count on is a painful lesson to learn, and not one easily forgotten.

Yet somehow, after only a week at Cade's side, I did. A total of seventy-five minutes spent in each other's presence, and he managed to make me forget.

I shake my head, forcing myself back to the books in front of me. The words on the pages blur, though, the code looking like a foreign language more than it ever has before. For two hours, I've been trying to focus on my homework, forget about seeing that bare wall again outside The Brewery last night. Pretend he didn't ignite a shred of light that grew and developed into the tiny wings of butterflies fluttering around in my stomach.

He didn't. He *didn't*.

I get two nights a week when I can focus solely on homework. Two nights when I'm not working, and I'm wasting one of them thinking about shit I have no business thinking about. I pack up my things, shoving my books and laptop in my bag before I heft it over my shoulder, my head down as I walk toward the front of the library. I'm nearly out of the building, the cool metal of the door against my fingertips, and I hear it.

That deep, rich voice that I've only heard for a handful of minutes but is burned into my memory. In my dreams, he says my name over and over again, just like he did the other night at the bus stop, and I want to slap him and gag him and bottle the sound to keep it forever. I close my eyes, hearing it repeat, a whisper growing stronger until suddenly it's right there.

"Winter."

# EIGHT

*cade*

Her back is rigid, her shoulders tight, hands clenched at her side—everything about her body language is screaming at me to leave her the fuck alone. But I can't back away.

"I, um—" I clear my throat. "I went by The Brewery tonight to see you, but the lady behind the bar said you weren't working." Winter remains silent, so I keep rambling. "I'm sorry I didn't come by the last couple nights. I had—"

She holds up her hand, stopping me. "You know what? It doesn't matter. You had to do whatever you had to do, and that's cool. I'll see you around."

And then she's gone, pushing through the door and jogging down the steps until all I can do is scramble after her, no thought to leaving behind my bag and books scattered across the table Jason and I were sharing.

"Wait. Winter! Wait . . ." I take the steps two at a time and quickly make up the distance between us, stopping to stand in front of her. I have my arms held out to the side, as if I'm approaching a scared animal. Which she might as well be.

Instead of stopping like I hoped, she dodges me, shifting to the side and ducking under my arm before she's cutting kitty-corner across the grass and toward the nearest bus stop.

I hesitate only briefly, looking back to the library, then to where she's getting farther and farther away from me. With a curse, I take off after her. Jason was roaming the library when I spotted Winter, so he's probably wondering where the hell I am. I don't even have my phone on me to text him. Hopefully he's got enough common sense to watch my things and stick around until I get back.

When I'm closer to her, I call out, "Hey, wait. Winter, please. Will you let me explain?"

"You don't have to explain anything."

"Obviously I do. It's pretty clear you're pissed."

"I'm not pissed. Why would I be pissed? You're just some guy who showed up every night, uninvited, and trailed me to the bus stop. That's it."

I grab her wrist, pulling her to a stop. Her entire face is a mask of indifference. Everything except her eyes. "It was more than that and you know it."

"What I know," she says as she pulls her arm free, that fire in her eyes blazing, "is that I'm going to miss my bus. Good-bye, Cade."

She turns and walks away just as the bus pulls to a stop against the curb, and she increases her gait, quickly climbing the stairs and disappearing inside. I don't hesitate as I follow her, hopping on the bus before the doors can close. I fumble with my wallet and shove some money into the slot at the front before I head to where she's sitting, all the way in the back.

When I take the seat across the aisle from her, my body turned toward hers, elbows braced on my knees, she doesn't even look at me, her attention focused out the window. "Some people would consider this harassment, you know," she mumbles.

"I like to call it using my resources. I have your undivided attention for however long it takes to get to your place."

Her silence greets me, but I barrel on. "I know you said you don't need an explanation, but I want to give you one. You deserve one. I didn't forget, okay? Or just say fuck it and decide to not come back. I wouldn't do that.

"I just . . . I had stuff I couldn't get out of. School and work and family stuff. I had to use the weekend to get caught up. I already don't have enough hours in the day to do all the shit I have to and still take care of what I need to—" I shake my head, clenching my fists as I stare down at the floor, knowing she doesn't need to have my burdens unloaded on her. "Never mind. That's not what I want to say. *Fuck.*" My shoulders slump, head dropping as I scrub a hand quickly over my hair, blowing out a frustrated breath.

"You only do that when you're nervous."

I snap my head up, meeting her gaze in the reflection of the window.

"Rub your hand over your hair, I mean."

And I can't help it. I smile. Because her noticing my stupid tell means she's been noticing *me*, and that whatever we have between us isn't just in my head. "Yeah, well. You make me a little nervous."

She remains quiet, and I can't tell if her lips quirk up on the side at my admission or if it's a trick of the light. She's definitely not going to make this easy for me, but after everything I know of her, I expect nothing less.

"I'm sorry, okay?" I try again, pouring as much sincerity in my voice as I can. "I'm sorry, and if I had your number or your last name, I would've called you or found your number to do so. I would've let you know I wasn't going to be there. And I didn't know if I'd get you in trouble if I called the bar looking for you. After everything that happened that first night, I didn't want to chance it."

"I already told you—you don't owe me an apology or an explanation."

"That's bullshit, and you know it. Even if we didn't quantify this . . . this . . . whatever the hell it is, that doesn't mean I'd be a complete asshole and just bail. I'm not like that. I don't bail on people. I especially don't bail on girls I'm coaxing into letting me make dinner for them."

After a minute of heavy silence, she expels a deep breath and says, "Okay."

"Okay?"

"Okay, I accept your apology."

"Damn, I was hoping that was going to be, 'Okay, I'd love for you to cook me dinner, Cade.' "

She's still facing the window, but I can see when she rolls her eyes, and this time I know I don't imagine the curve of her lips in the reflection. "You're awfully sure of yourself for a guy freezing his ass off, running after a girl he doesn't know onto a bus. You don't even know where we're going."

I glance down, realizing I'm in short sleeves, my coat left behind with everything else at the library, and I didn't even feel the chill of the early spring night. Shrugging, I say, "It was either grab my coat or follow you. And I don't care where we're going. I didn't hop the bus for a ride around town, Winter. I'm here for you."

She hums, but otherwise doesn't acknowledge what I said. By centimeters, she curves her body away from the window and toward me, and it's almost like witnessing ice melt. Little by little, the hard shell of her is fading away. I watch her as she watches me, her eyes tracking from my face, down, down, down, and if she's put off by my tattoos, nothing in her expression shows it.

After a minute, she says, "Your girlfriend won't mind that you're chasing after girls you barely know? Trying to get them to agree to dinner? Looks like you've been together a long time . . ."

My brow furrows as I try to follow what she's saying. "My girlfriend? What—"

Winter reaches out, tracing the letters on my forearm before she pulls away, and—*Jesus*—I'd give almost anything to feel her hands on me again. Dazed, I look down to where her fingers blazed a trail on my skin. Haley's name and her birthday sit interspersed with other designs weaving in and out.

I chuckle, running my hand over where she touched. "Um, no. She won't mind."

She raises an eyebrow. "Well, I do. Guys in relationships are off the table." She shrugs, glancing down at the tattoo again before meeting my eyes. "Too bad . . . I was going to say yes."

*winter*

A slow smile spreads across his face, his eyes dancing. There's nothing sweet about his expression. It's the look of a predator capturing his prey. And as much as the idea rankles me, I can't ignore the flare of excitement that grows low in my belly, the *awareness* he makes me feel in my body.

Everything about him is larger than life. His size, most notably, but there are other things I didn't pick up on before when the only illumination we had was the moon and passing streetlamps. But here, under the harsh track lights of the bus, everything is accentuated. He's imposing, even sitting there, his back curled as he leans toward me. His face looks like it was carved from stone, the angles of his jaw and cheekbones sharp and unforgiving. I feel like his shoulders are twice the width of mine, at least, though I know that's not possible. Probably. His arms are massive, roped with muscle and completely covered in ink. I'd seen hints of tattoos before . . . pieces here and there, but this . . . This is more than I anticipated. Designs cover both forearms, disappearing into the short sleeves of the shirt wrapped tightly around the bulk of his biceps, tiny whispers peeking out of the neckline.

I wonder where they stop. *If* they stop.

"I guess it's my lucky day then."

And his voice . . . low and deep and rumbly and so perfectly matched to the rest of him. I glance down once again at the name he's had permanently etched on him. The idea that someone—a girl—means enough to him to have her name forever branded into his skin is foreign to me. I can't imagine that kind of love . . . that kind of commitment. Not after the examples I've had in my life. The low hum of disappointment in my stomach at him being taken is a completely unwelcome sensation.

Meeting his eyes, I recall what he said and ask, "Why's that?"

He stares at me for a beat, his smile growing even more until his entire face lights up with it. "You just agreed to dinner."

I sit back in my seat, brow furrowed. "Um, no I didn't. What I said was I don't do committed guys."

"Right. And then you said, 'Too bad . . . I was going to say yes.' And you should know . . . this?" He runs a finger over the flowing letters that make up the girl's name on his arm. "Is my niece, not my girlfriend. That?" He points to the date. "Her birthday, not an anniversary."

I open my mouth to say something, anything, but nothing comes out. And then his hand is under my chin, coaxing my jaw up until my lips are no longer parted. With a single finger, he makes a path down the side of my neck, over my shoulder, down my arm to my wrist before he grabs my hand, and I swear to God, I'm on fire. Every nerve ending in my body is setting off a CODE-RED alarm, and I'm helpless to stop it. His thumb rubs back and forth on the inside of my wrist, his touch gentle and reverent, and I can't remember the last time someone's touched me so sweetly.

And I realize with clarity it's because I've *never* been touched this way.

When I meet his eyes again, they are open and honest and beseeching.

"So. What time can I pick you up?"

# NINE

*cade*

Tessa and Haley have the car tonight, so I have no choice but to pick up Winter on my motorcycle. I haven't ever asked her if she has a problem with it, and I wasn't going to now, too paranoid it'd give her a reason to say no. When I caught her in her words, I could see the panic in her eyes, trying to think up a plausible reason to go back on what she said. And I sure as hell wasn't going to give her one.

I roll to a stop in front of her apartment building, the outside rundown and unkempt. This isn't the nicest neighborhood, and it's farther away from campus than I would have figured she'd live, but if the exterior is anything to go by, the rent's cheap. I park and hop off, pulling my helmet off and setting it on the seat before I head up the front walkway.

The lock on the main door is broken, the speaker for the intercom system hanging open with wires spilling out. I let myself in, heading to the door marked *107* before I knock twice. And then I wait.

And wait.

I'm just about to raise my hand to knock again when the door swings open. "Hi." Winter's head is tipped down, and she won't meet my eyes. "Let me just . . . I'll grab my bag quick." She turns and walks farther into her apartment, not sparing me a glance, but that just gives me time to watch her. The jeans she has on hug her ass in the most amazing way, and when she spins back toward me, I notice the sweater she's wearing brings out the green in her eyes. Her hair is down, and her lips are full and pink, and I want to pull her to me and kiss her, if only to get her to stop fidgeting.

I step inside and lean against the closed door as I wait for her to get what she needs, trying not to add to her obvious nerves. Her place is . . . tiny. I have no doubt if I stretched my arms out on either side of me, I'd take up half the width of the room. She walks over to where a futon sits against one wall and grabs her purse. Save for a couple of TV trays set up—one with a laptop on it—there isn't any other furniture.

A door on the left probably leads to the bathroom, and to my right is the disgrace of a kitchen with its mini-fridge and two-burner electric stove.

"I'd give you the tour, but, well . . ." She shrugs, still avoiding eye contact.

"Hey." I reach out and grab her hand, tug her to stand in front of me. Bending my knees, I crouch until I catch her eyes. "You're not getting cold feet, are you? Gonna back out on me?"

"What? No." She shakes her head, her hair tumbling around her shoulders as she finally looks at me. "No, I . . . It's nothing. I'm fine." She gives me a tight, close-lipped smile, and after a moment of studying her, I decide not to press. I know I need to tread carefully with her, and I'm not sure how much I can push, how much she needs me to stand back.

"If you're sure . . ." I don't want to give her a reason to back out, but I also don't want to force her into something she's not comfortable with.

"I am."

I nod, stepping back. "Okay. Grab your coat. It's gonna be chilly."

"Why, taking me on a picnic?"

I chuckle. "Not tonight."

She pulls on a coat over her sweater as she leads the way out of her apartment building. I try not to watch the sway of her hips as she walks in front of me, but my gaze travels down without permission, once again taking in her ass in those jeans. I've seen her in less—far less—working at the pub, but there's something decadent about this. Knowing what she has underneath without being able to see it . . . I stifle a groan as my imagination goes to places better left for when I'm home, alone, and in my bed.

When we get outside, I gently coax her to my motorcycle, and I know the minute realization dawns, because she stops short in front of me on the sidewalk. She looks at me over her shoulder, eyebrows raised.

"Yep," I say in answer to her unasked question, holding out a helmet for her. When she just stares at it, I step closer, gently brushing her hair away from her face and pulling the helmet onto her head. I gather her hair, pushing it behind her shoulders and tucking it into the back of her coat before I hook the chin strap of her helmet. "Your hair will probably get tangled if you don't do that."

Just staring at me, she doesn't say anything. She looks

ridiculous with this giant-ass thing on her head, and all I can think is how much I want to kiss her. She's so close, her breath on my face, and I could just lean in, press my mouth to hers, slip my tongue between her lips, and finally taste her.

I step back, clearing my throat as I try to refocus. "Ready?" I straddle my bike, reaching out a hand to help her on.

Hesitantly, she closes the gap between us, and then she's behind me, her hands on my hips, legs flush against the outside of mine, body pressed against my back. Her husky voice echoes in my ear. "Ready."

And I know I'm utterly fucked.

*winter*

Freedom.

That's the only word that describes the feeling of being with Cade on the back of his motorcycle. It's chilly, the wind biting into me even with his massive body as a shield, but I don't care. It's exhilarating, this freedom.

I feel like I'm flying.

I grip his waist tighter, my arms clutching him as we round a corner, my head pressed to his shoulder. I close my eyes, getting lost in the movement of his body as he maneuvers us down a twisty path. My nerves have all but incinerated by the time he rolls to a stop in front of a sprawling ranch house in a nice part of town. I've forgotten all my reservations, my anxiety at what agreeing to this date means.

I don't do dates. I do random hookups once in a while, but I learned a long time ago that letting anyone in only ever has one outcome for me. Heartache.

I've had my whole life to perfect my defense mechanisms, the excuses and the brush-offs I'm so fond of, and yet I couldn't come up with a single one with his eyes imploring me, *begging* me to say yes.

And so I did.

Against my better judgment, against everything I've taught myself, I said yes.

Peeling myself from his back, I brace my hands behind me on the seat, not ready to stop touching him, but not ready to continue contact, either. "I can't believe you're actually going through with this whole make-me-dinner farce. You could've taken me to, I don't know . . . Where do people usually go on dates?"

A low chuckle rumbles from him, his shoulders quaking as he removes his helmet. Glancing back at me, he says, "You tell me, where do you go on dates?"

I use his shoulder to balance as I step off the bike. Suddenly, I'm feeling claustrophobic, and I need as much space between us as possible. "I don't."

He takes the helmet I offer him, one long leg swinging over as he dismounts the motorcycle. He doesn't stop until he's in front of me, mere inches away. "What do you mean you don't?"

I shrug, looking around his arm at the house spread out in the background, if only to give myself something to focus on. "I don't date."

"Never?" His voice is disbelieving, his eyebrows raised. "I thought you were just spouting off before when you told me that."

"Nope."

"Wow." He shakes his head, scratching at the back of his neck as he regards me. "Never."

Laughing, I step around him and walk up his driveway. "Is that so hard to believe?"

"Uh, yeah." He keeps step with me easily, his long legs moving at half the speed of mine.

"Why?"

He glances at me out of the corner of his eye. "Well, for one thing, you're gorgeous. For another thing, you're . . . what, twenty-one, twenty-two?"

"Twenty-two."

"Right, so even if your parents were super strict and didn't let you date in high school, you still had four years to work your way through the guys on campus."

"Well, now you just make me sound like a slut, whoring around." I laugh, though he's not entirely off the mark, even if the reasons aren't what he thinks. In high school, I was too focused on my grades, the necessity of getting a scholarship so I could do something with my life and get the hell out of California consuming my every waking moment. I couldn't even think about guys. Not that I wanted to intimately open up my shitty life to the judgment of others anyway. Especially then, being shuffled from place to place, never having a solid foundation I could count on.

And then college came, and I realized I could get male companionship without the strings. In fact, that was what most guys my age were looking for. I took advantage of it, taking pleasure from them and returning the favor with no emotions getting lost in the mix. It's a slippery slope I traverse, being lonely but still wanting to be alone. That arrangement was the perfect balance.

I know now more than ever why that was a good idea. Being around Cade, talking and laughing and walking with him, my emotions are all tangled up in him, and I don't know what that means for us. For *me*.

"What? No, that's not what I meant. I just mean . . . you know. Sowing your oats. Checking out your options."

"Well, I've done *that*. Dating? Not so much."

I climb the two steps onto his front porch, but before I can get any farther, he has a hold of my wrist and he pulls me to a stop. Turning, I'm eye level with him as he stands on the sidewalk. "That's not what I brought you here for, you know."

His thumb is brushing against my palm, his eyes boring into mine, and I want to fall into him. Forget all my hang-ups and my hesitations and just . . . fall.

"What, a date?"

"No, I definitely brought you here for that. But I meant sex. I didn't bring you here to sleep with you."

I can tell from the timbre of his voice, the constant eye contact, the reverent way he's touching me, that he's telling the truth. And the fact that this boy wants something more from me than my body is exhilarating.

And terrifying.

## *cade*

Winter is sitting on a stool at the island, her chin in her hand as she watches me prep everything. Her eyes are narrowed, and I can practically see the wheels spinning in her mind.

"What're you thinking about?"

She raises her eyes to mine. "I'm thinking you tricked me."

I move my knife against the cutting board without thought, trimming the asparagus before I look back at her. "How so?"

"I thought you were going to try to impress me with, like, spaghetti or something. You know, boil some noodles, pop open a jar, good to go. I didn't know you were gonna"—she gestures to the spread of fresh ingredients laid out on the island—"actually *cook*."

Concentrating once again on what I'm doing, I laugh. "I'd get ostracized by my mentor if I did that."

"Your mentor for what? I don't even know what you're going to school for."

"BA in culinary management."

"Really."

I glance up at her dry tone, her mouth hanging open. "Why, is that so hard to believe?"

She shrugs, her arms folded atop the counter as she leans toward me. "I don't know . . . I guess not. I just wasn't expecting that from you. Fireman? Professional bodyguard? Yes. Cooking? Not so much."

"Yeah, I get that a lot, though some of the guys in my program are tougher looking than me."

Her eyebrows lift as she regards me skeptically. "I find that hard to believe."

"That there are tougher-looking guys than me or that they're in the program?"

Laughing, she says, "Both, I guess. But I meant them looking tougher than you. You're pretty scary looking."

"You weren't scared of me."

"I didn't have time to be scared. I was too pissed."

I cringe, remembering our ill-fated first meeting. "Yeah. Have I mentioned I'm sorry? Even though I hate that we met like that, I'm sorta glad, too. I doubt I would've gotten under your skin if I'd just walked up and asked you for your number after those douchebags left."

"No, probably not." She tilts her head to the side. "Wait . . . you were going to ask me for my number?"

"Well, I was going to talk to you, at least. *Hopefully* get your number. But yeah." I look up and meet her eyes. "I noticed you as soon as I got there. And I was interested immediately."

She stares at me for a minute before dropping her gaze to the food stretched out between us. "I can't exactly say the same."

"No, I'd guess not. I was actually a little scared for my balls. You looked pissed enough to punch me right in the junk."

A loud, unrestrained laugh erupts from her, and I grin at her, making a promise to myself to do everything in my power just so I can hear it again. "You're not far off."

"I knew it."

She's quiet for a moment, her eyes tracking every movement I make as I trim the steaks and season the meat. "You make it look so effortless. Do you like it? Cooking?"

"I love it." I grab my cast iron pan and place it on the stove to heat it up before I get the steaks ready to go on.

"What made you decide to go to school for that?"

I turn my head, talking to her over my shoulder as I set the steaks in the pan, the answering sizzle interspersed throughout my words. "My mom, actually. She loved to cook. She didn't do it for a living, but I think she wanted to. She would've been amazing at it."

"Would have? She doesn't like it anymore?"

Once the steaks have char marks, I move my pan into the oven and set the timer. Wiping my hands on the towel slung over my shoulder, I turn back to Winter. "She loved it until she passed away a few years ago. Breast cancer." She doesn't say anything, and I don't give her a chance to offer platitudes. "She remodeled the kitchen shortly before she got sick. She loved being in here and saved to make it her dream kitchen. She got that, at least. Anyway, I think it was too big of a risk for her, being the only one to support Tess and me."

"Tess is your sister? Haley's mom?"

"Tessa, yeah."

"Your dad's not around, either?"

"Ah, nope. He died in a car accident when I was ten."

"Wow." Something in the small catch in her voice makes me glance up from what I'm doing. Her lips are curved down in the corners, frown lines creasing her forehead. "So you're all alone."

Something in the tone of her voice makes me pause. I clear my throat before I say, "No, I'm not. I have Tess and Haley. They mean the world to me. Things didn't work out how I thought they would, but we're doing okay."

*winter*

*Doing okay.*

From where I'm sitting, looking in, he seems like he's doing a hell of a lot better than okay. He got into one of the best art schools in the country, so I know his grades are above average, and he doesn't slack off. His house is well kept, big, and in a neighborhood I would kill to even just live *next* to.

He's like me in so many ways—navigating his life completely without parental guidance—yet so utterly different in others. In all the ways that matter. Above all, he has it together. What will it take before I feel like I'm doing anything other than floundering, barely treading water?

I study him as he focuses on dinner, his brow creased in concentration, lips a tight line. He's so confident. So sure of himself and his abilities.

I'm just trying to get by.

"Hey, where'd you go?"

His voice pulls me from my thoughts, and I refocus on his eyes. "Nowhere. Just thinking." Not wanting to get into all my insecurities, I say, "Your sister and niece live here, too?"

"Yeah, just made sense for us after my mom died. Plus it's easier for me to help while Tessa works . . . Shuffle Haley to preschool or dance or whatever. And to look out for them."

"You do that a lot, huh?"

"What's that?"

"Look out for people."

He smiles, keeping his focus on the block of cheese he's grating. "Yeah, I guess I do."

I think about how different my life would've been if I had someone looking out for me as well as he looks after his sister and niece. If I had someone who cared about me, about my life, where would I be now? Thousands of miles away from where I grew up, just so I could put as much distance between me and that time as possible? Or would I have stayed there, not trying with every ounce of myself to run from everything I knew?

Would I be happy?

It's too much to think about now, on top of everything else he seems to bring out in me. I take a drink of the wine he poured, willing it to relax me, make my thoughts muddled so I stop thinking so much.

"When is this fancy dinner going to be ready? I'm starved."

"Soon." He reaches into the oven and pulls out the pan, the scents of everything he's making hitting me at once. "The meat just needs to rest for a bit. I'll get the asparagus going. Can you last ten minutes?"

"I don't think I'll wilt away."

He removes the steak and places it on a platter, then uses that pan for the asparagus. I'm mesmerized by his sure movements, his confidence and ease when in this environment. He commands the kitchen when he's in it. I can't imagine how hot he must look with his chef's coat on, eyes focused, face flushed from the heat of the kitchen.

His sleeves are rolled up, the muscles in his forearms flexing under the designs inked there. I never really gave much thought to male chefs, but there is something delicious about this giant of a man—imposing and dark and looming, complete with tattoos and a piercing—with an apron tied around his waist as he prepares me dinner.

I must zone out for longer than I intend, because suddenly a plate is in front of me, the biggest meal I've eaten in years displayed in the center like a piece of art.

"Since you're already settled, I figured we could just eat in here instead of the dining room, if that's okay. And I didn't even ask if you were a vegetarian. You like steak, don't you? And asparagus?"

"In here's fine, not a vegetarian, and yes." I offer him a small smile.

"Thank God. I'm clearly new to this whole impress-a-girl-by-cooking-for-her thing."

"You mean this isn't in your usual repertoire?"

He laughs, shaking his head as he sets his plate next to mine. Reaching out, he grabs my wineglass and refills it with the bottle he uncorked a while ago. "You are the first."

"Really."

"Hard to believe?"

"Yeah, a little. Don't guys usually use whatever arsenal they have in their possession to get girls?"

He opens his mouth to say something, then drops his eyes to his lap, shaking his head, lips lifted at the corner. "Anything I say here will undoubtedly make me sound like a pig, so I plead the Fifth."

I smile as he takes his seat perpendicular to me. The scents coming from my plate accost my senses, and I look down again, my mouth watering. "Wow. I had no idea this was what I was getting tonight, or I might have agreed to this a long time ago."

"Next time I'll print you a menu when I ask, maybe add some pictures. And you should probably taste it before you start spewing things like, 'Wow.' "

"You're right. I mean, it doesn't look or smell very good . . ." I crinkle my noise in mock disgust, trying not to laugh at the look he gives me.

With narrowed eyes, he says, "Careful. Insulting my cooking is worse than challenging my manhood."

I laugh. "I don't think anyone would be stupid enough to insult your manhood." I grab my fork and ask, "So what is this exactly?"

"Marinated hanger steak topped with butter and shaved blue cheese, with a side of grilled asparagus."

I stare at him for a minute, mouth dropped. "Wow, even your description is elaborate. I seriously don't think I've eaten anything this fancy in my entire life." I cut into the steak, making sure to get some of blue cheese and butter with it, as well.

He smiles but his focus is on my mouth, on the bite that's an inch from my lips. I don't want to tell him my normal menu consists of ramen noodles and boxed macaroni and cheese, so whatever he made will no doubt be a million times better than what I'm used to. As soon as I slide the first bite in my mouth, I know it wouldn't have mattered what my standard fare is. The flavors burst on my tongue. It's incredible. "Oh my God."

"Good 'oh my God' or 'oh my God, how could you feed me this shit'?" he asks with raised eyebrows.

I roll my eyes, saying around another forkful of food, "I'm sure people tell you how awful your food is all the time."

Laughing, he shrugs, spearing his own bite. After swallowing, he says, "Every time I cook, it's me on that plate, you know? It's always nice to hear if someone likes what I've made for them."

I meet his eyes, and he's absolutely sincere, not fishing for compliments but waiting for my approval. And I can't believe I see nervousness written all over his face, but it's there. Seeing it eases whatever worries were lingering even with the alcohol doing its job. "It's amazing. Seriously."

With a tip of his head in my direction, he spears another bite. "You never said what you're going to school for. I know you're not in culinary school."

"How do you know that?"

He meets my eyes, a slow smile spreading across his lips. "Believe me, Winter. If you were there, I definitely would've noticed."

I don't know what to do with myself when he says things like that. Part of me wants to run, to escape because things are getting too close, too comfortable, too intimate, and I don't *do* close or comfortable or intimate. I do quick and anonymous and thoughtless. I do not do butterflies and anticipation and *hope*.

Clearing my throat, I spear a piece of asparagus. "I'm in web design and interactive media."

"Wow. Really? I wouldn't have guessed that."

"Why not?"

"I don't know . . . It just seems more technical than I thought you'd be. I mean, I know jack-shit about web design, so I guess it could be fly-by-the-seat-of-your-pants and I wouldn't know any different. You just seem uninhibited. You do what you want, speak your mind. Doesn't fit my perception of a web designer, I guess." He shrugs. "You seem . . . free."

I suck in a breath. I don't feel free. I feel trapped, suffocated under the piles of baggage I've had strapped on my back for so long, it feels like they've melded to my very soul. I'd give anything for a moment of peace. To be able to *breathe*.

"Do you want more?" He points at my plate, and I glance down, realizing the only way I could've gotten it any cleaner would've been if I had picked it up and licked it. Which I actually contemplated.

"Oh, no, thank you. It was delicious, but I'm so full."

"I hope not too full for dessert."

"Dessert, too?"

"Nothing fancy, just cookies. My mom's recipe, actually. It was the first thing she taught me to make. I can't bake worth shit, normally, but these I've perfected."

I smile. For some reason, that brings a warmth to my chest, that he'd want to share that with me. He's so open, so transparent, and I feel like I'm hiding every ounce of myself behind walls too thick to be infiltrated.

But as he looks at me, smiling, his eyes dropping to my lips for the briefest moment, my heart stutters and trips, my stomach doing back flips, and I wonder.

Will he be the one to finally get through?

# TEN

*cade*

Winter helps me clean up, even though I tell her she doesn't have to. She pulled back into her shell right after dinner, and I'm not sure what I said to make her take a step back. I want to ask her, but I also don't want to force her further away. I don't know what it is about this particular girl, but she makes me want to know more about her. She makes me want to know *everything*.

The back door bangs open, then, "Uncle Cade!" My sister calls for Haley, the door slamming shut behind them, but my niece pays no attention. She tears into the kitchen, completely ignoring Winter, as she crashes into the back of my legs, wrapping her arms around my thighs as far as she can.

"Hey, short stuff. How was school and your play date?"

"Good. Smells yummy. What'd ya make me?"

I dry my hands on the towel and turn, bending to grab her and throw her into the air before I hold her at my side. With my other hand, I tickle her stomach. "You're hungry? I thought you already ate dinner. Where do you put all that food?"

Her giggles turn to gasps as she twists and squirms on my arm until I relent. With a deep sigh and a couple leftover chuckles, she wraps an arm around my neck, then notices Winter standing against the island, watching us.

"What's your name?" Haley asks, her head tipped to the side.

Winter smiles, offering a small wave. "I'm Winter."

"Really?" Haley's face brightens, her eyes wide. "I love winter! It's my favorite. I do snow angels and make snowmens and go sledding. Do you?"

"Do I what?"

"Like that stuff?"

"Um . . . I'm not sure. I guess I've never tried."

"Never?"

"Nope." Winter shakes her head. "They didn't have snow where I grew up."

Haley's eyes go wide, like it's the worst thing she can imagine. "That's *awful*."

A breathless laugh escapes Winter, and I smile at the sound. "Yeah, I guess it is."

Ignoring Winter again, Haley turns to me, hands on my cheeks until she's turned my head to face her. "Mama says I have to leave you alone 'cause of your date, but I really, really, really, really, really want you to read our story tonight. Will you, will you, please?" She leans closer with every word until she presses her nose to mine, her eyes wide as she stares at me.

I shift my focus to the side, trying to get a read on Winter, but Haley just moves her head until she's once again filling up my entire line of sight. A soft laugh comes from the corner of the kitchen.

"It's fine, Cade. Go read to the poor girl."

I try to catch her eye only to be intercepted by Haley's head once again, so I lift her, flipping her over my shoulder and gripping her by the backs of her legs, her little fists pounding into my lower back as she laughs. Winter's watching us with a wistful expression on her face. "You're sure?"

"Yeah. Definitely."

"Okay. I shouldn't be too long. I'll take you home after."

She nods and I carry a squealing Haley down the hall, meeting Tessa just as she's coming out of her room.

"Hey. Sorry, I had to change. Little Miss Ants in Her Pants dumped juice all down the front of me at dinner. How's it going?" She tips her head in the direction of the kitchen.

"Good. I think. No, it's going good. She's laughing. So that's a plus, right?"

"Definitely. Unless she's laughing *at* you . . ."

"Funny."

Before she can respond, Haley interrupts, her fingers jabbing into my lower back. "Hurry up, Uncle Cade!"

"I'm going to read to her for a bit before bed. Winter's in the kitchen." I narrow my eyes at my sister, pointing a finger at her. "Do not embarrass me."

"Oh, please. Me?" She flutters her eyelashes and offers an innocent smile I know is nothing more than an act.

"I'm serious. Remember all the dirt I have on you," I call out to her retreating figure. Her laughter drifts back to me, even as she rounds the corner into the kitchen. I hear her greet Winter, and all I can do is hope she shows an ounce of restraint.

*winter*

Cade's sister isn't what I expected. Where he's dark and imposing, this giant of a man with a cloud of "don't fuck with me" constantly surrounding him until you get to know him, his sister is nearly the opposite. She's shorter than me, which is saying something, her smile vibrant as she introduces herself and pulls up a stool next to me.

"What'd he make you?" Her elbow is on the table, chin resting in her hand as she focuses on me.

"Um . . . I can't remember what it's called. It was sliced steak with butter on it. And some asparagus."

"Mmm . . . one of his specialties. I'm not surprised. Cade doesn't bother if he can't hit it out of the park."

I think about what I've come to know about him. How he throws everything he has into whatever he's doing, giving it his sole attention. Giving *me* his sole attention. "I'm learning that."

"Don't let that hard exterior fool you, though. He's soft as a marshmallow inside. He plays tea party with Haley . . . even lets her wrap him up in feather boas and put those ridiculous hats on him. If the tutus would fit him, she could probably talk him into wearing one of those, too."

The image of him in a pink feather boa and tutu is too much, and with the wine making me mellow and relaxed, the laugh flows from me without restraint. Tessa nods her head and smiles, like she's reading my mind.

"He really is a great guy. Dependable and loyal. And I'm not just saying that because I'm his sister, though I've definitely seen it more than anyone. When I found out I was pregnant with Haley, it was only a month after our mom passed away." She shakes her head, a sad smile on her lips as she stares where her finger is tracing an invisible circle on the counter. "I was such a bitch, acting out however I could. And I knew Nick—Haley's dad—got under Cade's skin, so of course I kept seeing him, even though he was a player and an asshole. I was only seventeen and so goddamn stubborn."

She glances behind her down the hallway, then turns her attention back to me, her words coming quickly, like she wants to get everything out before Cade comes back in. "But even when I told him, he didn't get pissed, didn't lecture me. Didn't say I told you so when Nick bailed. Just asked what he needed to do. He went with me to every doctor's appointment. Lamaze and breast-feeding workshops . . . I mean, can you imagine him sitting in on those classes?"

I shake my head, but not only because of the image of *him* at any of those things, but the thought that there are people—families—who care enough about each other to do that. To help out and support one another. To stand by them when they need it.

"I know, without a doubt, I couldn't have gotten through it without him."

Haley's muffled voice calls for her, and she smiles and stands. "It was nice to meet you, Winter. Hopefully we'll see you around here again."

I'm not sure what to say—whether to confirm or deny she will, because, honestly, I don't know myself—so I don't say anything, instead just offer a tight-lipped smile.

She turns to go, then stops, looking back at me. "Guys like him don't come around often, Winter. I'd give anything to find someone as strong and caring and loyal as him. I know he can be a little much sometimes, but just . . . give him a chance before you write him off."

Her words penetrate my defenses, seeping in until they're all

I can hear, playing on a loop in my mind. I stare at the leftover dishes from our dinner, at how welcoming everything was here tonight, at being included in something, and how terrifying that is. This whole night, everything, is *too much*. He's getting in, and though I've tried everything I know of to stop it, thrown up another layer of bricks, he's still chiseling away at them. The problem is, I don't know whether or not I want him to.

The flutter in my stomach as he comes down the hall, smiling at me before he grabs our coats tells me I do.

I do.

## cade

I wonder if she realizes I've taken the long way to get to her apartment. Even though it's April, that doesn't mean shit in Michigan, and it's cold out this time of night, the wind bitter against me. My coat and gloves don't even keep the chill out, but I don't care. Winter's body hugs mine, her breasts pressed flush to my back, her legs against the outside of my thighs. I slipped Winter's hands under my coat before we left so she'd stay warmer. And I won't deny the appeal of her touching me with a few less layers between us.

She's been driving me crazy all night. Her cheeks flush when she gets tipsy, and she chews on the inside of her cheek when she's thinking or nervous, the act making her lips even more prominent. And, Jesus Christ, those lips. I think about them wrapping around her fork, pressed to the rim of her wine glass, plump around her teeth as she offers me a shy smile . . . If I'm going to hold it together, refrain from pushing her further than she's ready, I need to stem those thoughts immediately.

As soon as I stop at the curb in front of her place, her hands are out of my jacket and she's off my bike, holding out my helmet before I can even kill the engine.

"Well, um, thanks. For dinner. And the ride. Good night." She spins and hustles down the sidewalk to the front door, yanking it open without a backward glance.

"Winter, wait." I go after her, following her into her building, down the stairs, and around the corner into the hallway. "Hey, what's up?"

She turns, her eyes wide as she watches me until I'm standing in front of her, just outside her door. "Nothing. You didn't need to come in."

"Why'd you take off like my bike was on fire?"

"I didn't . . ."

I cock my head to the side, brow furrowed. "Did my sister say something to freak you out?"

She shakes her head. "No." She sighs, closing her eyes. "Yes. I don't know. It wasn't anything I wasn't already aware of."

"What's that?"

Leaning against the door, she blows out a deep breath. "This was just dinner. It's not anything else. It *can't* be anything else."

"Why the hell not?"

"We're different, Cade. I'm not . . . I don't do this."

"This . . . what? Dating?"

"Yeah."

"Why?"

"I just don't. I never have. I'm not good at it, and I don't like it."

"If you've never done it, how do you know you're not good at it or you don't like it?"

"Don't attempt to spin this around in your favor. It's not going to work."

"Well, I'm sure as shit going to try." I reach out, even though every inch of her body is coiled, warning me not to touch her, and grab her hand. "I like you, Winter."

"You don't even know me."

"Yes I do. You're a web design major. You work five nights a week at The Brewery. You spend the rest of your time studying. You never go out, don't have many friends, and hide in your apartment when you're not at school or work. You love to be alone, but you're lonely. You're stubborn and strong and determined, and you don't like taking help from other people. How am I doing so far?"

Her eyebrows are drawn down, her face pulled into a scowl. "Don't be smug."

I bend my knees so we're eye level and tug on her hand until she meets my gaze. "I don't know what we could have. It might be nothing. But I'll be honest . . . I haven't felt like this in a long time, and that's enough for me to know I want to see where it goes. Can't we just see where it goes?"

With a deep sigh, she says, "I'm not right for you, Cade."

"How about you worry about if *I'm* right for *you*. Let me decide the other."

And then before she can stop me, before she can utter another word of opposition, I slide my hand up her arm, over her shoulder, until it's wrapped around her neck. With my other hand, I swipe a piece of hair back with my fingers, and then lean in, brushing my lips against hers. After only a moment, I pull back just enough for her to be able to tell me to stop. When nothing comes, I close the distance between us once again, taking her bottom lip in between mine. I brush my tongue against it, coaxing her mouth open, and she breathes this sexy little gasp as I slip inside. She tastes like cookies and wine, and I want to fucking devour her.

She grips my shirt with both hands, clutching me to her, and I stop holding back and press every inch of my body against hers, groaning as my cock presses fully against her. The moment a whimper comes from her, I know she feels it. And I can't muster up any embarrassment, because I *want* her to feel it. Even with all her brass balls and fuck-everything attitude, something tells me she needs reassurance, so I give it to her. In every stroke of my tongue against hers, every brush of my thumb along her jaw, I show her how much I want her.

When her chest is heaving, her lips parted and swollen and so fucking hot, I trail kisses down her neck, seeking out every inch of skin that's uncovered. Her head thumps back against the wall, one of her hands gone from gripping fistfuls of my shirt. Instead, she's holding my head to her, and I don't want to stop. I want to kiss and lick every inch of her, slip my hands under the material of her sweater, unbutton her jeans, and not stop until I feel her soft wetness against my fingertips.

But the knowledge that she'll regret it if I don't stop forces me to slow down.

I pull back, loosening my grip on her and putting an inch of space between us. I kiss the corner of her mouth, her cheek, and then her ear. Against it, I whisper, "Don't say no."

There's a beat of silence. Two. Three. And then she says the sweetest word I've ever heard.

"Okay."

# ELEVEN

*cade*

The mornings in my house are always chaotic. Tessa is trying to get herself plus Haley ready. Orders are given too loudly, followed by indignant squeals and the frustrated protestations of an almost-four-year-old. I usually use the time to catch up on homework, writing recipes for class or researching some new cooking method my instructor wants us to try that week.

This morning, however, silence greets me. Blissful, beautiful silence that means maybe, just maybe, I can avoid my sister's third degree for a few more hours. In reality, there'll be no escape. I know my sister better than anyone, and I have no doubt she'll corner me at some point, demanding to know more about Winter and what she means to me. Though the answer to that is probably pretty obvious to her. Considering I've never brought a girl home, and I've never, ever cooked for one. Not in such an intimate setting anyway. At the restaurant for class, obviously, and if I'm making something and Tessa has a friend over, sure.

But a dish I planned and executed with the sole purpose to try and impress someone I was interested in? Nope.

It's too personal, like putting my entire soul on a plate for the judgment of others.

I roll out of bed and know I'm going to be paying for sleeping in later. The day's barely started and I'm already behind on what I need to do, but I can't dredge up an ounce of remorse. I needed to sleep in later because I got to bed late. I got to bed late because I got home late. I got home late because I had Winter pressed against the wall—then the door and eventually her couch—until all I could think, hear, *breathe* was her. Her name, her scent, her sexy-as-hell, breathless gasps when I pressed against the length of her, nipped at that spot on her neck . . .

After taking a very necessary lengthy shower, I get dressed, then pad toward the kitchen. I have my bistro class today, and I usually like to have some time in the kitchen before everyone else gets there to get my head in the right place. There's nothing worse than being the one lagging behind, dragging everyone else down with you. And right now, my mind is racing with a million things, none of them food related.

When I round the corner in the kitchen, I stop short, seeing Tessa sitting at a barstool, laptop open in front of her as she sips a cup of coffee. When she looks up at me, it's with a predatory smile on her face.

"What're you doing home?" I shuffle over to pour my own cup of coffee.

"My first appointment canceled. It was a cut and color, so I've got loads of time. Thought I'd swing back here quick and see how my dearest brother was doing." Her smile grows, and I know there's absolutely no getting around this line of questioning.

But still, I try.

"I'm good. And I'm late. Gotta run." I attempt to sneak out, even willing to sacrifice my coffee and breakfast if need be, but she stops me, blocking my path out of the kitchen.

"Why are you running so late? You don't normally sleep in." Her head's tilted to the side and her eyes are bright, her smile nearly blinding.

"Jesus, Tess, just ask what you want to ask and get it over with." I sink back to the counter, resting my ass against it as I sip my coffee, eyebrows raised like I have nothing of interest to discuss.

"Oh, I have a lot of questions." I snort and roll my eyes, and she continues as if I've done neither. "But what I really want to know is . . . why now . . . why her?"

Hoping to be spared, I make a last-ditch effort to get the focus off me. "I could ask you the same thing. Updating your dating profile?" I tip my chin in the direction of her computer. "I don't know why you think you need to be signed up with one of those places."

She huffs. "Why are you being such a shit? Don't push this back on me. We've had this discussion, and I *told* you why. I'm tired of only meeting losers. I don't want to bring home guys who are only looking for a piece of ass when I have Haley to think about. See? That wasn't so hard. Now it's your turn. Why?"

I shrug. "Why not?"

"Please, Cade, I know it's not that simple. And you probably burst a couple blood vessels in your eye from pretending like she wasn't anything important. I think you're forgetting who you're talking to here. I'm not some friend you see a couple times a week in class or once a month at a bar when you actually peel yourself away from your self-appointed responsibilities long enough to go."

Forgetting what we were talking about in the first place, my

spine straightens. This is the main argument we have, and it
seems to be happening more frequently. She's just slammed me
full force on the defensive, and I don't try to soften my tone.
"Self-appointed?"

"Yes."

"Oh, like what? Bringing Haley to dance? Picking her up or
dropping her off at preschool? Making the three of us dinner?
Watching her when you go out with your love-dot-com losers?
Are those all my *self-appointed* duties?"

"I acknowledge what you do for us, and I appreciate it, Cade.
You know that. But I don't like seeing you sacrifice your own
happiness for the sake of us. At the expense of yourself."

"When have I ever said I was unhappy?"

"Well, you're certainly not the person you were five years ago."

"Oh, and you are? Fucking hell, Tess. It's not like we had any
major changes during that time or anything. So I'm not the guy
who screws around, getting into trouble over dumb, juvenile shit.
I had to grow up. Who else was going to be there to take care of
you and Haley?"

"Believe it or not, I'm actually quite capable. I can remember
to lock the doors at night, shut off the stove when I'm done using
it . . . I can even cook a few things so we won't starve."

Dropping my chin to my chest, I groan, scrubbing a hand over
my face. "Why are we even talking about this? I don't want to
fight with you, Tessa. Not this morning."

"I don't want to fight with you, either."

I lift my head to glare at her. "Then why the hell did you bring
it up?"

"Because I wanted to know if you like her."

"Of course I like her. I brought her here. That's seriously all
you wanted to know?"

She leans forward, elbow on the counter, chin in her hand. "Well, no, but I have a feeling you won't open up enough to tell me everything."

"Once again, you are correct." I turn, dumping the rest of my coffee down the drain before I grab my keys, wallet, and bag. "I'll see you tonight."

"You can take the car—I'll grab the bus."

"S'okay. It's supposed to warm up today. I'll be fine." I pass her, feeling her eyes boring into me, so I glance over. "What?"

She raises her eyebrows. "Not self-sacrificing at all, huh?"

Rolling my eyes, I pat her head and stride to the front door. "Take the car, Tess. It's no big deal. I'll see you tonight."

Before she can say anything, I'm out the door and on my bike, revving it to life. The air's cool, but the trip to school is only five minutes. It makes the most sense for me to do this, especially considering it's Tessa's night to get Haley from her after-school program. If she took the bus, she'd have to add on at least thirty minutes, if not more, to her commute. And then there's the fact that they'd be on the bus by themselves later at night. We live in a nice neighborhood, but sometimes that doesn't mean shit.

After all the loss we've suffered, the heartache and pain, I'd think Tessa would understand why I like to be around to make sure they're safe. Why is it so hard for her to understand I don't want to take chances with them?

I *can't* take chances with them.

*winter*

I wake up a different person. My futon isn't quite as uncomfortable as usual, my studio apartment not quite as small, my bathroom not quite as dingy. It's like he brought his light and painted it into every crevice, every crack in my life.

And it terrifies me.

Last night, my defenses were down, my walls weakened, and I agreed to something I normally wouldn't give a second thought to. But he wanted me, that much was obvious. Even after seeing the shithole I live in, even after watching me run away. He came after me, erasing all the doubt I had, as though the toxic thoughts never crept in in the first place.

They're there now, though. Whispers trying to tell me why this won't work, why it can't work. He's too different, too big and bold, too *good*. All I can hear are the harsh words from my mother, the soundtrack to my childhood, saying I don't deserve something so perfect. Saying it'll never work. It'll never last.

I keep to myself more than usual as I trudge through my classes on autopilot. I wave off an offer of being included in a study group during my free period, and instead find myself in the library once again. As I'm supposed to be going over my notes for a test tomorrow, my mind wanders and I wonder what would have happened if I'd left a little earlier or a little later that night Cade approached me here and followed me home . . . if he didn't see me slipping out. Would he have come back to The Brewery? Would he have sought me out as he planned to? Or would he have forgotten about me altogether?

All through my day, negative thoughts eat away at me until it's all I can think about—that it was a mistake. That I should've said no. That opening myself up to him will only bring me heartache. Opening myself to anyone will *always* bring me heartache.

By the time I walk through the door for work that night, my mood is shit. When Annette calls me over, her voice soft, her eyes softer, it's clear I'm not being as subtle as I hoped.

"Hey, sugar. How was your night off?"

I shrug, sliding over the drink order from table five. "Fine."

She avoids looking at me as she prepares a mojito, and I tap my fingers on the bar, counting down the minutes until close with equal parts dread and anticipation.

Will he be there waiting for me? Do I *want* him to be?

As she passes me the glasses, she says, "I thought maybe your guy would take you out somewhere."

I pause in placing the drinks on my tray, my eyes snapping up to hers. "My guy?"

"Yeah, the same one who's been waiting for you nearly every night."

I try to swallow but my throat's too thick, my voice weak when I answer her. "He's not mine."

She tips her head to the side, eyeing me seriously. "Not because he doesn't want to be."

I shake my head and reach to grab my tray full of drinks. Before I can turn away, her hand is on my wrist, stopping me. Glancing up, I look into her imploring eyes.

"You see a lot of people while working this kind of job. A lot of assholes walk through those doors. Guys who only want a piece of the young girls we've got working here, who only want to see some skin, touch, and push their boundaries until they get you all ruffled. Do you know how long I've worked here?"

I shake my head.

"Fifteen years. After that long, you learn pretty damn well how to get a read on people."

She doesn't say anything else, just refills drinks for a couple people sitting at the bar.

When she makes her way back toward me, I ask, "And all that means . . . what? Are you trying to say Cade's one of the assholes?"

"Oh, honey." She smiles softly at me and pats me on the arm. "You already know the answer to that one. You're just a little scared to admit it."

## cade

When she walks out of the pub, her eyes automatically cut to me, like she hopes I'm there, but the surprise plainly shown in her expression proves she doesn't expect me. She shuffles toward me, her eyes wary, and I wonder what could've happened today to make the boneless, blissful girl I left at her apartment last night this stiff, buttoned-up, nervous one in front of me now.

"Hi." Her voice is low, her eyes downcast.

I reach out, tug at her arm, and pull her in between my wide-set legs as I lean back against the brick wall. "Hey." I slip my fingers around the nape of her neck under her hair, coax her chin up with my thumb, ready to make her tell me what could've changed so much in such a short period of time. And then a startling thought hits me: What if this expression doesn't have anything at all to do with me, and instead has something to do with the shithead patrons who frequent this place? White-hot rage fills me, and I have to make a conscious effort not to tighten my grip on her in my anger toward something completely out of her control. "Did you . . . did something happen tonight?"

She looks at me, her brow furrowed, and I jerk my head to indicate the pub. "In there. Did someone touch you again?" I work to make the words come out soft so she doesn't know I'm edgy, ready to beat the shit out of whoever laid a hand on her.

"Oh, no. They don't touch me, Cade. You don't have to worry about that."

Except I know they do—I saw it with my own two eyes, and replaying it still makes me feel like I want to crawl out of my fucking skin.

She doesn't elaborate, but I can see the honesty on her face, and I'm mollified only slightly to know it wasn't anything that happened on her job. "So it is about me, then."

"What's about you?"

I reach up with my other hand, smoothing my thumb against the creases on her forehead, the pinch of skin between her eyes, trying to soothe away her worries. "This. You didn't think I'd come, did you?" Her silence and the aversion of her eyes prove my point. "Doubting me so soon? I figured I'd have a couple months, at least."

"*Months?*" Her eyes are wide when she snaps them to me. "I thought we were taking this one date at a time. That's what you said last night." Her voice is accusatory, and I can't help but smile. There's my spitfire. Not the unsure girl I saw a moment before. I like her fiery and feisty. I know how to react to that.

I slouch down the wall a little more, forcing her closer between my legs. With one hand against the small of her back, I bring her forward until she has her hands on my chest and the rest of her pressed as close as she can get. "Well, yeah, one date at a time that will hopefully lead to months of many, many dates. And besides, you agreed to that one date at a time thing in the hall-way . . . before."

"Before what?"

I stare at her, my eyes dropping to take in her full lips. Thoughts of what those lips did last night . . . of what they *could* do if given the opportunity, assault me. Not able to resist any-more, I lean forward and press my mouth to hers. With her top lip between both of mine, I swipe my tongue softly against her but pull away before I get too worked up. If I don't, I'm afraid I'll have her spun around, sandwiched between me and the rough brick, pushing her boundaries more than she's ready for. Lips still brushing against hers, I say, "Before I had you against the wall and then the door and then underneath me on the couch."

She shivers, her eyelids drooping, and I don't wait another second before I have her lips between mine, my tongue in her mouth. Moaning, she presses closer, the hands at my chest gripping fistfuls of my shirt. I can't get enough of her, this complicated girl who fell into my life. I want to know everything about her. Her quirks and her fears and her hopes and dreams, the tiny things that make her *her*. I want to know what she thinks about before she falls asleep at night and what she thinks about first thing in the morning. I want to know what she does on a Wednesday night when she doesn't have class or work. I want to know what her favorite song is, what movie she could watch a hundred times and never get sick of. I want to know what her skin feels like under my fingers . . . under my tongue. I want to know the sounds she'll make when I'm inside her.

As she melts into me, going boneless once again, I just hope whatever whispered voice telling her this won't work is quiet long enough for me to prove to her it will.

I kiss her twice more, holding her face between my hands as I pull back. Her eyes are heavy, her lips swollen, and *fuck*, I want to do unspeakable things to this girl. She drives me fucking crazy.

"About that date," I say, my voice coarse.

Her eyes focus sharply on me, and she reaches up to grip my forearm. "What date?"

"The one of many you promised me."

"I said one at a time, not one of many."

I shrug, unconcerned. "Logistics. When's your next night off?"

"Sunday."

The weekends are usually when I'm able to catch up, not having bistro class or to serve in the restaurant, but I can still make it work. I'll just have to juggle things around in the days leading up to it. And after the coaxing I had to do to get her to agree, I'm sure as hell not going to say no now. "Perfect. I'll pick you up at seven."

"Where are we going?"

Gripping her hips, I push her back slightly so I can stand upright, then lead her to the car I drove instead of my bike. I open the door for her, and once she's settled in her seat, I lean down and say, "You'll find out on Sunday."

# TWELVE

*winter*

I've never been this nervous in my life. My first day on the job at The Brewery, complete with my lack of uniform to hide behind, has nothing on me waiting for Cade to arrive for our date. And while, sure, he cooked me dinner and probably considered it a date, it didn't feel official or real.

*This* feels real.

I wipe my sweaty palms on my jeans again, wearing a three-foot path on the floor of the only open space in my apartment. I already spent longer than I care to admit going through my clothes and deciding what to wear—not that I have a bursting closet to choose from. In the end, I settled on jeans and a soft sweater, figuring I couldn't go wrong with either.

If I can't work up the nerve to actually go through with this, it won't matter what I'm wearing. Staring at my phone, I contemplate for the fifth time calling him and canceling. Now that I actually have his number, it's taunting me, and the little voice in my head is begging me to use it. The same voice that's telling me this is a bad idea, that nothing good can ever come from it.

Before I can hit send on my phone, there's a knock at the door, startling me. With wide, panicked eyes, I glance over, knowing without looking exactly who's on the other side. He's ten minutes early, and I wonder if a part of him worried about me backing out. I'm frozen, my feet stuck to the floor, and I can't make myself move.

He knocks again, harder this time, and immediately after, my phone rings in my hand. I glance down at it, seeing Cade's name flashing across the screen. From the other side of the door, he says, "I can hear the phone ringing, Winter. Just pick it up."

Chewing the inside of my cheek, I press the talk button and hold the phone to my ear.

"Hey," he says, like this is perfectly normal first-date behavior. "A little nervous?"

I blow out a harsh breath. "Yeah. Am I that transparent?"

He chuckles softly, and it's like a caress in my ear. "On most things, no. But on this? Yeah. You worried I'm going to take you to, like, a deserted warehouse or something?"

"Well, I wasn't until *now*."

"Open the door, Winter." His words are soft and soothing, just the right amount of force behind them to make me comply. And the way my name rolls off his tongue . . . I love how he says it. How he makes the one thing I've always hated, the one thing *she* gave me that I could never get rid of, sound beautiful. It's like he caresses it every time it leaves his lips, and I want to listen to it on repeat.

Somehow, I find myself in front of the door, the knob turning under my hand until he's standing in front of me, phone up to his ear. His mouth is turned up at the corner, his eyes doing a quick sweep down my body, and I can't help but return the favor. He's dressed casually like I am, jeans and an untucked button-up shirt under his opened coat.

"Think we can put away the phones now?" His voice echoes in my ear as I hear him say it in front of me, and I nod. He slips his phone in his back pocket, then steps through the threshold. "You need to grab your purse? And you should probably get a jacket."

"Right," I say, snapping myself out of my daze as I dart around and grab both, my stomach a chaos of nerves. God, I feel like I'm fifteen.

When I have everything, I meet him back at the door. "Do I need gloves for the ride?"

"Nope, got the car. Tessa and Haley are already home for the night." He smiles and pulls the door shut behind me, double-checking to make sure it's locked.

As I start walking down the hall, he grabs my wrist before I can get too far, tugging me to a stop and pulling me around to face him. He doesn't stop until I'm directly in front of him, the tips of our shoes nearly touching.

"Hey." He brushes an errant strand of hair away from my face with his thumb, tracing along the curve of my jaw until he tugs at the corner of my mouth. The inside of my cheek is raw from biting it, my nerves getting the better of me all day. Like he read my mind, he says, "You don't need to be nervous. Technically this is our second date, so you're a pro at this whole dating thing."

I blow out a breathless laugh, rolling my eyes. "Yeah, feels like it."

"I wouldn't be much of a date if I didn't take your mind off it." Even as he's saying the words, he's moving, pressing his back against the wall as he pulls me between his legs. His hands are on me, one cradling my head as the other settles on my hip, holding me to him.

"This is all for me, then, huh?" I ask when I'm close enough to see the flecks of gold mixing with green in his hazel eyes.

"Definitely. I don't even want to kiss you, really. Do you see the sacrifices I'm making just for your comfort?" He speaks the last words against my lips, and then he's kissing me, his mouth barely a whisper against mine, but I melt into him all the same. His hands tighten on me, a soft groan rumbling from his throat as his tongue sweeps against my bottom lip. My hands settle against his chest, the crisp cotton of his shirt clenched between my fists as I feel the nerves that were holding me captive all day fade away.

When we're both breathless, he pulls back, hunger in his eyes. "We need to go if I plan on showing you anything other than the hallway of your building."

At this point, I'm not sure that's such a bad thing, but I still nod and follow him out to the car. When he's settled in the seat next to me, I try to get him to tell me where we're going again, but he won't divulge.

"You're going to see for yourself in, like, five minutes."

"Exactly, so why can't you just tell me?"

"Well, at first, because I wanted it to be a surprise. But now it's kind of fun to taunt you."

"Jerk." I laugh, looking out the window. Nothing and everything looks familiar, this neighborhood like a hundred others in the city. He could be taking me to a million different places, and when he pulls up in front of a hole-in-the-wall restaurant I've never been to, it catches me off guard. All day I wondered where he was planning to take me, and I was anticipating something big, over the top, considering the dinner he made for me last week. That was where part of my nerves came in.

He comes over to my side of the car and opens the door for me, offering me a hand to help me out. "What's that surprised look for?"

I snap my eyes to his, hating that my thoughts are displayed so plainly for him to see. "I was just expecting something . . . different."

"Well," he says as he opens the door to the restaurant for me, "you said you'd never been on a date before. So tonight, it's cheesy first-date activities. Dinner and a movie, followed by ice cream."

Stopping just inside the door, I stare at him, struck by the kindness he's showing me. I realize now I'm not just a chase for him. He listened to every pointless and inconsequential word I spoke to him, cataloged it all away as he got to know me in ten- and fifteen-minute increments.

He mistakes my silence for disapproval. "Don't tell me you hate movies. Or you're allergic to ice cream."

Shaking my head, I squeeze his hand. "No, neither. It sounds good."

Perfect, I amend in my head as the waitress leads us to a table. It sounds perfect.

*cade*

"It's probably too cold for ice cream, but there aren't a lot of choices for dessert this late."

She shakes her head, following me into the small ice cream shoppe. "It's never too cold for ice cream. I can't remember the last time I had some."

"Really? Tessa lives on the shit, I swear. If I go to the store and don't get a pint of her favorite, it's like World War Three at our house. She's *ruthless*."

After selecting our flavors, we settle into a corner table in the back, away from the few people inside. Around a bite of ice cream, she asks, "Have you and your sister always been close?"

I shrug, scooping a spoonful of chocolate. "Sort of. I mean, she was always that pain-in-the-ass younger sister. Even after my dad died, it was like that. But then when my mom got sick, things just . . . changed. The shit we used to fight about seemed pretty fucking pointless, you know?"

She nods, looking down at the table.

"What about you? Any brothers or sisters?"

"Ah, no. Only child."

"I used to wish for that when I was younger. When Tessa did something to piss me off, I'd tell her I was going to sell her to the circus and use the money to redo her room into an arcade." I laugh, remembering her rage. "That was probably my favorite thing to torment her with. But yeah, I used to wish it was just me."

"Gets lonely," she mumbles around her last bite of ice cream. Before I can ask her any more about her family, she turns and stands up. "Gonna throw this away and use the bathroom."

I nod as she walks away, watching her go. Our conversation wasn't stilted at all the whole night, but any time I asked a question too personal, she deflected, bringing it back to me or avoiding it altogether. It feels like I know a lot about Winter *now*, but I don't know anything about what made her into the person she is. I don't know anything about her time before The Brewery or school.

And I can't shake the feeling she doesn't want me to.

She walks back after I've already tossed my garbage, and she smiles tightly when she gets to the table.

"Ready?" I ask.

Nodding, she allows me to grab her hand as I lead her out and to the car. When she's settled inside, I walk around to my side and start the car, pulling into traffic. The ride is short, and Winter is quiet the whole time, staring out the window. Once we're parked in front of her building, I shut off the car and turn to her. "So how was your first date? I do okay?"

She twists to look at me and smiles, and this time it's genuine. "It was nice. Thank you for this."

"Don't thank me yet. You've got one more first date milestone."

"Oh, really?"

"Mhmm," I murmur as I lean across the center console. She meets me halfway, her lips pressed softly against mine. And even though I've kissed her harder, longer, I keep this soft and sweet, exactly what she'd normally experience on a first date, had she ever had one.

When I pull back, she keeps her eyes closed, her lips parted, and it takes every ounce of restraint not to throw my chivalry out the fucking window and kiss her like I want to, pull her into my lap or push her against the door and feel her tongue slide against mine, feel her hands under my shirt or mine under hers. Feel everything until there's nothing separating us but air and I'm between her thighs, pressing into her.

And then she opens her eyes, stares right at me, and I'm done. I will do anything . . . let her set the pace completely, just to see that look in her eyes when she's with me.

I walk her inside, going past the broken lock on the front door, the busted intercom system, and I hate that she lives in such a shithole. Once her door is open and she's braced on the door frame, leaning to the side, I kiss her again, as softly as I did in the car, offer a quiet good-bye, and walk backward away from her.

"I'll see you tomorrow night."

She shakes her head, but there's a ghost of a smile on her lips, and she doesn't voice the rebuttal I know is perched on the tip of her tongue, the one telling me she doesn't need a ride home from work. Probably because she knows I won't listen.

In the short weeks we've known each other, she's already getting to know small details about me, uncovering bits of me here and there, though I've never pretended to be a closed book. I'll tell her anything she wants to know. With her, it's completely different. If I think I'm getting to know her better, I'm just fooling myself. Because the more I uncover about her, the more I want to discover. But I don't want to dig out the answers, chisel away until she crumbles. I want her to trust me enough to tell me on her own.

# THIRTEEN

*winter*

It's getting warmer now, my walk across campus as I hustle to my next class not as chilly as it was even a week ago. I wonder what it will be like to ride on the back of Cade's motorcycle when I don't have the ever-present chill nipping at my exposed skin. And a part of me—a part I've tried to keep locked up tight, but has slipped out anyway—can't wait to find out.

I dodge groups of students scattered around on my way into the building. This is, by far, my most exhausting day of the week. With a full schedule of classes until three thirty, then work from four until midnight, I have no break. When I squeeze in time for studying and homework, I'm a walking zombie by Wednesday.

As if all that wasn't enough, now there's a maybe . . . What? Boyfriend? Can I even call him that? A week ago, I would've said hell no. A fresh wave of hives would've popped up all over my skin at the mere idea, but now . . . Now it doesn't send me running in a panicked frenzy like it might have only a few days ago.

Rather than troublesome, his presence in my life is comforting. And after twenty-two years of nothing and no one, of doing it all on my own, it feels damn good to be comforted . . . wanted.

My phone buzzes in my pocket and I wait until I'm inside the building before I pull it out of my jeans pocket, fighting the smile that wants to spread across my lips when I see Cade's name on the screen.

*When's your next break? Can I see you?*

A week or two ago, I might've tried to find excuses not to go out, not to interact, but now I find myself wishing I actually had a break in the day, if only to sneak off for five minutes just to say hi.

Frowning, I type out my reply.

*Class all day. No time to meet.*

I put my phone back in my pocket and climb the steps to the third floor, making my way down the hallway and into the classroom. Several people are inside already, scattered all over the room, a couple offering me waves, which I return. When I'm seated at my desk, I check my phone again to see if he replied.

*Tonight?*

I glance at the clock, seeing I still have a couple minutes before class starts and type out a response.

*Work*

*Be there at 12:30*

*It's ok. Bus.*

I know my reply will fall on deaf ears, but the prideful part of me still feels like I need to say it, just to prove—to myself more than anything—that I don't *need* him. I stare at my phone, waiting a minute for a reply. Before anything comes through, my professor arrives and gets started with class. My phone is forgotten in my bag, my books and notes spread out in front of me, but

I can't focus on anything the man at the front of the classroom is droning on about.

Instead, my mind is across campus in the kitchens of the culinary school with a boy who consumes my thoughts. I figured the first few nights he picked me up after work following our first true date were a fluke. But he's continued to show up, and now I'm certain he's planning to be there every night when I get off. I try to dredge up the indignation I should feel at him thinking he can just push his way into my life and do whatever the hell he wants.

But it's nowhere to be found.

Where my normally impenetrable ice-cold heart sits, there's a warmth blooming at the fact that this boy is interested. In *me*, just as I am. Enough to come see me every night, to take time out of whatever he has to do to greet me after work, kiss me breathless, and drive me home to make sure I get there safely.

His attention makes me nervous. Nervous and unsure and . . . weightless. Feeling this way is addictive. *He's* addictive. Though the intelligent part of me knows this is bad, very, very bad—especially with only forty-eight days left—the overwhelming majority of me is basking in the feeling of finally being wanted.

*cade*

I leave the house late, having fallen asleep face-first on top of the recipe cards I was working on that were strewn out across the table. The late nights are catching up to me, but our conflicting schedules don't allow for much time otherwise. Knowing there generally aren't any cops between my house and the pub, I speed the whole way, trying to get there before Winter is out and headed to the bus stop. I never responded to her earlier text when she told me I didn't need to pick her up. I figured the best thing was to just show up, so she couldn't tell me not to come. The last thing I want is for her to think I bailed. She's skittish enough, and I don't want to do anything to exacerbate that.

I pull into the parking lot just as the back door bangs open. Winter walks out with Annette and another girl I've seen a few times. I watch as they step into the parking lot, talking as they go. Before they've even taken three steps, a guy comes to the doorway, the lights from the bar illuminating him from behind. In the darkness, I can't make out his face. I narrow my eyes as I watch him watching the three women walk toward their cars, or in the case of Winter, toward nothing or no one. I'd like to think he's doing it to look out for them, make sure they get to their cars safely, but in all the times I've been back here to pick up Winter, I've never once seen him, and something uneasy churns in my gut.

Winter glances to the spot I usually wait at, and I can see the moment she realizes I'm not there, her face falling. Before she can turn to go, I step out of my car. As she turns back around to head to the bus stop, she sees me and freezes mid-step. After only a moment's hesitation, she changes her trajectory and walks toward me. I keep my eyes on her until she's in front of me, stopping on the other side of my opened door. Glancing over her shoulder, I see the guy still in the doorway and my apprehension increases.

"I told you that you didn't need to come."

I shrug, tilting my head toward the other side of the car, gesturing her that way. "You know me well enough by now to know I don't listen. Go get in. I'll give you a ride."

She smiles, just barely, and shakes her head, but makes her

way over. With a quick yank, she pulls open the car door and slides in, shutting the door just as I duck into my seat.

"You know, I did this by myself for more than a year before you came along." Her voice is teasing, but I hear an edge of discomfort skirting along the fringe.

"I know. And I hate the thought of it." I lean in, not giving her a chance to respond, and I capture her mouth in a kiss. Even as her tongue brushes against my lips, I feel eyes on us, and I pull back to glance out the windshield toward the restaurant.

"Who is that?" I ask with a tip of my head.

She turns to look, squinting into the darkness. "Randy, I think."

"Your boss?" She hums in confirmation, and I continue, "Does he always make sure you guys get to your cars okay?"

Snorting a laugh, she eases back into her seat and buckles her seat belt. "No, never. I don't know what his deal is tonight."

While she doesn't seem worried about it, I can't shake the uneasy feeling I get as he continues to stare at us. Wanting to get her home and away from him as quickly as possible, I shift into gear and drive us toward her apartment.

After we've driven a couple blocks in silence, she says, "So this is your plan, then?"

I glance at her before looking out the windshield again. "What?"

"Picking me up every night after work . . ."

"Why not?"

She doesn't say anything for a few moments, and when I look over at her, she's already staring at me. "You can't be serious."

"Again, why not?"

"Cade . . ." She sighs my name, and I can tell she's frustrated, but my mind goes places it definitely shouldn't go. Like what else

I could do to make her say my name like that. "Am I just, like, a project or something?"

Brow furrowed, I pull up in front of her building, parking before I look over at her. "What do you mean, a project?"

"You know, help the girl who's all by herself and can barely afford groceries, let alone a car?"

I'm waiting for a trace of sarcasm to pop up, a hint of a smile to play at her lips, but she shows none of that. Her eyes are serious, the corner of her mouth dipping in slightly. She's biting the inside of her cheek again, her one dead giveaway for her nerves or uncertainty.

Sighing, I shut off the car, then turn to face her. "Winter . . . anyone who thinks of you as some helpless girl is obviously an idiot who hasn't spent more than five minutes with you. I do this because I *want* to. Because I like you. Because even though this"—I gesture between us with my hand—"is still new, the thought of anything happening to you drives me fucking crazy."

I reach out, brushing the hair back from her face, tracing my thumb down her cheek to her jaw. "Why is it so hard for you to let me be there for you?" I don't even realize how badly I want her answer until I ask the question. I want her to open up to me, even just a little.

She doesn't say anything as she looks at me, and not for the first time, I wonder who she lets in. Who looks out for her—if anyone does. She lives in a shitty apartment in a shitty part of town, busts her ass to get good grades, and works every minute she can just to afford food. Everything about her life tells me she's alone. When I told her my parents passed away, she didn't say anything. Didn't commiserate with me or share her own experience. If they aren't dead, where they hell are they?

Her quiet voice cuts through my thoughts. "It just is. I'm not used to all this."

"Well, you better get used to it. I'm not going anywhere unless you kick my ass out."

The uncertainty in her eyes kills me, so I lean in, capturing her mouth with mine, sweeping my tongue across the seam of her lips until she opens to me. I move to get closer to her, but we're in an awkward position with the center console between us. Without breaking the kiss, I reach down and grasp her hips, tugging her up and over the console until she's sprawled across my lap, her knees on either side of me. A soft moan comes from her when she settles flush against me, against where I'm hard and aching for her.

I slide my hands up the outside of her thighs and over the curve of her hips until I slip under the material of her shirt, finding miles of smooth skin underneath. Going slow, I brush against her stomach, stopping for a minute when I get to the band of her bra. When she doesn't tell me to stop, I continue, bringing my hand up to cup her through the lace covering her breasts. She gasps when I run my thumb over the hard peak waiting for me, then moans when I lift her shirt up just far enough to expose the front of her to me. I dip my head, taking a nipple in my mouth through her bra. With my other hand at the small of her back, I press her as close to me as I can get. I want to feel all of her—every fucking inch of her skin against mine, against my lips and my tongue. But not here. Not in a car in the middle of the street.

I slow my kisses, trailing them over the tops of her breasts, pulling down her shirt and tilting her face to mine as I press my lips to hers softly. "I need to leave."

She shakes her head, her mouth brushing against mine as she does so. "No, not yet."

"Yes, now. If I don't—" I groan as she shifts in my lap, my

hands squeezing her hips to still her. Closing my eyes, I swallow and start again, "If I don't, this is going to go further than either of us expected."

She breathes deep, her eyes fluttering closed. "Right now, I'm not sure I care." And, *Jesus Christ*, the raspy timbre of her voice nearly sets me off again, and I have to remove my hands from her completely to get a fucking grip.

My voice is too low, too rough when I respond, and I'm too far gone to censor my words. "As much as I'd like that, when I take you for the first time, it's not going to be in a goddamn car like we're a couple of sixteen-year-olds sneaking around."

She leans into me, her hands resting against my chest, and if she shifts her hips once more, I'm going to have a huge problem on my hands. Or in my pants, at least. "Oh, really? Where will it be?"

"My bed, your bed, the shower, the living room floor . . ." I trail off, my head back against the seat as I peer at her through half-lowered eyelids.

"Thought about this, have you?"

"Once or twice."

She traces unknown designs on my chest through my T-shirt as I take a moment to just stare at her. Her dark hair is a wild mess, thanks to my restless fingers. Her already pouty lips are red and full from my hungry mouth, her cheeks flushed, eyes bright.

I remember the first night I saw her in the pub. It seems like forever ago I thought her eyes were dead, only coming to life with a fire in them at her anger. But now . . .

Now they're filled with a brightness I've never seen before. And if I thought seeing the fire in her eyes from that first night was amazing, it has absolutely nothing on seeing the light in them now.

I always want to put that light in her eyes.

# FOURTEEN

*winter*

I'm lost in miles of code, my focus completely on the laptop in front of me. Students shuffle around me in the library, but with my earbuds in, I pay them no attention. My classes are getting more demanding, and I'm not sure if that's a result of this being the last quarter of my final year and the mounting pressure, or of the fact that I've been spending more and more time with Cade and less and less time on homework.

I've got an hour until I have to be at work, and I'm hoping to get caught up enough that I don't need to crack open my computer at 1 a.m. when I get home. My nights have become later and later—or earlier and earlier, depending on how you look at it—and it's showing in my gradually declining grades for my early classes.

I'm so lost in my work, I don't notice the person in front of me until a hand comes into my line of sight, knuckles rapping on the table. I jump, yanking the headphones out of my ears as I look up. I recognize the guy as Cade's friend from that first night at the pub. The one I gave the money to, along with a handful of colorful words.

"Hey, Winter, right?"

"Yeah, hi."

"I'm Jason. I figured I should come over and introduce myself since the only time we really met was when you were yelling at me to tell my best friend to fuck off." He grins, pulling out the chair across from me without asking, and plops into it, his backpack dropped on the floor by his feet.

I cringe, offering him an apologetic smile. "Sorry about that."

He shrugs, leaning back in his chair as he stretches his long legs out underneath the table, his arms crossed against his chest. "Not the first time someone's wanted to tell Cade off. Not even the first time someone's done it through me. He can be a little . . . overbearing."

I think back to the first night we met when he swooped in without me asking for help, how he's taken it upon himself to give me rides whether I want them or not, how he coaxed me into agreeing to try this whole dating thing. "That's putting it lightly."

His mouth lifts on one side as he studies me. "Something tells me you can handle him."

I return his look, settling back in my chair. "You're probably right. Holding my own's never been a problem."

His smile grows until it takes over his whole face. "I can see that."

Now that I'm not mad enough to spit nails, I take a minute to look him over. His brown hair is perfectly mussed—the kind of style that looks like he just rolled out of bed, but in actuality probably took him twenty minutes to perfect. His eyes are dark, lashes darker, and his smile is disarming, somehow both boyish and naughty. His body language is open and friendly. Charisma practically pours off him.

"Sorry if I made things difficult between you and the girl you were with that day."

His eyebrows lift, a smirk settling on his lips. "You definitely didn't. In fact, you might have helped."

I roll my eyes, shaking my head, but I can't stop the smile from tugging at the sides of my mouth. "Figures."

"I'll still take the numbers of any of your pretty single friends, though."

A laugh slips out of me before I can contain it as I stare at him in disbelief. When he doesn't crack a smile, I say, "You can't be serious."

"Hell yeah I am."

"Isn't this something you should be asking Cade for?"

"Please, that jackass hasn't been my wingman in years. I'm just out here, floundering all by myself."

"I somehow doubt that."

"Okay, you're right. But I am all by myself because he's absolutely useless. Now more than ever because he's so wrapped up in you, he doesn't even pay attention to other girls anymore."

My stomach flips and squeezes, and I don't know what to do with all these conflicting emotions constantly battling inside me.

Jason continues rambling, "So really, the least you can do for taking all his attention is toss me a bone."

"Has anyone ever told you you're a little bit of a pig?"

"A time or two, Winter. A time or two." He stands, his grin showing I didn't offend him in the least. "I'll let you get back to"— he leans forward, looking at my screen before he makes a face—"advanced scripting. Had that last semester. I feel your pain."

"Yeah, thanks."

"I'm sure I'll see you around. Keep him on his toes." He winks, grabs his bag from the floor, and saunters off. As he goes, I notice a handful of girls watching him, their expressions ranging from mildly interested to looks so thinly veiled in their want, I wouldn't be surprised if they left a trail of clothes through the library just for a chance with him. No wonder he's so full of himself.

Full of himself and bluntly honest, if my instincts aren't leading me astray. Our conversation plays on a loop in my mind until I realize I'm going to be late if I don't get moving. I shove everything in my bag as I think about what he said . . . how Cade's completely preoccupied with me. I've never had someone's undivided attention like he's given me. I'm worried I'm getting wrapped up in it, consumed by it, and while the attention often makes this warmth spread through my body, it's also absolutely, completely terrifying.

*cade*

"Cade, where are my pesto fries?" the head chef for this week yells from his workstation, irritation ringing loud and clear in the tone of his voice.

"I've got them. Give me two minutes."

"I don't have two goddamn minutes! Your ass is dragging tonight, and you're bringing everyone else down with you. Get your shit together!"

I curse under my breath, wiping the sweat from my brow with the back of my sleeve. I focus on plating and garnishing the fries, trying to block out the murmurs of frustration from my classmates

and fellow workers at the bistro. Even though this is technically a class and not a job, regardless of the fact that people pay
to eat our food in the restaurant, I've always treated it as though
I'm getting paid to be here in the kitchen. Every week, every
rotation, I act as though this is my job, that it's my career. Because
it will be. And when it is, the executive chef isn't going to wait
around for me to get my head in the game. I'll get fired if I can't
pull my own weight.

That propels me faster, and I get the plates out in record time.
I force thoughts of Winter to the back of my mind, knowing that's
what's slowing me down. Since the first night I saw her over a
month ago, I've been slipping incrementally, and in the last week,
I've stopped slipping and instead have fallen straight over a fucking cliff. I need to find a way to compartmentalize everything or
I'm going to fail this class. And it would be more than failing a
class. It could fuck up my entire career if I can't get a recommendation from this.

The smart thing to do would be to call this thing with Winter
off. To end it now before we get too involved, too deep. The only
problem is I'm scared of how deep I already am. She takes up
nearly every waking thought. She's seeped into my life, her presence bleeding into everything I do, showing up everywhere I go.

I should be focusing on making an outstanding portfolio to
show prospective employers, perfecting my techniques, learning
everything I can from my mentor. I need to be garnering contacts
in the industry, polishing my attributes, working on my hin-
drances. Graduation is in four weeks, and I planned to have a
dozen possible prospects already lined up. As of now, I have none.

And while I know what I *should* do, I just can't bring myself
to. Forget the fact that she's wormed her way so far under my
skin I can't get her out . . . I can't do it to her. Even though she's

told me nearly nothing about her childhood, it's obvious she's been left on her own. In what capacity, I have no idea. But it doesn't matter. Whether she's been abandoned completely or just financially, I can't leave her, too. Not after getting to know her. Not after getting her to let me in, little by little. I can't . . . not when there's so much more of her I want to learn.

# FIFTEEN

*winter*

I can't quite get used to this . . . whatever this is that Cade and I have. Despite my protests, Cade's been by work every night I have a shift to pick me up. And I'm still conflicted. I want him there—with his wide smile and his warm arms and his soft lips and his *everything*—but a part of me is scared to get too invested, too lost in him. Everything I've ever known my whole life has warned me against exactly that. But the feeling I get when I'm with him . . . I've never been freer. It's ironic, really, that it's only present when I'm tied to someone else.

I assumed the feeling would be immediate when I moved out here, getting away from California and all the ghosts of my past. I thought once I got as far away as I could from the years of my childhood, I would finally, *finally* be free of everything. The years of heartache and abandonment. The fucking baggage I've had my whole life. That they would just . . . float away. Disappear.

But they didn't.

It was the same . . . everything was the same, except I was really, truly on my own. This weight was still on my chest, this ache in my heart that had me wondering if this was it. If this was all there was to life.

Amazing that I finally get a glimpse of that freedom I've been searching for—*craving*—my whole life when I open up to someone else.

With graduation looming, classes are demanding more of our time, especially since we're both seniors. Our final projects are time consuming and can't be neglected or pushed aside. But even still, Cade's found a way to pick me up every night after work. I haven't asked him what has changed to allow him the free time. I'm a little scared to hear the answer. I'm not sure I could handle it if he was pushing his other responsibilities to the back and moving me first and foremost. Or if his schoolwork was suffering for it. For *me*. After watching him cook, it's obvious that's his life's calling, and he'll be incredible at it. I don't want to get in the way of that.

At the same time, there's a small part of me that likes it, the dark shadows that thrive on knowing I'm so important to him after such a short period of time. Nearly my entire life, people only had me around so they could use me in some way or another. For sympathy from my biological mother's friends, for a paycheck from the state for foster families, for a warm body from men who found me attractive and didn't want to work too hard for anything more than sex . . .

But Cade . . . Cade wants me for *me*. For the first time in my life, I feel good enough, as is. No improvements needed—he takes me as I am without an ulterior motive.

The timer in my kitchen goes off and tugs me out of my thoughts. I pull the tiny pizza from the oven and cut it into fourths before I make my way over to my futon, munching as I go. My laptop is open in front of me, Dreamweaver up on my computer as I work on my final project. I focus on my screen, creating pieces of what I envision for my final site, and startle when I hear a knock at the door. Brow furrowed, I glance at the clock, seeing it's a little after eight.

Haley had a spring program of some sort tonight for preschool, so I wasn't expecting to see Cade at all. I can't deny the flurry of butterfly wings that erupt in my stomach at the sight of him standing on the other side of my door, arms raised above him, hands resting on the doorjamb. He leans forward, kissing me, before he strolls inside and shuts the door behind him.

"Smells like shitty pizza in here."

I laugh, rolling my eyes. "That's because I made shitty pizza."

"I wish you'd have told me. I would've brought over some of what I made tonight." He walks farther into my apartment, and I take a minute to appreciate the way his dark gray cotton shirt hugs every inch of his upper body, the way his jeans are slung low on his hips, the sight of his muscular legs encased in soft, faded denim.

I swallow down the bubble of arousal that always seems to be present when he's around. "Which was?"

"Lemon shrimp scampi."

Looking over at the remaining pieces of pizza on my plate, the pale red sauce barely covered by scraps of cheese, I sigh. "Next time."

With a nod, he leans in for another kiss. "Thank God you don't taste like it. I'd hate to stop doing this."

I grab a piece of the pizza and bring it to my lips, smearing the bland tomato sauce around my mouth, raising my eyebrows in challenge as I drop the crust on my plate.

He narrows his eyes, debating for a moment before he finally relents. Leaning forward, he cups my face in his hands as he traces the outline of my lips with his tongue, then captures first one, then the other between his, sucking lightly. "Mmm . . . pizza sauce tastes good on you."

I smile, placing a hand on his chest to create some space between us. He's so easy to get consumed by. Sometimes I feel like I lose myself when we're together. "What're you doing here?"

He shrugs, walking over to the futon and pulling me along behind him. "The program didn't go as long as they thought, so I got all the work done I needed to."

I raise my eyebrows and regard him skeptically. "I doubt that."

"Okay, so I got *most* of the work done I needed to." He pulls me down onto his lap, my legs straddling his, knees bent as I hover over him. With widespread hands, he palms my outer thighs, the heat coming from him seeping through the thin cotton of my pajama pants. "I wanted to see you. And with school kicking our asses, I knew we wouldn't get another real date for a while."

"Oh, you think you're gonna get more real dates out of me, huh?"

"I'm fairly confident, yes." He grins, his fingers tightening against my legs.

"I didn't think you were coming, otherwise I would've . . ." What? Cleaned? Not tossed in a crappy frozen pizza that cost a buck? Worn something other than hot pink plaid pajama pants and a penguin tank top, sans bra? *God.*

"I'm glad you didn't know. I like catching you off guard. Seeing you like this." He traces a finger along the scoop neck of my tank, his eyes following the movement. His other hand moves up my thigh, over my hip, light fingers pressing into the small of my back until I lean forward to kiss him. He captures my lips with his, his tongue slipping into my mouth the moment I part my lips. Pulling me closer, he cradles my head in one hand as he urges my hips forward with the other. I feel him hard and ready through the thin cotton of my pants and the thinner cotton of my underwear, and I rock against him instinctively, needing to feel the evidence of his want for me.

"Winter . . ." He breathes against my cheek, his lips blazing a trail to my ear, across my shoulder, and down my chest to the neckline of my tank. With fluttering touches, he traces the edge with his tongue, teasing me. Winding me up until all I can think about is his mouth on me, his hands touching me everywhere.

*Everywhere.*

When his fingers ghost under my tank top, hands sliding up, I don't stop him. I utter no protests as he slowly pulls it up, up, up until it's off and tossed somewhere across the room. I do the same to him, wriggling my hands under his shirt until it's over his head and on the floor at our feet. His eyes are transfixed on every inch of my skin he's uncovered, and my nipples tighten in response. His eyes caress me as I use that time to take in the bare chest in front of me. While we've made out, things going far enough that he's had my nipples in his mouth, we've always kept at least one layer of clothes between us, usually his. I've never had the pleasure of seeing anything more of him than his bare forearms and a glimpse of his biceps in a short-sleeved T-shirt.

The thoughts of what he's had underneath has been fantasy fodder from the moment we met, wondering how far his tattoos went, if his chest and shoulders and back were covered in them, as well as his arms. I wondered if he had so many, it'd take me hours to map the designs on his skin. And now that he's before me, nothing separating us but air, I realize I *could* spend hours memorizing the tattoos, though his body isn't covered in them. The art on his arms carries up and extends across his sculpted shoulders, tracing just barely up the sides of his neck, but his chest is bare. Bare and broad, defined with muscle, his abs rippling under my touch as my fingers ghost along them until I'm skimming the trail of hair that disappears into the waistband of his jeans.

With a harsh groan, he pulls me to him, my nipples brushing against his chest, and I shiver. Tilting my head up to him, he fists his hand in my hair as he kisses me, slow and sweet. After a moment, he pulls away, his voice gritty and deep as he says, "I didn't come here for this."

The echo of what he said on our first date settles over me, and just like then, I have no doubts of his sincerity. "I know," I whisper. And I do. I know he'd never come here for the sole purpose of getting in my pants. Especially after the heavy makeout in his car a couple weeks ago, and the subsequent ones we always seem to find ourselves engaged in. He could've had me any of those times—I certainly wouldn't have stopped him—but he was the one to put the brakes on. Always.

But now, I think we both realize there'll be no stopping tonight.

He captures my lips again, his mouth hungry, his tongue insistent. As soon as his lips start their path toward my breasts, the tip of his tongue tracing a nipple before he engulfs it in his mouth, my hips start rocking against him. I moan and gasp when he hits that spot that makes me see fireworks, and he replies with a groan, my name uttered among the *Gods* and the *fucks* and the *shit, yes, right theres*.

Somewhere between our breathy moans and oaths to God, there's an unspoken agreement between us. I don't know how it happens. If he reached for the waistband of my pants, or if I undid the button of his jeans, or if we did it simultaneously, but somehow we're naked and he's on top of me, his forearms braced on either side of my head. We stretch out on my tiny, shitty futon, and I'm too far gone to suggest we pull it out so we have more space. I'm not even sure he'd allow me to move from underneath him long enough to do so.

He shifts away from me, but never so far that his lips aren't caressing some part of my body. Innocent parts that still manage to set me on fire—my neck and shoulders. My wrists, the insides of my elbows. And then the not-so-innocent parts that have fireworks bursting behind my eyelids and erupting under every inch of my skin—the undersides of my breasts, the insides of my thighs, the very center of me.

This isn't the first time I've been naked in front of a guy, not even close, but it feels like it. While I've been naked before, I've never been *bare*. Not like I am with him. I feel like he can see every bit of me, every ugly, unlovable part of me I've tried for years to hide away.

He sees me.

And he wants me anyway.

## cade

I move up until I'm hovering over her, so hungry to feel her around me I can hardly fucking breathe. She is . . . indescribable. Her eyes are glassy, but I can read the uncertainty behind them, the corner of her mouth tucked in as she bites on the inside of her cheek. Wanting to reassure her, I brush the hair back from her face, tracing her flushed cheeks, running my thumb across her bottom lip.

"God, baby, you're so beautiful." It sounds lame and inade-
quate, and I want to create a new word just for her. She deserves
a new word. Hell, she deserves a whole fucking language.

She lies under me, her breasts the perfect size for the palm of
my hand, the dip of her waist the perfect curve for my fingers to
grip. I duck my head, taking a nipple into my mouth as I trace
up the inside of her thigh with my fingertips. She shivers under
my touch, and I want this to last forever, to spend the whole night
getting lost in her body and her gasps and the way she looks at
me when I'm above her. I can't wait to see what she looks like
when I'm inside her.

I slide my fingers up until I find her hot and wet, ready for
me. She arches into me as I stroke her pussy, slipping a finger
inside until she's panting and writhing, her fingernails digging
into my forearms. I watch her face as I continue to pump into
her, rubbing circles around her clit with my thumb, and then she
tightens around my finger, her entire body going taut as she calls
out my name and God's until she's a boneless heap under me.

Her fingers relax, the sting of where her fingernails dug into
my skin barely a blip on my radar. I lean down and capture her
lips again. I can't get enough of this girl. "Seriously, so fucking
beautiful."

"Cade . . ." She reaches down, grips my cock, and it's all I
can do not to blow my fucking load on her stomach right now.
I've never been this turned on, this ready to go, in my entire life.
She does that to me. Makes me lose sight of everything but her—
her eyes filled with a light only I can seem to bring out, her lips
curving into a smile, her body under my hands—until I'm consumed by her.

Blindly, I reach down to the floor for my jeans, pull out the
foil packet I stuck in my wallet after the incident in the car. Just

in case. I tear open the wrapper, unroll the condom down my length, and settle between Winter's thighs again. I brace myself on my forearms, cradling her head in my hands.

Before I take it any further, I have to be certain. I couldn't live with myself if she had regrets. "You're sure?"

"I wouldn't be lying here naked if I wasn't sure." She curls toward me, her shoulders off the futon, and grabs my lower lip between her teeth, giving a tug. Her hands on my hips pull me closer until I'm flush against her, pressing into her. I ease inside, rocking forward and back, forward and back, until she accepts me completely into her body, her heat engulfing me.

"*Christ*. Winter . . ." My throat feels raw, my voice scratchy and deep, and I swallow harshly as I look down at her. "Okay?"

She stares at me, her eyes wide as she gives me a short nod, and I know she feels it, too. Whatever this is between us, this want, this *need* to be around her, to have her in my arms . . . it's not one-sided.

With the subtlest pressure of her hand on my ass and a shift of her hips, she tells me without words to move. And I do. Slow and deep at first, reveling in the soft moans that fall from her lips, the sight of her breasts moving under me with every thrust I make into her body.

Seeing her like this, completely unguarded, utterly open, is my new favorite side of her. She's always beautiful, especially when she has that fire in her eyes, but seeing her like this, eyes glazed in pure bliss, body boneless and vulnerable beneath me, nearly does me in. That she feels comfortable enough, safe enough, with me to let go like this makes me feel fifty fucking feet tall.

Our slow, steady pace soon grows into something more, her fingers digging into my ass, her back arched, neck exposed, head pressed into the cushion of the futon as she pants and moans, groans out my name. I kiss and suck at every inch of her I can reach. With frantic movements, I slip a hand between us, stroking her until every sound coming out of her mouth is unintelligible.

I grit my teeth, trying to stave off my orgasm until she comes again, but it's too much as she tightens around me. I come in a blinding rush of light, my thumb losing the rhythm against her as my body releases and I call out her name. When I've caught my breath, the whooshing in my ears receding, I become aware of her hands gripping my biceps.

"Don't stop. God, don't . . ." Her hips roll restlessly under me, and I touch her again, circling my thumb around her clit until she gasps, body arched, breasts pushed up, and comes around me.

I kiss her, trying to keep my weight off her so I don't crush her. After a few minutes, I head to the bathroom, take care of the condom, and make it back out to find her in the middle of the now-extended futon. Her eyes are closed, one arm thrown above her head, the other resting on her stomach. She pulled on a pair of panties, but otherwise is gloriously naked.

Settling in beside her, I pull her close, running my fingers through her hair and tracing my fingers down the line of her spine. She's soft and supine in my arms, and I'm stiff and rigid, completely tense as I wait for the moment she slams her walls back up and sends me packing.

After a few minutes, I can't stand it anymore and ask, "How long do we have?"

"Before what?" she mumbles against my chest.

I press my lips to her forehead. "Before you freak out."

She pulls back, cracks open an eye. "What makes you think I'll freak out?"

I just stare at her, eyebrows raised, and she eventually blows out a breath. "Point taken." She moves to snuggle into my chest again, ignoring my question completely.

"So?"

"So I think the next time we do this, it should be at your place. If that's what you can do on a shitty old futon that isn't even pulled out, I'd love to see what you can do in a bed."

I open my mouth to say something, but she reaches up, pressing her fingers to my lips. "Shh . . . it's quiet time."

A slow smile spreads across my mouth, and I let myself relax, hopeful that I'm knocking down the fortress surrounding her, one wall at a time.

# SIXTEEN

*cade*

"So what you're saying is you're pussy-whipped." Jason takes a pull of his beer, and he's lucky I don't smack the bottle out of his hand.

"What I'm saying is you're about to get my fist in your face if you don't knock that shit off."

He holds up his hands in a sign of surrender, leaning back in his chair. "All I did was ask how your girl was doing. Jesus, Cade, I didn't ask how her blow job skills are, for fuck's sake."

I glare at him and the asshole just laughs, pointing an accusatory finger at me.

"See? That's what I mean. If you didn't want me talking about her, why the hell did you drag me to the place she works? It's like you *wanted* me to give you shit over it. I mean, Christ, you're staring at her like a little lost puppy."

"Fuck off."

He laughs, slapping his hand on the table as he shakes his

head. "Goddamn, I never thought I'd see the day you were whipped over a girl. And before Adam, too. Figured for sure it'd be him that fell into the black hole first."

I flip him off before picking up a few fries from my plate. "For all you know, he's as whipped as they come. It's not like we Skype every night with him. Or maybe you do? Maybe that's why you're not pussy-whipped. Too busy chasing dick?"

He laughs, repeating my earlier sentiment. "Fuck off. You remember that pact we took in, what, fifth grade? No girls, *ever*. It was gonna be just the three of us for life. Roommates right out of high school and we were gonna spend our days doing nothing but eating chips and playing video games. What a bunch of dumbasses we were. I mean, I love you guys, but I also love girls. And boobs. A lot."

I snort, shaking my head as I take a pull of my beer. "We'd kill each other if we lived together. You need a fucking revolving door on your bedroom. And I don't even wanna know what you'd do to my kitchen counters, you pervert."

"Oh, Christ, not this again. That was *one time* and I was sixteen! What the hell was I supposed to do?" He takes a big bite of his burger, talking out of the side of his mouth as he chews. "Tell Sherri Campbell I didn't want her to suck my dick, and hey, thanks for offering to have sex with me in my friend's kitchen, but no thanks. My buddy'd be pretty pissed if we did anything on his precious counters. I'll just jack off after I bring you home . . ."

"Well, fucking hell, you could've at least told me before we ate on them an hour later." I shudder, reliving that night all over again.

"Maybe you need to have impromptu sex on a counter just

once and then you'll stop harassing me about what my hormone-addled brain couldn't say no to seven damn years ago."

"Who says I haven't?" I haven't, but he doesn't need to know that. "Just because you insist on replaying every gory detail of your sexual adventures doesn't mean I do."

His eyebrows lift as he leans forward, his forearm braced on the high table, a grin on his face. "*Really*. Spitfire?"

With a scowl, I flip him off again and take another swig of my beer. Knowing he's picturing her like that sends a wave of anger through me. "I'm not talking to you about this."

"You've always talked to me about it before." He shrugs, feigning nonchalance, but his eyes focus sharply on me. "What gives?"

"She's . . ." I shake my head, looking down as I pick at the food on my plate. "I don't know, man. She's different. She's . . . *important*."

He's quiet for a minute, and when I look up at him, his mouth is hanging open. "Holy fuck, dude."

"What?"

"Are you . . . I mean . . . do you *love* her?"

I open my mouth to respond, but snap it shut when I realize I don't have an answer. I haven't given it much thought—or any thought, really—but I know I love being around her. I can't wait to see her at the end of the day, if for only fifteen minutes to make sure she gets home safely. And the nights she doesn't work and we both use to catch up at school, I miss her. Her smile and her sense of humor and her strength.

I've never been in love before, so I have no idea what any of what I'm feeling means. But I'm smart enough to know that if I'm not already in love with her, I will be.

Soon.

*winter*

It's hard keeping my mind on my customers when Cade's just across the restaurant. I knew he was doing something with Jason tonight, but I didn't know they were planning to come here. His laugh draws my eyes over to their table, and he looks so relaxed, so happy. I've never had a friend with whom I could relax completely, actually be happy.

Or I didn't until I met him.

It's not too busy tonight, and I'm able sneak in a few minutes here and there to work on some design sketches in the back during my downtime. I'd be in serious trouble if Randy caught me, but Annette's good at keeping watch, and the other girls have been doing the same thing. Finals are coming up, these last few weeks kicking everyone's asses, and I need every extra minute I can get.

I head over to one of my tables, a group of eight—five guys, three girls—celebrating a birthday. They've been boisterous but harmless, with the exception of one of the guys, whose hands have roamed the few times I've been to his side of the table.

"Anyone need another round?" I ask, doing a quick scan of the table to see who could use another. They're all still nursing their drinks except for the one whose hands have a mind of their own.

He holds up his drink, shaking the lonely ice cubes in the glass. "Keep 'em coming, gorgeous."

I paint on my fake smile, grabbing the glass from him and skirting away before he can touch me.

When I'm at the bar, I say, "Hey, Annette, can I get another Jack and Coke?"

"Sure thing, sugar." She grabs a glass, tossing in some ice and mixing the drink. "How is it tonight?" she asks with a tip of her chin to the group.

"Not bad. One of them seems to think he's my boyfriend, though."

"I have faith you can handle him," she says with a wink, sliding the drink across the bar top to me. "Put him in his place like you always do. Careful, though, you've got an audience tonight." She says the last part quietly, her eyes flitting to the back briefly. Without turning around, I know Randy is standing in the hallway to his office, looking over everything. He's been doing that more and more over the last couple of weeks, and it's starting to creep me out.

I tip my head in thanks and turn to make my way back to my table and the guy who ordered the drink. Keeping as much physical distance between us as possible, I lean over and place the glass in front of him. Unfortunately, no matter how much space I put between us, these outfits aren't meant to conceal anything, and his eyes linger on the scoop neck of my shirt, getting an eyeful of the small bit of cleavage my less-than-ample breasts show.

He pushes away from the table slightly and leans back in his chair, patting his knee and giving me what I'm sure he thinks passes as an inviting smile. "Why don'tcha sit down for a minute, honey?"

I offer him the fake smile I use like a weapon in here, the corner of my mouth turned down as if the thought is tempting but I just can't. "Sorry, my boss is kind of a stickler with not letting us sit with the customers. He likes to keep us up and moving."

"I can see why. You look mighty fine up and moving." His gaze drops to sweep over me head to toe, and I'm crawling under my skin. "But I'm sure he wouldn't mind, just this once." This time, he reaches out, his hand skimming up the back of my thigh until his fingers are centimeters from the curve of my ass. From the corner of my eye, I see Cade stand at his table. His hulking frame takes up so much space, and I don't have to look at him to know there's murderous rage on his face at the sight of this guy touching me.

I move to step away from the guy who can't keep his hands to himself, but he slips his hand around my waist and tugs. Caught off guard, I lose my balance, toppling into his lap. His sour breath is in my face, his lips against my ear. "There, that wasn't so hard, was it?"

Before I can answer, Cade is next to me, body looming and tensed for a fight. I shoot him a sharp glare and subtle shake of my head, warning him to stay back as I remove the hands around my waist and stand up. Turning a falsely sweet smile to the guy whose lap I just got out of, I say, "Now you're gonna get me in trouble. You better behave the rest of the night or I'll have to get Annette"—I point to her and the glare she's offering this guy—"to fill in for me. And believe me, she's not as nice as I am."

He holds up his hands, grinning, his eyes drooping in a drunken haze. "Okay, okay. I'll be good."

I tip my head and turn to go, narrowing my eyes at Cade as I head to the bar. "Annette, I'm gonna take a fifteen-minute break. I need some air."

She looks over my shoulder to where I assume Cade is standing, glowering, then gives me a knowing look. "No problem. I'll keep an eye on your tables."

Looking once again at Cade, I turn and walk into the back room, not stopping until I'm out the door and against the brick wall of the building. No more than three minutes later, Cade's in front of me, eyes still blazing.

My temper is simmering, the frustration I felt that first night when he plowed his way into my life sparking again. I poke a finger into his chest, tilting my head back as he looms over me, and speak through gritted teeth. "What the *fuck* was that?"

He looks stunned for a minute, his head snapping back as he stares, mouth agape. "What do you mean what the fuck was that? That was some asshole with his fucking paws all over you, *again*, and me coming to stop it!"

"Goddammit, Cade!" I yell, my hands thrown in the air. I shove hard at his chest, though he doesn't move an inch, his body too tense. "Do you even listen to me? Haven't we already had this discussion? Didn't we have this same exact issue the first night we met?"

"This wasn't some fucking misunderstanding, Winter," he says, his voice low, his anger barely restrained. "This wasn't me misinterpreting some asshole's hands on you. This jackass pulled you, *unwillingly*, into his lap. His fingers were about an inch from your tits, and you expect me just to sit back and watch as some guy does that to *my* girlfriend?"

I don't even have time to contemplate his comment and the fact that he's claimed me as his, my anger boiling out of me in a rush of words. "Yes, that's exactly what I expect you to do if you come into where I *work*. Have you learned nothing in the weeks we've been seeing each other? I *need* this job. It sucks sometimes, yeah, but I can handle it. I've been handling it for a long time, and I've done it all without you by my side. I'm not some poor, incapable girl who needs someone to swoop in and rescue her. And if that's all you're here for, you can go find someone else, because I don't need it." I turn away, ready to go back inside, but he snakes an arm around my waist, pulling me against him. His chest is heaving against my back, his breaths harsh in my ear.

"You think that's all I'm here for? That I have some fucking knight in shining armor complex? Jesus Christ, Winter, I can't stand the thought of anyone putting their hands on you, and it drives me fucking crazy every night I'm not here knowing they might—that they probably *are*. But to *see* it? To see it and just sit there, not doing anything? I'm not the kind of guy who can just sit back and watch it happening—to *anyone*, let alone the woman I'm in love with!"

Every ounce of breath in my lungs vanishes in a long exhale, all the rage evaporating as confusion and terror and, dammit, hope take its place. His declaration hangs in the air between us,  and I'm afraid to move, to breathe. In all my twenty-two years, this is the first time I've ever heard those words spoken to me, and my brain is in overdrive, all the ways this could come crashing down around me flashing through my mind.

Breaking the silence, Cade groans, his forehead falling to my shoulder. "Aw, fuck. I didn't mean to say that."

His honesty is refreshing, even as I'm frozen in uncertainty, and a breathless laugh escapes me. My throat is tight as I say, "Just what every girl wants to hear after declarations of love."

"Forget I said anything."

"I don't think it works that way."

"Sure it does. Just go back to three minutes ago and pretend I kept my mouth shut and nodded after your tirade."

"I *know* I can't do that—you don't keep your mouth shut about anything."

After a deep exhale, he says, "Don't even think about slinking away and never returning my calls."

I reach down, patting his arm locked around my stomach, clutching me to his chest. "I don't think I could escape even if I wanted to."

"And you don't? Want to?"

I take a deep breath and stare at the rough brick of the building, finding it easier to share my feelings without his eyes on me. "I'm not going to lie and say it doesn't scare me. It does. This is all new for me, Cade. I don't know how to do this, and I'm afraid I'm going to screw it up." The thought of what we have, what we could have, fills me with more hope than anything, and for once, I think I'm ready to try. "But my fight-or-flight response didn't kick in, so I think maybe we're good."

He's quiet for a minute before he lifts his head, his hand sweeping my hair behind my shoulder to bare my neck. He settles his cheek against my temple, his mouth by my ear. "Yeah?"

I close my eyes, praying I'm not making a mistake. That I'm not taking the first step to heartache. I nod. "Yeah."

He presses his lips to my ear, then my neck. His breath washes over my collarbone, warming me from the outside in. "Good. Because I'm not ready to let you go yet."

# SEVENTEEN

*cade*

I toss the pizza dough into the oiled bowl and cover it, setting it aside for later. Ever since going to Winter's apartment and seeing her eating that shitty, fake-ass pizza, I've wanted to make her some of mine, and tonight I'll finally get the chance.

The clock reads just before five, so I wash my hands and peel off my apron, grabbing my books and laptop and setting them out on the island. Just as I open my computer, a knock sounds at the door. I make my way over and open it, smiling at Winter.

The strap of her bag is slung over her shoulder, and she has a couple books in her hands. She's chewing on the inside of her cheek again, and I wonder what it will take before she stops being nervous. I can never quite reconcile what, exactly, makes her apprehensive. It's not me, because it doesn't happen every time we're together. She's only been to my house once—that very first time—and maybe that's what's making her so anxious.

"Hey," I say, reaching out with my other hand and tugging

her inside. "I wish you'd let me come pick you up. Seems stupid for you to ride the bus when I have a perfectly good set of wheels."

She smiles and adjusts her bag at her side. "You can hardly drive me everywhere I need to go, Cade. I don't know why you think you have to."

"I don't think I have to. I *want* to. That's a big difference." I reach for the strap of her bag, slipping it from her shoulder as I carry it into the kitchen. I pull Winter behind me, her finger hooked in mine.

"Still. I need to do some things on my own. And you need to let me." Her voice is firm, and though I want to argue with her, tell her all the reasons I want to be there for her, to protect her, I realize it's a battle I won't win today.

Instead, I keep my mouth shut and heft her bag on the counter. "You really thought we were gonna study, huh?" I say, pointing to her overflowing bag.

She raises an eyebrow, staring at me. "Did you bring me here under false pretenses?"

With a hand to my chest, my eyes wide, I gasp in mock offense. "Me? Never."

"Mhmm." She doesn't sound convinced as she settles into the chair I pull out for her. "Where are Tessa and Haley?"

I take a seat next to her, grabbing the books I'm using for research on my term paper for Cajun and Creole cuisine. "Haley had a play date. They'll be back in a couple hours."

"So we're all alone, then? I have to tell you, this 'study date' is sounding shadier and shadier."

Leaning closer to her, I sweep her hair over her shoulder then slide my hand down her back until I tuck it into the waistband of her jeans, my fingers settled on the top curve of her ass. With my lips by her ear, I whisper, "Would that be the worst thing?"

She doesn't say anything, just the subtlest shake of her head as she tucks her chin to her chest. When I pull away, she's smiling into her lap, but her body is still tense, her shoulders rigid, hands fidgeting.

"You okay?"

Turning her head, she looks over at me, her eyes darting between mine. She doesn't say anything, just nods, but I can read the tension radiating off her.

"Bet I could get you to relax." My lips are against hers, brushing with every word. I slip my tongue out, licking along the seam of her mouth. She opens to me, meets me halfway, and I groan at the first taste of her. She always tastes so fucking good.

She doesn't protest as I move to stand, sliding her from the high bar stools and lifting her up against me. Her arms go around my shoulders, her legs around my waist as my hand settles on her ass, holding her to me. Gripping my face in her hands, she kisses me as I walk us down the hall to my bedroom, kicking the door shut behind me, and locking it for good measure. While I don't expect Tess or Haley for a while, I sure as fuck don't want to take any chances that we get interrupted while Winter and I are getting naked in my room.

Once we're in front of my bed, I drop her in the middle, her hair in a wild disarray around her. She's so fucking beautiful. I want to spend hours studying every nuance of her. The cluster of freckles just under her collarbone, the indentation of her waist, the faint, paint-splatter birthmark on her hip. From the look she's giving me, the pure hunger in her eyes, she feels the same.

I reach back, tugging on the neck of my shirt as I pull it over my head and toss it aside. Her eyes track down my body, and I've never been so grateful for the grueling hours of football or basketball, the days spent in my basement whaling on the punching bag, as I am when her eyes rake over me. Her breathing gets faster, her lips part, and as I shift my focus lower, I can see the evidence of her excitement in the two points pressing against the front of her shirt.

With a quick flick and a tug at the fly of my jeans, I have them off and on the floor in a pool next to my feet. I crawl over her, gathering her hands in mine as I pin them above her head.

"You forgot a piece . . ." she says, laughter in her eyes as she moves her leg to rub her thigh against the boxer briefs I still have on.

"I didn't want to give you too much of an advantage. I just stripped for you, woman, and you didn't take off anything."

She raises her eyebrows in challenge. "Maybe you should rectify that."

"I think I will." I slide my hand under her shirt, palming the expanse of her stomach. She clenches underneath my fingers, goose bumps covering the skin I've touched. I take my time as I remove her shirt, then her jeans, leaving her spread out on my bed in nothing but her underwear. They're nothing special, nothing sexy—a mismatched set of different colored cotton, but the way my body reacts to it, to *her*, the way my cock twitches at the sight of her, you'd think she was in the sexiest lingerie I've ever seen. I stand at the foot of my bed, taking in her gorgeous body. I want to lick every inch of her.

"Quit staring." Her voice is low and throaty, the tone it always takes when she's turned on and ready for me.

Glancing up to her face, I smile. "Quit being so beautiful and I will."

She rolls her eyes, but I can see the color bloom in her cheeks. Reaching out, she beckons me closer, and I comply until I'm close enough for her to trace along the tattoos on my arms and over my shoulders, watching her fingers as she does. The corner of her cheek dips in again, and I bring up my finger to tug it out of the prison of her teeth.

"What's got you chewing on your cheek? We've done this before . . . don't tell me you're nervous now. My size intimidate you since you know what you're in for?"

She laughs, shaking her head. "How do you walk around with such a big head?"

A grin curves one side of my mouth as I lift my eyebrows at her double entendre. "It's tough, not gonna lie." I place my hands on either side of her head and lower myself over the length of her, arms bent as I hover inches above her. Her hands clench my biceps, her eyes staring up at me. I dip to capture her lips, then pull away before she can slip her tongue into my mouth. All teasing gone from my voice, I say, "Seriously. What's up?"

Her eyes dart to the side, to the ink on my arms. "I was just wondering about these." She traces my skin as she says it, the story I've had forever imprinted on my skin. "Will you tell me about them?"

She looks so nervous, so unsure, and I take this for what it is: her digging deeper into my life, seating herself a little more permanently in it. And it thrills me. "Anytime, baby." I place another kiss on her lips, lowering my hips into the cradle of her thighs. "But maybe after? I'm a little busy at the moment . . ."

Her laugh cuts off as I bend to trace her nipple through the cotton of her bra, her fingers digging into my arms. "Cade . . ."

"I'm here."

I remove the rest of our clothing, taking time to study the parts of her I wanted to. I detour to all the good spots—the places that make her gasp and moan and giggle. The side of her neck, the tips of her breasts, the dip of her waist. I grasp the insides of her thighs, spread her wide for my tongue as I get lost in the taste of her. I don't stop until her thighs clamp over my ears, her hands gripping my head as she says my name over and over again.

I don't think I'll ever get sick of hearing her call my name as she comes.

Crawling up her body, I press my lips everywhere I can reach. I'd like to do nothing but kiss every inch of her, get lost in the softness of her skin, but I know our time is running out before we won't have the house to ourselves anymore, and I don't want Winter to be uncomfortable in front of Tessa if she were to get home before we're done. Instead, I kiss her, tease her with my tongue as she cups my jaw in her hands. Pulling back, I flip her over until she's on her stomach, her head turned to the side as she cranes her neck to look back at me. I place openmouthed kisses on the backs of her knees, skimming my fingers down the length of her legs. Standing, I reach into my drawer and pull out a condom, quickly rolling it on before I climb on top of her.

"Okay?"

She answers in a hum, her ass lifting a little. Enough to know she wants it. She wants me. I pull back and guide myself to her, one hand gripping her on the dip just above her ass. The comforter is pulled tight between her clenched fists as she moves her hips restlessly. Lips parted, thighs spread, eyes glazed, she looks fucking sexy.

I sink into her, slow and steady, until I can't go any deeper. "Fuck. *Winter.*"

With a breathy moan, she pushes back against me, and I start a rhythm, pumping into her as fast as I dare. I don't want to lose it—she feels too fucking good—but the sight of her underneath me, spread out and completely giving up power to me, is nearly my undoing. I make the mistake of looking down to where I'm disappearing inside her, seeing myself move into her body, seeing the evidence of how much she wants me each time I pull out, and I groan. Taking my hand from her waist, I bring it up, stretching myself over the length of her body as I cover her with mine. I reach for one of her hands, interlocking our fingers together as I hold myself over her with the other. I probably weigh twice as much as she does, and I don't want to crush her under me.

Brushing my lips over her shoulder, I say, "Kiss me."

She complies, twisting her head and straining back to reach my mouth. Her gasps and moans punctuate the press of her lips, the slide of her tongue. When I shift and push into her again, her eyes roll back, her fingers tightening around mine. "God, right there. Don't stop."

I smile against her temple, continuing with my pace. "Did I find the spot, baby?"

"Yes. Yes, yes, yes . . ." She drags out the last word. "Oh, God."

Then words fail her, her mouth opening in a silent scream as she goes completely taut underneath me, her pussy clamped around me, until she releases, a long, deep breath whooshing out of her as she shudders, then goes boneless.

"Holy fuck." I've never seen anything as sexy as Winter when she comes. She loses all inhibitions, the shadows I see lurking in her eyes are suddenly gone. She's free and she's gorgeous and she's mine. It's this thought that pushes me over the edge, claiming her as I finally give in to my body's need for release.

# EIGHTEEN

*winter*

I didn't think it'd feel like this. In all the times I let myself go down this path, indulge in this daydream, I thought there'd be waves of panic, a crushing weight on my chest, shackles chained to my ankles from being connected to someone. From being on the receiving end of someone's love. There's too much responsibility, too much faith lying in your actions, too much possibility of heartache.

I didn't want *any* of it.

And then Cade came, sweeping his way into my life, imposing and relentless and persistent, and I'm not the same.

That's the only possible conclusion I can come up with. I'm not the same, because as I lie with him in his bed, his fingers trailing up and down the bare expanse of my back, I don't feel the need to flee. The urge to run, to hide, doesn't overcome me, even after experiencing what we just did.

I've had sex before. Plenty of sex with guys I knew and some

I didn't. And it was always fine. Sometimes I got off, sometimes I didn't, but it was never anything more than just sex—two bodies meeting for a common need. With Cade it's so different. It's emotional and all-consuming. It's . . . transcendent.

"What're you thinking about?" His voice is low and throaty, his lips brushing against my temple as he speaks.

And even though I saw the look in his eyes while he was inside me, even though I know he feels this crazy connection like I do, I can't share this with him. Not yet. I might be changed, but old habits die hard. He told me he was in love with me, and I still haven't mustered up enough courage to reciprocate. I'm not sure I'll *ever* be able to say it back. I don't even know if I feel it, because I've been too scared to take stock of my emotions.

What if I don't?

What if I *do*?

Instead of divulging my thoughts, I say, "You lured me over here for homework, and somehow we wound up naked in your bed."

His lips curve against my head as he smiles. "I was studying."

I snort. "Studying what, how many different ways you can make me come?"

"Yes," he says as he turns over, pinning me to the bed. "I've counted five so far. Are there more?"

Laughing, I push against his shoulders, and he rolls off me easily. "You are impossible."

"Irresistible, you mean." He's on his back, completely naked, arms spread over his head. My eyes are drawn once again to the designs on them, and while I want to know, while he said he'd tell me about them anytime, I'm not sure I'm ready to hear their stories. Because I know, with Cade, it's going to be deeply personal. I don't know if I can handle that so soon after what just happened between us. If I have any hope of not ruining this thing between us, I need to move in baby steps.

"You *did* promise me study time."

"I think I also promised you food." He climbs out of bed and pulls on a pair of jeans, and the fact that he's going commando is going to haunt my thoughts as I attempt to focus on schoolwork. When he has a T-shirt pulled over his chest, he gathers up my clothes for me, depositing them on the bed, and waits until I'm dressed before he leads us into the kitchen.

My laptop sits open on the island, his books and computer set out next to it. I'm glad we got back out here before Tessa and Haley returned, because there's no way what we were doing wouldn't be completely obvious. And yeah, we're grown adults, but I just don't quite know how to act around his sister, don't even know what she thinks of me. I want her to like me, I realize as Cade slips around to the other side of the island. I've never cared much about what people think of me—my own personal deflection technique—but I do care what his family thinks.

I don't want to dissect that too closely, so I settle in on the high stool at the island, in front of my computer. "What are you making for me tonight?"

"Nothing fancy since I figured we'd be busy with homework. Just homemade pizza, a salad, and some garlic knots."

"I think you forget what I normally eat. That *is* fancy."

He smiles at me over his shoulder as he preheats the oven, then grabs a couple stainless steel bowls from back on the counter. "Yeah, what you normally eat is exactly why I'm making this. What kind of chef boyfriend would I be if I didn't show you what real pizza was supposed to taste like? Not that cardboard shit with canned tomato sauce and fake cheese you've been living on."

After everything that's happened between us, him referring to himself as my boyfriend shouldn't set off a flurry of tornadoes spinning in my stomach. I've seen him nearly every day, we've slept together, and he's told me he's in love with me. A silly, inconsequential word like *boyfriend* shouldn't mean anything.

But it does.

Never once did I plan on having one. I assumed I would go through my life single and happy, kicking ass in my field and loving every minute of being on my own, of being the only one I counted on. I took comfort in that.

I had no idea what I'd be missing.

The movement of his hands catches my eyes, and I turn my attention to him as he concentrates on prepping our dinner. He flours the counter, then flips a ball of dough out of a bowl before pressing into it with both hands.

"What's that for?"

"The pizza crust."

"Wow, when you said homemade, you really meant it."

"What'd you think I was going to do, get one of those crusts in a tube and feed you that?"

I shrug, resting my chin in my hand, elbow propped on the counter as I forget all about my homework and focus on his actions. "That would still be gourmet to me." I watch him for a minute, his movements mesmerizing as he pushes and pulls and flips the dough before repeating his actions. "Why are you doing that by hand instead of using your fancy machine?" I ask, pointing to the huge stand mixer behind him.

He looks up at me with a grin. "So I can impress you with my muscles."

I laugh. "I think you successfully accomplished that when you did a push-up over me just to get a kiss." And even though he's teasing, he isn't far off. I watch as they strain and flex under the ink covering his forearms as he kneads the dough. I don't take my eyes off him as he manipulates it into the shape he wants, then transfers it to a pizza stone.

"Do you have any topping preferences?" He opens the fridge and pulls out an armful of fresh ingredients. "I was going to do a white pizza, if that's okay?"

"What's on that?"

"The base is a mixture of cheeses, then I'll top it with shallots, fresh basil, spinach, and some sliced tomatoes."

"I've never had one, but that sounds amazing."

He smiles and pulls down a cutting board, quickly and efficiently chopping the shallots, then slicing the tomatoes. I love watching him cook, seeing his brow creased in concentration.

"You want to help?"

My eyebrows shoot up to my hairline. "Really?"

"Yeah, come around here." He jerks his head and smiles at me, and how can I say no?

"Do I need an apron?"

"Nah, I won't get you too dirty." The grin he shoots me speaks volumes, and I shake my head at him, though I can feel the awareness sparking in my body.

"Okay, what should I do?"

"I've already got the cheese base mixed together, so go ahead and spread that all over the crust, then we'll top it with the rest of the ingredients."

I do as he asks, then we layer the onions, basil, and spinach on before topping it all with the tomato slices. "It looks delicious." My stomach grumbles as I say it, and he laughs, swooping down to steal a kiss.

"Soon, baby."

I wash my hands as he tips the other bowl he grabbed earlier, flipping more dough out onto the floured countertop.

"That's for the garlic knots?"

"Yep. C'mere, I'll show you how to make them, too."

Sliding over to where he's standing, I wait as he cuts off a chunk of dough and proceeds to roll it out until it looks like a rope.

"You need to roll them until they're about ten inches long. Then you just tie 'em in a knot and put them on the pan."

I watch as he does this, his too-big hands delicately working the dough into perfect knots. He repeats the process a second time, and I stare, the juxtaposition of him mouthwatering. Here he is, this huge, linebacker of a man with a facial piercing and arms covered in tattoos, donning an apron and delicately twisting tiny pieces of dough into knots with a pair of hands nearly twice the size of mine.

A laugh escapes me, and he turns his head to glance at me, his eyebrow raised, the silver through it glinting under the kitchen lights. "Something funny?"

I shrug, leaning against the counter. "A little. Never in a million years would I have guessed this is what you do." I wave a hand toward him as he carefully twists a third knot to perfection. "You don't scream soft and gentle."

With his hands covered in flour and dough, he leans over, his mouth by my neck as he kisses me there. His breath brushes against my ear as he says, "You know exactly how soft and gentle I can be."

I turn my head back toward him, my mouth brushing his cheek as he pulls away, my lips catching on the rough scrape of stubble. He looks at me, heat radiating from his eyes, a cocky grin lifting one side of his mouth, and I know he's thinking about what we did earlier.

"Come on, it's your turn." He cuts off a hunk of dough for me, then moves behind me as he places his hands over mine. His chest is broad and solid against my back, radiating heat, and I try not to lean too far back into him. His arms are around me, capturing me in place, and the panic I'd normally feel at being trapped is suspiciously absent.

"Okay, we're gonna roll it out first, kind of like you used to make a snake with Play-Doh as a kid."

I don't have the heart to tell him I never played with Play-Doh. When I was young enough to be interested in it, my mother wasn't exactly a domestic queen. Toys weren't something that were part of my world. Instead, by the age of four, I was well acquainted with beer bottles and ashtrays and the sounds my mother made when she had a man over.

It was a miracle, really, I didn't starve to death or die of neglect before I escaped her care. I was feeding myself by the time I was old enough and smart enough to figure out how to get into the cabinets. I was lucky I was able to scrounge up cereal most days. Dry cereal, because there was rarely milk, and if there was, it was usually sour. But I was resourceful, even then. I had to be.

So, no, growing up like that, Play-Doh wasn't exactly at the top of my priorities. By the time I was tossed into the system, I was too old, too jaded, too hurt to care or ask for stupid, superficial things like that.

He's still talking, his chest rumbling against my back, his chin barely brushing the top of my head with every word, and I focus on him once again. ". . . then you just twist like this." He grabs my hands, trying to help me turn and fold the dough in on itself, but between my clumsiness and his huge hands, it's a mess by the end. We both stare down at the chunk of dough on the counter, no longer even resembling a Play-Doh snake.

Chuckling in my ear, he says, "Okay, so maybe I'll finish these off so you don't starve to death." He moves from behind me, quickly rolling the dough out again and knotting it with ease. Glancing over at me, he offers me a smile. "But someday, I'm going to teach you how to do these."

I stare into his eyes until he breaks contact and works on another piece of dough. The certainty in his voice sends a rush of feeling over me.

*Someday.*

The only somedays I ever planned for were the day I turned eighteen, the day I graduated high school, and the day I will graduate college.

But now . . . Now I think I could see a someday with him.

It's scary and exhilarating and exciting, this unknown that awaits me. I have no idea what I'm getting myself into—if there will be anything for me at the end of this path but heartache and pain and darkness—but for the first time in my life, I'm willing to try.

For him.

"All right, I'll get these in the oven and it shouldn't be too long." He turns and places both pans into the oven before going over and washing his hands. I follow behind him, then watch as he unties his apron and sets it loosely on the counter. As I'm drying my hands, he says over his shoulder, "Should probably get busy on your homework, baby. Don't think I'm not going to drag you away from it later. Better get your ass in gear now."

I roll my eyes, shaking my head as I settle back in my seat, but images of what he plans to drag me away for drift through my mind, taking up valuable space I need for studying. If his intention was to make me focus more, it's having the opposite effect.

Before I can picture any more decidedly inappropriate situations, the back door opens, Haley's sweet voice ringing through the house. "Uncle Cade! I'm home! Whatcha makin' me?" Her feet pound on the floor until she's in the kitchen, running at full speed into Cade's knees.

He laughs, picks her up, and tosses her in the air, then plants a thousand kisses all over her face until she's a fit of breathless giggles. And while this picture should fill me with nothing but happiness, my heart actually hurts to see it. To see what a family could be like. *Should* be like. Being there for one another, even when you don't have to be. It's not about obligation or guilt, ultimatums, and crushing, unwanted responsibility. It's not the death sentence my mother always told me it was.

Unlike her, Cade wasn't saddled with this responsibility because of poor decisions. This is a choice he made. To help his sister as much as he can in raising Haley because he *wants* to. He doesn't have to, but he's here because he loves both of them beyond measure. He's the most amazing, wonderful, giving, selfless man, and I love him.

I love him.

# NINETEEN

*cade*

"Cade, stay for a bit after, would you?" Chef Foster says as he passes my station before continuing on.

I nod without looking up, focusing intently on the food I'm plating. It's my first class since last week's shit show, and I've made it a personal mission not to fuck up again. It's not something that's ever happened before—even when I was first starting—and I'm pissed as hell at myself that I allowed my personal life to seep into the kitchen. I can't let it happen again. I have too much riding on this class. And the last thing I want to do is disappoint my mentor, especially after all the advice and guidance he's given me. I know that even with our personal relationship going years back, he isn't going to go easy on me.

I get my plates out on time today, the line moving smoothly and efficiently. I'm in my groove, the rhythm of my actions soothing as things continue like this for the hours-long class and restaurant service. For a while, I let myself indulge in my biggest dream—this is *my* restaurant, these are my ideas we're plating and serving to customers. They're paying for *my* food.

I have years until I'll get to that point—if I ever will. After graduation, I'm more than likely to get a position as a prep or line cook. And I'd be happy with either of those, working my ass off and climbing the ladder. I don't have a problem paying my dues, and there's little doubt in my mind I'll have to.

It's about talent, of course, but so much of getting placement after graduation is being in the right place at the right time . . . knowing the right people in the right positions. It's nearly unheard of to land something as prestigious as head or executive chef right out of school. Sometimes students get lucky, stumble upon a sous chef position at an up-and-coming restaurant, but I have no false aspirations this will happen for me. I'll be happy with whatever I can find, so long as I can be in a kitchen, creating incredible food.

When class ends, the restaurant closing as the last customers file out, I stay behind, making sure my station is clean to a meticulous degree. I pack away my knives and wait for Chef Foster. He hasn't said anything to me since last week's fuckup, and if I had to guess, I'd say that's why I'm here right now. To get my ass chewed. And while I know he gave me several days' buffer so he'd keep his head on straight and not ream me, I almost wish he would've talked to me immediately after instead of having to wait days to get ripped into like I know I deserve.

"Cade," he says. His eyes are sharp behind his wire-rimmed glasses, his shoulders straight as he walks toward me like he owns the kitchen, the very tile I'm standing on. I have probably six inches and sixty pounds on him, but the respect he commands in here is undeniable.

"Chef Foster."

"I think we both know why I had you stay behind, so I'm just going to cut to the chase. What the fuck was that last week?"

I blow out a long breath through my nose. There's nothing I can say that doesn't sound like an excuse. I know exactly what happened. Her name is Winter and she's the best thing that's happened to me in a long fucking time.

Somehow, I don't think he'd like to hear that, though.

"I'm sorry I let you down, Chef. My mind was elsewhere. It won't happen again."

"You're damn right it's not going to happen again." He crosses his arms, staring me down, clenching his jaw. He's pissed, even with his cooling-down period. I don't think I've ever seen him this mad, but it looks like it's more than just frustration. I see disappointment lurking in his eyes, too, and that kills me.

Shaking his head, he pushes his glasses up the bridge of his nose. "You are one of the brightest, most talented chefs I've ever had the privilege to teach. And to see you making stupid mistakes this late in the game? Well, it irritates the piss out of me, to be honest. And it's unacceptable."

I nod in understanding, knowing I can't say anything to refute him. He's right.

"You want to run your own restaurant someday, don't you?"

"Yes, sir," I answer without hesitation. It's been the only dream I've allowed myself to truly indulge in, to actually strive for. While I have other dreams—going to Italy, cooking in Rome and Tuscany, I know those will never happen. I can't leave Tessa and Haley. Winter. But my own restaurant is something that can happen here, at home.

"You think you're going to get there by falling behind, dragging an entire fucking kitchen down with you?"

"No, sir."

"You think there are going to be people as goddamn nice as I am there to pick up your sorry ass and shove you back on your feet?"

"No, sir."

"That's right. I'm going to look like your fairy fucking god-mother compared to everyone else out there. This is a cutthroat industry, and if you fail, there are a hundred chefs that will stand in line to get your position. They will climb over you and not look back. Do you understand?"

"Yes, sir."

"You have the talent, Cade. Pure, raw talent. You have the drive. I know what you want for yourself, and I don't have a doubt you'll achieve it. But in the last few weeks, you've been lacking focus. I realize you've got a lot of shit to deal with at home, shit you didn't count on for yourself, but that's nothing new. I'm not sure what's been happening in the last few weeks, and I give zero fucks what it is. What happens in here doesn't have anything to do with what happens out there. Do whatever you need to get that figured out, *outside* of my kitchen. Think about it before you walk through that door," he says as he points in that direction, "and again when you leave, but while you're here, in my fucking world, you think about nothing but food, you got me? *Nothing.*"

"Yes, sir." I nod. "I'm sorry."

"I don't want an apology. I want your performance back up to par with what I've come to expect from you. Don't make me regret talking you up to several contacts. I don't put my ass on the line for just anyone."

The shame that I let him down hangs even heavier now, the

disappointment I know he feels obvious. That he thinks enough of me to put his reputation on the line? I can't let him down again. I won't.

"Amazing things are going to happen for you, Cade. But you have to *want* them."

"I do. I'm all in."

"Good." He reaches out, claps his hand over my shoulder, and turns to leave. "I'll see you tomorrow, and you better be ready to bleed sweat on this floor."

"I will be."

*winter*

As soon as I walk out the back door after the pub closes, Annette by my side, my eyes immediately find Cade. He's at the far end of the parking lot, just a shadow of a man, but I know it's him. He's straddling his bike, and my stomach kicks and twists and flips at the sight of him.

"See you tomorrow, sugar."

"Have a good night, Annette."

Before I can get too far, I hear my name called from the doorway of the pub. Turning around, I see Randy standing there, leaning against the door frame.

"That your boyfriend?" he asks, tipping his head in the direction of Cade.

"Yeah."

He hums, staring at the dark shape of Cade in the corner. "He's been in before, hasn't he? Big guy, lots of tattoos? Some metal through his fucking face . . ."

My shoulders tighten, hearing someone refer to Cade that

way, I know that's how people see him—as nothing more than an imposing, scary guy with too many tattoos and a facial piercing—but I've never been on the receiving end of that judgment. And I find myself ready to tell this guy off—tell my *boss* off—over his wrong impression.

I have enough sense to bite my tongue against the flurry of venom I want to spew in his direction. Tell him all the ways Cade's amazing and kind, but I don't. I don't care what this asshole thinks of him. Or me. Instead, I merely nod.

"Yeah . . . I had a customer come in the other day and complain about him, says he just about broke his fucking arm." His face is blank, giving nothing away, and I don't know if he's lying or not. My gut churns with apprehension, whispers floating through my mind that this is just one more thing he's going to use to hang over my head.

Swallowing back my unease, I say, "That customer had his hand on my ass, and Cade saw it. Stepped in."

"He had no business doing that."

"If you'd get a couple bouncers in here, the patrons wouldn't have to get involved when one of your waitresses is groped."

He snorts, completely unfazed. "You want bodyguards, princess? Go to Roxy's. You can't handle yourself in here, go find another place to work."

My entire body goes rigid. "Are you firing me?"

Stepping closer, his voice drops. "Not yet. I'm telling you to keep your freak of a boyfriend away from my business, you got that? All these little instances are adding up—you being late, mouthing off to the customers, your boyfriend roughing them up—and pretty soon we're going to have an issue."

With a jerky nod, I turn and head to Cade, my skin crawling as I feel Randy's eyes along my back, on my ass as I walk. When

I get to Cade, his jaw is clenched, his eyes focused at the building behind me. "What'd he say to you?"

"Nothing. Let's just go." I move to take my helmet, but he stops me with a hand on my wrist.

"Winter."

Blowing out a deep breath, I say, "He's pissed about the guy you bothered that first night. I guess he complained."

He stares into my eyes, waiting for me to continue. When I don't, he says, "What else? There's more."

"You can't go in there anymore, Cade, if you're going to cause a scene every time. He's cataloging everything I do, and you by extension. He's going to fire me."

"Fuck," he snaps. "If he'd hire some goddamn bouncers, I wouldn't need to worry about it. Does he think his scrawny ass can deal with a situation if it comes up? Fucking *asshole*."

I look over my shoulder, seeing the outline of Randy still in the doorway. Putting my hand on Cade's arm, I squeeze. With my voice lowered, I say, "Cade. Stop. He's still out here. I don't want to give him any more ammunition, okay? Let's just go."

"Go? You wanna just *go*? What happened to the Winter who bites my head off when I step in? Where's she at when her boss is being a complete shithead?"

"She's standing right in front of you, worrying about what would happen if she lost her fucking job. How she'd pay her bills. Well, guess what? She can't. I need this job. You know that." I step into him, grip his face in my hands. "It's not for much longer. I just have to make it until graduation and then find something in my field." His jaw is tight under my fingers, his eyes still blazing. I smooth my thumbs over his jaw, a little bit rough from his stubble. "Okay?"

"I hate that fucking guy," he grumbles, but accepts the kiss I place on his lips. Finally snapping out of it, he grips my hips, pulling me closer to him as he slants his mouth over mine, his tongue slipping between my lips. After a few minutes, he pulls back. "Let's get out of here."

I tie my hair back, slip my helmet on as I slide in behind him. With my legs pressed tightly on the outside of his, my arms locked around his waist, my head tucked to his shoulder, I get lost to everything but the feeling of his strong body in front of mine, of the wind surrounding us, and the feeling of freedom that's always present when I'm on this bike with him.

## cade

I park in front of her building, waiting as she gets off the back of the bike. When her helmet's off, her hair loose again around her, I ask, "When's your first class tomorrow?"

"Nine, why?"

"Can I come in for a while?" I know it's late. She's just worked eight hours, probably wants to wash off the night, then crash immediately. But after the talk with Chef Foster, and then seeing Winter's asshole boss harassing her, I'm too keyed up to go home and sleep.

I need something. I need *her*.

Standing to the side of my bike, she stares at me for a moment, before nodding her head and turning to go. I reach for her hand before she can get inside the front door, and she lets me hold on, twining our fingers together. She slides me looks out of the corner of her eye as she leads us down the hallway and into her apartment but doesn't ask why my shoulders are so tense, why my jaw is clenched. Once inside, she drops her bag, and I lean back against the door, scrubbing a hand over my face.

"Hey," she says as she steps between my legs. "What else is going on? This isn't just about Randy, is it?" She reaches up, smoothing her thumb between my eyes, along my forehead. "If it is, you can't let him get to you so much. He's an asshole."

As I stare at her, it's hard to believe this is the same girl from a few weeks ago. The one with the dead eyes and false smiles. I can hardly remember her, the mystery girl I wanted to know, however she'd let me. She's softened, just a little. Just enough to let me in.

I grab her hips, pulling her tight against me as I drop my head on her shoulder. "It's been a shitty day."

She rubs her hand over my hair, up and down, up and down. "Yeah, I got that. Why's it been so shitty?"

Turning my head, I press my nose into the crook where her neck meets her shoulder and inhale. Open my mouth over the juncture and suck, my tongue flicking out to taste her. "Later," is all I say as I continue peppering kisses over her skin.

"No, Cade. Wait. Tell me."

"After."

"I stink like the pub."

"Better get you in the shower, then." I don't wait for her response before I grab her ass in both hands, hauling her up against me as I walk to her bathroom. I strip her quickly, then myself, and tug her into the shower before the water's even heated. She yelps as the cold stream hits her, shooting me a glare over her shoulder.

She probably wants slow. Easy. Soft and sweet. She deserves it. And I want nothing more than to give it to her. But I can't. My mind is a tornado of chaos, thoughts about fucking up at school, letting my mentor down, of doing something with my life after I graduate so I can still help Tessa and Haley . . . So I can help provide for them like they deserve. As if that wasn't bad enough, seeing Winter's boss talk to her after work was the last fucking straw. I was far enough away that I didn't catch everything he said, but I heard enough to know I wanted to climb off my bike and slam him up against the wall, see how tough he was when he was facing off with someone other than a hundred and ten–pound girl.

I focus back on Winter, my eyes traveling down her body. I'd love to get on my knees for her here. Press her against the tile and lift her up until her thighs were on my shoulders and my mouth was on her pussy, licking every bit of her. But not tonight, not when all I can think about is fucking out everything I have boiling in my veins.

I lift her easily, guiding her legs around my waist as I kiss and lick every part of her I can reach. Dipping my head, I suck a nipple into my mouth, letting my teeth scrape over it, giving her just a bit of pain to go with her pleasure. She gasps, her head falling back as her hand clutches me to her. I switch sides, repeating the treatment on her other breast until she's grinding against me. She shifts enough that the head of my cock slips just inside and we both freeze, our panting breaths the only movement between us.

"Don't move. *Fuck*. Don't move."

Feeling her like this, even this tiny bit, without a latex barrier between us is un-fucking-believable. I've *never* felt this. I've always worn a condom, never once gone without. But Jesus, feeling her heat, how wet she is . . . I want nothing more than to be with her like this, skin to skin. To feel her sweet pussy gripping me, pulsing around me when she comes. When *I* make her come.

"It's okay. Cade. It's okay." She pulls back, smoothing her hands down my cheeks, brushing aside the rivulets of water trailing down. Her eyes are so intense, so bright and full and *alive*. "It's okay. I'm safe, and I'm on the pill."

And fucking hell, is she actually contemplating this with me? Just the thought has my words coming out jumbled. "Same. Me, too. Christ, I mean, I'm not on the pill obviously, but I'm safe." I'm a bumbling fucking idiot with the prospect of pure, unencumbered sex in front of me.

"I know." She frames my face, places the softest of kisses on my lips, her eyes still open. "I trust you." It's whispered into the space between us, nearly lost among the sounds of our breaths and the water beating around us and my heart pounding relentlessly in my chest.

And while I came in here to take her, to pound into her until I fucked out every ounce of anger and frustration I held from the day, I can't.

I can't.

Not when she's looking at me like I'm her whole fucking world.

"Winter . . ."

She nods in response, our lips touching, shared breaths mingling between our parted mouths. With our eyes locked, I grip her tighter, shift her lower until all I can feel is her. She's everywhere. Surrounding me. *Consuming* me.

"I love you." I capture her lips in a kiss, slow and deep, sweeping my tongue into her sweet mouth, tasting her as I move slowly into her. She's hot, *Christ*, so fucking hot. She takes me easily, her body ready for me, and if I don't pause, go slow, this is going to be over before it's even begun, because the feel of her—nothing *but* her—is unlike anything I've felt before.

Her arms are around my neck, forearms braced against the back of my head. Her legs are clamped around my hips, her breasts and stomach flush against me, and I yet want her closer. I press her into the shower wall, taking her mouth in another kiss as I keep my rhythm slow and deep for as long as I can. But when her fingernails bite into my back, her teeth nipping my lips, her hips restless against me, I know she's ready for something else.

"What do you need, baby? Tell me."

"Faster, *God*, faster, please."

"Thank Christ." I speed up, pushing into her and shifting my hips until I hit the spot inside her that makes her legs tighten around me, her mouth go slack, her eyes roll back in her head.

"Cade . . ."

"I've got you. Let go, I've got you."

Her moans are soundless, just whispers of breath as her entire body goes taut, inside and out, until she throbs—and *fucking hell*, feeling her come with nothing between us is better than I could've imagined. I grit my teeth, holding back just so this lasts a few minutes longer.

When she's caught her breath, she lifts her head, her eyes locking with mine, open in their intensity, and even though she hasn't said the words, even though she hasn't told me she loves me, I can see it in her gaze. Feel it in the way she holds me to her, the way she clutches me with everything she has.

And I'm gone.

# TWENTY

*winter*

I almost said it. I was so close, the words sitting on the tip of my tongue, ready to jump off, but I couldn't. When I stared into his eyes, shining with everything he feels for me, I froze.

He's so open and honest, so forthcoming with his thoughts and his feelings, and I'm not. I'm closed off and jaded and angry at the world. And he deserves someone who's so much more. Someone like him, who can love him freely and openly, who isn't afraid to say those three little words.

I'm not that girl. I don't know if I'll ever be that girl.

After our shower, he dried me off then brought me to my bed, folded it down, and pulled me into the middle with him. Now he's playing with strands of my damp hair, picking them up, rubbing them between his fingers before moving on to another piece. His chest is warm under my cheek, his heartbeat my own personal lullaby, and I don't want him to leave.

I don't want him to leave me.

His lips are on my forehead, pressing a soft kiss there, then brushing against me as he speaks. "Why'd you get so tense?"

And what am I supposed to say? That fears I've had my whole life are eating me alive? That all I can think about, all I worry about, is the day he gets tired of putting up with my closed-off bullshit and decides I'm not worth it?

But I can't say that, so I do what I'm so adept at. I deflect. "Don't make this about me. You said you'd tell me after. Well, it's after."

"Maybe I meant after round two . . ."

I reach up, pinching his nipple.

"Fucking *hell*, Winter! Shit . . ." With a scowl on his face, he rubs the spot I just grabbed. "Christ, that hurt."

"Don't be such a baby. You're six-three, two-twenty. Don't tell me a titty-twister is gonna make you cry."

"Six-four, two-thirty, and no." He huffs, reaching down to slap my ass. "Fine."

"You'll tell me what happened before? Earlier today?" I tilt my head back so I can see his face.

He reaches up, traces his finger down the line of my nose, brushes over the outline of my lips. "I will." I settle back into the crook at his side, until he says, "But you have to answer a question from me."

I stiffen in his arms, thoughts of all he could ask me flying through my mind. *How'd you end up here? Where are your parents? When will you let me in?*

*Why are you so broken?*

The hard lump in my throat refuses to go down, even after swallowing hard. I hope my voice doesn't sound as shaky as I feel. "Do I get a veto?"

He hums, contemplating my request. "Fine, yes. One. But if

you veto the first question, you have to answer the next. No excuses."

I take a deep breath, my fingers tracing the lines of the tattoos on his forearms. I still don't know what they mean, and I've been too scared to ask again, to listen to that part of him that I know will be a glimpse into his very soul. Afraid he'll want me to reciprocate. Like now. Even so, not even twenty minutes ago, I told him I trusted him. I need to start living up to that. I want to. "Okay."

His chest deflates as he blows out a long breath. "Okay. You better not be fucking with me."

Smiling against his chest, I say, "Promise."

His fingers start back up on my hair, his voice echoing under my ear as his body rumbles with his words. "In class earlier, my mentor asked me to stay behind. I . . . last week, I fucked up."

"How so?"

"When we're in the kitchen, we need to work like a cohesive machine, everyone doing their stuff on time, in the right order, and not holding anyone back. Well, my mind wasn't there and it showed. I fell behind and dragged everyone with me. It was a complete clusterfuck, and it was my fault."

He's so tense, his muscles tight and bunched even under my fingers as I rub back and forth on his chest and stomach. I know how much pride he takes in his work, in his food, so knowing he screwed up, affected everyone else on top of it, has to be hard on him.

"Anyway, he called me on it today, said he expected more from me. And he's right. I know that, and I knew it last week, but to see the disappointment in his eyes? It just fucking killed me, you know? He's more than just my mentor. I've known him for a long time. He was friends with my parents, was there when my mom was going through chemo and I was trying to do everything on my own. I mean, fuck, I was only seventeen when she was diagnosed, eighteen when it got really bad. I didn't know what the fuck to do, so I just did the best I could. I made sure Tessa went to school every day and did her homework, ran the household. Mark—Chef Foster—was there if we needed it, always told me that, but I hated the idea of someone being dragged into our mess. And I hated the idea that it was something I couldn't do on my own." He squeezes me, and I know he's thinking back to all the conversations we've had where I've said pretty much the same thing to him. Pride is a bitch.

"So we got by without him. I graduated and put off going to college. I always knew I wanted to be a chef, so I applied to Le Cordon Bleu before my mom got sick and got accepted, but after, I just . . . I couldn't. None of it mattered, you know? I just wanted her to get better, and there was no way—no fucking way—I could've packed up and moved away to school while she was going through that by herself.

"He was the one who pushed me to finally go, after my mom died. Since my dad's accident, Mark's been pretty much the only male influence in my life, and to know that I disappointed him . . . it *sucks*." He blows out a deep breath, shrugs his shoulders. "So that was my shitty day before I came to pick you up, and then to see that asshole boss of yours go off on you . . . well, it just all sort of piled on top of me. Which was why I came into your apartment like a brooding asshole and dragged you in the shower to have my way with you. Sorry about that."

I smother a laugh against his skin, and he squeezes me tighter. Settling closer to him, I trace my fingers over the indentations of the muscles in his stomach. "I'm sorry, Cade. About your mom, but also about what you've given up. I know it's not easy to lose the person who's supposed to watch out for you. It doesn't matter that it happened after you were an adult or not."

"I've accepted it now. I did the best I could at the time. And the three of us are doing okay now. That's what's important to me, being there for them."

Pushing away, I lean onto my elbow, my face above his. "But what about you? What do *you* want?"

"I want them to be safe and happy. I want that for you, too."

"I'm not talking about us. I'm talking about you. Be selfish for a minute. What do you want?"

His hand pauses in my hair, his eyes flitting back and forth between mine. After a moment, he admits, "I want to go to Italy. I want to work for a year or two, learn everything I can. And then I want to come back, here maybe, or close, and open a restaurant. My restaurant with my food."

"Okay, then why don't you?"

His brow furrows, like it's the dumbest question that's ever tumbled out of my mouth. "Why don't I just fly over to Europe for a couple years? Forget all my responsibilities here?"

"Cade. Your sister is an adult and Haley is hers to worry about. You can't put your dreams on hold for them. I don't know Tessa very well, but from what you've told me about her, I think I know enough to realize she'd hate it if you did that, to know she's stopping you from what you really want."

"What I really want is right here. Them. *You.*"

"But—"

"Nope, I answered. It's your turn."

*cade*

Her eyes go wide with panic, and I almost tell her she doesn't have to answer my questions. Almost. I brush my thumb over her lower lip, trying to soothe her nerves.

"What secrets are you hiding that make you so nervous about this?"

I don't expect her to answer, but she does. "Too many."

"You can tell me, you know. Anything. Nothing you say will change the way I feel about you."

She nods her head, but the uncertainty in her eyes is clear. I reach up, smooth the hair away from her face. I want to know more about her—I want to know *everything* about her. But I don't want to push her into anything she isn't prepared for.

"You ready?" I ask.

The corner of her mouth is pulled in, her eyes filled with fear and dread. And I hate that she still feels this way around me. Instead of asking any of the dozens of questions flying through my head that I've had weeks to think about—what her family's like, where she goes over the holidays, what her life was like before she came here to school—I ask one I know is safe. "What do you want to do after you graduate?"

It takes her a moment before the lack of complexity of my question registers, and her breath rushes out of her in a whoosh. "That's what you want to know?"

No. "Yes."

She settles on top of me, her entire body melting in relief. Her arms are folded across my chest, her chin on her the back of her hand. "That wasn't what I thought you were going to ask."

"What'd you think I was going to ask?"

"Well, I'm not giving you ideas."

"Believe me, baby, they're there. You're just not ready for me to ask them."

Her eyes widen the tiniest bit before she looks down, clears her throat. "I want to do a hundred things, see a hundred different places. I'd love to get in a car and just drive, with no agenda, just go. I can design from anywhere, but I've always wanted to go to New York or Chicago. Philly, maybe. Florida. I don't care. I just want to go. Somewhere other than here or . . . home."

The last word is barely a whisper, and it's on the tip of my tongue to ask where home is, but the expression on her face, the sorrow in her eyes as she flits them back up to mine, stops me.

Instead, I say, "Then you should."

She smiles then, her real smile. The one that crinkles the corners of her eyes. "With all my extra money, huh?"

"I don't mean take off right the fuck now. I just meant someday."

"Tell ya what . . . I'll have my someday when you have yours. When you go off to Italy, I'll hop in a car and just go."

All her fear evaporates in a minute, the panic that was present in her eyes only a moment before replaced by determination and challenge. A challenge she knows I can't accept.

# TWENTY-ONE

*cade*

"Okay, now add the flour, but—" It's too late, a puff of white exploding in Winter's face before I can get the words out or reach to flip the switch. "You need to turn the mixer to low."

She spins around, her cheeks covered in random white spots, some of the flour dusting her hair. "You couldn't say that before 'Now add the flour'?" Her voice is low, her eyes narrowed, and I take a step back.

"Well, yeah, I guess I could've, but I just sort of figured you'd know enough not to add loose flour to a wildly spinning mixer."

"Oh, you figured I'd know enough for that, huh? Even after I told you I've never made cookies before? Even then?"

She's advancing on me now, and I shouldn't be retreating like a scared animal. I have more than a foot on her, a hundred-plus pounds, but she looks pissed. And that glint in her eye tells me she's up to something. I glance down at her hand, seeing a measuring cup half filled with flour, and I realize what she's going to do a split second before she does, but not soon enough to dodge it.

A cloud of white powder hits me straight in the face, and I cough as I inhale some. Wiping away the dust from my eyes, I say, "I can't believe you did that."

"Oh, well, I just figured you'd know enough to duck." She shrugs and offers me a saccharine smile.

"I don't think you want to start this with me, baby."

"In case you missed the flour in your face a second ago, I already started it, *baby*."

I stare her down, then reach over, grabbing the bowl of melted chocolate—my mom's secret ingredient in her cookies—and dip my fingers into it. Winter narrows her eyes at me and takes a step back. "Don't you dare."

"Where you goin'? I thought you wanted to get messy."

"No, I wanted *you* to get messy. I didn't have a choice with this," she says as she gestures to where the flour hit her. She darts her eyes down to the bowl of chocolate, then back up to my face. "Don't, Cade. You're going to get me dirty, and I have to be at work soon."

"You maybe should've thought about that before you threw a scoop of flour in my face." I don't wait for her response before I smear the chocolate down her cheek to her jaw, then all the way down her neck and into the deep V of her shirt, stopping when I feel the swell of her breasts. "Whoops."

"You did not just do that."

"Looks like I did." I shrug, putting the bowl back on the counter before I lick the chocolate from my fingers. She focuses on the act, her lips parted. I lean closer to her, drop my voice, and gesture to the spots of her skin that are covered. "You want me to clean you up, too?"

Glaring, she gives a jerky shake of her head, but a flush works its way up her chest to her neck—one of the tells she's getting turned on.

I step closer, backing her into the corner until she's pressed against the cabinets behind her. "Sure about that? It wouldn't take much. Just a lick or two. Maybe a couple sucks. We'd probably have to take your shirt off, though, and your bra, too. I really got down in there."

Her head's tilted back as she stares up at me, her chest rising and falling in quick succession from her labored breathing.

I lean into her space, lick up a path from her neck to her ear. "I think you do. I think you want my tongue all over you, don't you, baby? I got you all dirty. Seems only fair I clean you up." Before she can respond, my mouth closes over her shoulder, my tongue tracing along the chocolate I smeared there. By the time I've dipped into the neckline of her shirt, my tongue in the valley of her breasts, her nipples are pressed tight against the material, and she's got a white-knuckled grip on the countertop behind her.

"Want me to stop?"

I wait a second. Two. And when she gives the slightest shake of her head, I take. Gripping her face in my hands, my mouth covers hers, my tongue slipping inside. She groans into the kiss, her hands finally coming up to clutch my forearms.

"Wait." She wrenches her mouth from mine, turning her head to the side. "Cade, wait. Your sister."

I focus on licking every stray ounce of chocolate I can find, her hands a counterpoint to her words as she holds me close. "Not home. Gone till four."

"Shit! Four. I have to be at work at four!"

"We've got time. Now stop talking."

I peel her jeans and panties off, then lift her onto the counter, desperate to feel her around me. With one hand, I fumble with the button of my jeans, the other busy between Winter's thighs, rubbing soft circles around her clit, getting her ready for me. She's moaning, her head resting back on the cabinets, and the sight of her there, half naked in my kitchen, is too much. Too fucking much, and I can't get my goddamn jeans off.

When she notices, her hands are there, opening my jeans and yanking my boxers down just far enough to pull me out. Her hands are around my cock, pumping slowly, and I need inside her now.

*winter*

It just gets better. Every time, it's better than the last. Will it always be like this? In a month, will I be having sex so utterly mind-blowing in its awesomeness I can't even comprehend it now?

I wonder if it's him. Maybe sex for him is always like this. Maybe he's just that skilled that he can make the women he's with go off in three seconds, can make their nipples hard with a glance, their clits ache from the brush of his lips anywhere.

Or maybe it's us.

Maybe it's the way we move together, the way our breaths mix and mingle in the space between us. The way we give and take, push and pull, until we're both out of our minds with pleasure and need.

I stroke him, gripping and twisting my hand over the head just how he likes, until he's so far gone, so frenzied to get inside me, he doesn't even bother with the rest of our clothes. With his jeans still around his hips, he pulls me to the edge of the counter, my ass barely on it, and then drives deep.

And it's good, so good, so good.

His name leaves me in a breath as he fills me completely, pulling out slowly and pushing in again. Three or four or five times, until my fingernails dig into his ass and my teeth clamp down on his shoulder. He groans, his hips moving faster now, like he can't get far enough inside me, like he wants to crawl right into my body and never leave. Forehead pressed to mine, he looks down to where we're joined, seeing himself disappear inside me with nothing between us. No barriers, just us, and it's terrifying and intoxicating and freeing to give myself over to him like this, just like the first time in my shower. Give myself to him in a way I've never done with anyone else. I've never *wanted* to with anyone else.

He moves his hand between us, his thumb on my clit flicking back and forth, and then he sends me into a tailspin before I even know I'm at the precipice. I clutch at his shoulders, legs locked around his waist, as I'm thrown headfirst into oblivion.

"Baby . . . *Fuck*, Winter . . ."

And then he's there with me, his body tight and coiled, his muscles so hard under my caressing hands, his breaths panting against my neck as he stills inside me, and I want him like this always. Always, I want to be this close to him, this connected, this free from the doubts I carry with me endlessly except when he's inside me. I want the freedom he gives me *always*.

When we've both caught our breath, he pulls away, his forehead sticking on my skin where he licked the chocolate from me.

"Ewww . . ."

His chuckle is low and deep, rumbling in his chest. "Just what every guy wants to hear after sex."

"I think you got chocolate in my hair."

"Sorry I'm not sorry."

I laugh and push him away, glancing at the clock as I do. "Oh, fuck! It's almost three thirty. Cade! Dammit, I'm going to need to shower now, too." I scramble off the counter, grabbing my underwear and jeans from where they're scattered around the floor.

"Go use mine. I'll drive you to work. It'll be fine."

"If I'm late—"

"You won't be late, unless you stand here and keep arguing with me." He grabs my shoulders, turns me toward his bathroom, then slaps my ass. "Go. I'll clean up in here and be ready to go whenever you are."

I take the fastest shower known to man, thankful I brought my uniform with me, just in case. I slip into it, pulling my jeans and hoodie on over it. I find a comb in the drawer and yank it through my hair until it's acceptable. When I'm as ready as I'm going to get without any of my normal shit with me, I run back into the kitchen.

"Let's go, let's go!"

"Hi, Winter."

I whip around, seeing an amused Tessa sitting at the island, chin in her hand. "Oh, hi. Hey. Sorry about the—" I gesture to the now spotless kitchen and realize there isn't anything to apologize for. She raises an eyebrow like she knows exactly what I did with her brother in here a few minutes ago. Glancing down, I offer a quiet, "Sorry."

Her answering smile makes my face burst into flames.

"Ready?" Cade comes up behind me, his fingers on the back of my arm.

"Yeah, we have to hurry."

"I know. It'll be fine."

"Cade, he told me—" I shake my head, lowering my voice to a whisper. "I can't be late. You know I can't lose this job."

"You're not going to get fired because you're five minutes late. And I'll speed the whole way."

Once we're in the car, the inside of my cheek is raw, my leg bouncing as I watch the clock tick closer to four o'clock, and then watch the minutes accumulate as it passes. He reaches over, settles his hand on my jittery leg.

"Should I go in with you?"

I snap my head to him and see that he's dead serious. "Cade. *No.* You should not go in with me. God, I'm a grown woman. If something is going to happen, I don't need my boyfriend there to bail me out of trouble."

"Okay, okay. I was just asking." He holds up a hand in surrender. "I just . . . I don't like that guy. He's nothing but a sleazy asshole."

"Yeah, well, that sleazy asshole's my boss, and he doesn't like you, either. If I get in trouble, you'll only make it worse. He probably won't even be out front anyway." Except I know he will. He will. He always is. Ever since he talked to me that night after work, he's been watching. Every day when I come in, every night when I leave, and all the times in between. I can feel his eyes on me through the glass mirror to his office as I'm working, waiting on customers. Knowing he can look at me whenever the urge strikes while I'm wearing glorified underwear sends a shudder through me.

I barely wait until the car stops before I lean over, give Cade a quick kiss, and slip out the door. Cars litter the parking lot, and I hope there are enough people inside to mask my arrival. When I push through the front door, I keep my head down, walking to the back and clocking in before stripping out of my jeans and hoodie in record time.

Once on the floor, I go straight to the bar, finding out what tables are mine for the night so I can get started right away.

"You've got four through ten tonight, sugar." Annette's eyes keep flicking to the back of the restaurant, and my heart sinks.

"Did he see?" I whisper, though I already know the answer.

She gives a small nod. Leaning toward me, she lowers her voice. "I don't know what his deal is lately. It's like he's just waiting for you to screw up. He can be an asshole, but this is a little much even for him."

I nod, swallow, and push away from the bar, trying to ignore the pit in my stomach as I start my night.

IT'S JUST PAST ten when Randy comes up to me. My last table has cleared out, and my entire section is empty, the only people still inside sitting at the bar.

"Winter. My office." He doesn't wait as he walks past the mirrored window and into the open door settled in the middle of the dark hallway.

I glance back at Annette, her eyes focused on us, then steel my shoulders and follow after where he went. When we're both inside his tiny office, he closes the door behind me. I've been in here before, of course, but seeing it now—this late at night, when the entire restaurant is spread out like a buffet for him, half a dozen barely dressed college girls prancing around for his unencumbered eyes—sends a wave of unease over me.

His desk is dark and cluttered with paperwork and garbage. A ratty brown couch sits against the far wall, directly in front of the mirrored window that looks out onto the floor, and I feel dirty all over again at the thought of him back here, watching us at his leisure.

He stands against the front of his desk, his legs out in front of him, arms crossed. He looks the same as he always does—black pants, gray button-up shirt, dirty blond hair parted and combed to the side. Generically handsome if you don't notice the small, beady eyes, a slightly crooked nose, and a goatee that looks out of place on him. But now . . . he's got this air of malevolence I've never felt around him.

"You were late tonight."

I swallow. Meet his direct stare. "Yes. Less than ten minutes."

"I don't care *how* late you were. Late is late, and we've talked about this before, haven't we?" His voice is low, controlled, as he focuses on his shirt, flicking away a piece of imaginary lint.

Clenching my teeth and my hands, I force myself to remain calm. "Yes. I'm sorry, and it won't happen again. I can stay late tomorrow or come in early, without pay, to make up the time."

He doesn't say anything, just stares at me. Then his gaze drops, his eyes taking a slow perusal of my body, and the hairs on the back of my neck stand on end, trepidation rippling through me as disgust settles in. "Things are tough for you at home, aren't they?"

"I'm not sure what you mean."

"I mean, making rent, paying your bills. This isn't just extra spending money for you, not like it is for Jenny or Tara or Eve. You *need* this job. Right?"

My entire body is taut, my spine ramrod straight, and I force myself to give a jerky nod. There's no use lying about it. That first night when Cade came in and I had to ask for an extra shift, I alluded to as much. I had no idea it would come back to bite me in the ass.

"That's what I thought." He pushes away from his desk, walks over to me, so close I can feel his sour breath against my face. I try not to recoil, try to hold my ground, but it's difficult. The sense of smell is remarkable. How an inconsequential hint of something can transport you back to a time or place, regardless of whether you want to go or not. And everything about him right now—the hint of cheap aftershave, an undertone of ciga-rette smoke, and the undeniable scent of whiskey on his breath—shoves me full force back to my childhood. To dark rooms and lonely nights and listening to things no five-year-old should have to listen to. And when he touches me, his finger tracing circles on the back of my hand, I can't control the shudder that racks my body.

"I don't want to fire you, Winter. I like you. The customers *definitely* like you. But I can't have you coming and going as you please, setting a bad example for the other girls. Pretty soon I'll have employees showing up two hours late to work or not at all, and then what will I do?" He shakes his head, steps even closer. "But I think we can work this out. I'm just going to need a lit-tle . . . incentive to keep you on."

It takes me a moment to register what he means as his finger trails up my arm, over my shoulder until he's tracing the scoop neck of my low top, the cut of it so deep his fingernail scrapes against the top swells of my breasts. It's only a moment—four or five seconds of time where I'm frozen, my feet glued to the ground—but it allows him to touch more of me than he ever should. Coming back to myself, I reach up and slap his hand away before stepping back, my body shaking with fury. "What the fuck are you doing?"

He raises his eyebrows at me, holds his hands in the air. "I'm not doing anything. *You're* saving your job."

My anger is building, bubbling up until it's spilling out of me, no thought for the repercussions. No thought of what I'll do tomorrow or next week or even in five minutes. "Is this where you tell me to get on my knees if I expect to work here anymore?"

"I was going to let you stand, but your knees work fine for me."

I scoff, rolling my eyes, hands clenched at my sides. "Did you actually believe this would work? You think I need this job that much? You, what, thought I'd be so thankful you wanted to give me another chance that I'd fall at your feet and open my mouth, suck your dick for you? Just until the next time I was two minutes late, though, right? Or until my boyfriend showed up and had a problem with your customers feeling me up and decided to step in because you're too cheap or just too much of an asshole to hire bouncers to protect us. Or until I broke a glass or messed up a ticket or forgot to punch in just once. Then I'd be back in this office, on my knees in front of you, sucking your too small dick. Am I close? Did I get it right? Well, *fuck you*," I spit, jabbing a finger at him. "I'd rather live on the streets than have any part of you anywhere near me."

I don't give him a chance to respond, don't wait to see if he'd force me into something against my will before I tear out of his office, passing the scattered customers along the way. I feel Annette's eyes on me as I blow past her and into the back room without a glance. Before I can get all my things from my locker, yanking my belongings out and struggling to cover myself, she's there, her hand on my back.

"Winter . . ."

I shake my head, focusing on the buttons of my jeans as I cover up the uniform I'm never going to have to wear again. If I look up or speak, I'll break. I won't break here. Not because of him.

"I can't believe that asshole. He fired you?"

A humorless laugh slips out. "No, that was all me. He said he'd let me keep my job if I sucked his dick."

Her hand pauses on my back, her fingers curled into the material of my sweatshirt. "Bastard," she spits under her breath. "I had no idea . . . I mean, I knew he was always a slimeball, but I had no idea he'd do that. I never would've let you go in there alone. I shouldn't have let you . . ."

Turning back, I look at her, her troubled eyes begging for forgiveness for something she had no part in. "There wasn't anything you could do, Annette. And if he thought I was going to sit there quietly without anything to say about his *offer*, he got a surprise." I gather up the rest of my things, stuffing the couple of items I kept in my locker into my bag.

"You'll be okay. You're strong, Winter. You'll get something figured out."

I give a jerky nod, hoping she's right. Thoughts of what this means are trickling in, and panic is hovering on the edges. I have to get out of here so I can think. So I can plan.

"Here." She slips a cocktail napkin into my hands, her messy scrawl across the stark white. "That's my number. You call me, you understand? If you need anything, you call me."

I stuff it into my jeans pocket and settle the strap of my bag across my chest.

"No, I mean it." She grabs me by the shoulders and turns me, forces me to stare into her eyes. "If you need anything, sugar. A ride, a place to stay for however long . . . you call me. Promise me."

I stare at her, her eyes sad and tired, her face showing more wear than it should at her forty-something years. Swallowing, I say, "Okay."

"I'm counting on that."

"Thank you."

She squeezes my hand and then I'm out the back door, the weight of what happened finally crashing down on me. I don't have a job. I just walked out on my means for rent, for groceries . . .

Oh, *God.*

I have to find another job. Immediately. One that pays as well, that works around my school schedule, where I can make what I was making in the hours I was putting in at the pub. A dozen options flit through my mind, a couple stashed away as possibilities.

By the time I'm sitting on the bus, I've already calculated how much money I have against how long it is until rent's due. How long I can stay without paying the next month's bill, but I already know. I've seen eviction notices all over the building, constantly. There is no leeway. I think about what corners I can cut, what I can skimp on, what I can go without to save money. I contemplate applying for unemployment until I can find something else, and then remember I was the one to walk out rather than being fired and kick myself all over again for doing so.

It doesn't take long before I come to the conclusion that I'm fucked.

Even if I get a job tomorrow, my paychecks aren't going to start rolling in soon enough that I'll be able to skate by. Annette's napkin burns a hole in my pocket, and for one second, I think about calling her. About how easy it would be to just . . . let someone else help for once. To not carry the burden on my own. How freeing . . . how weightless it would feel. I shove that thought down, knowing I'll get by on my own, like always.

I don't even realize where I'm headed until the bus pulls up a block from Cade's house. I descend the steps and start the walk to his place, and before I've really thought it through, I'm at his front door. I don't know if I should be here, if I should burden him with this, especially with everything else he has going on that he should be focusing on. But he's so deeply seated in my life now that I don't know where else I'd go. And though I know I'll get through this on my own, just having someone to talk to about it, having someone I can share my fears with, is more than enough.

It's more than I ever thought I'd have. *He's* more than I ever thought I'd have.

I close my eyes, take a deep breath, and knock. It only takes a minute before the door is pulled open, and Cade's standing there, his brow creased in confusion.

"Winter? What are you doing here so early? I thought you closed tonight." He glances down to check his watch, the lines in his forehead deepening. "I was about to text you to see how it went with your boss."

And I don't even know how to find the words. How do I tell my boyfriend that my asshole boss told me I had to suck his dick or lose my job? In the end, I don't have to say anything. Cade takes my hand and pulls me inside, through the living room, and down the hall until we're tucked away in the privacy of his bedroom. He moves to sit on the bed and pulls me to stand in front of him, his hands wrapped around the outsides of my thighs.

"Baby, what's going on?"

I take a deep breath, blow it out. Close my eyes and say, "Turns out I can get fired for being five minutes late."

He's quiet, and when I open my eyes, his jaw is unhinged, his eyes wide. "That fucker *fired* you? Are you kidding me?"

"Not kidding."

"He just fired you."

Blowing out an exasperated breath, I say, "Yes, Cade."

He opens and closes his mouth, shakes head, his forehead creased in confusion. "He fired one of his best waitresses for being five minutes late? That doesn't make any sense."

And I don't want to tell him the real reason. I *can't*. I don't want Cade to see me like that. Dirty and trashy and no better than the mother who left me. He was the one person—the *only* person—who looked past all my bullshit and didn't care about the dark parts of me. Just remembering the words Randy said has shame pouring over me. I wonder how many times my mother was in that exact position. How many times she did it to get her next fix, for a place to stay, for a bottle of Jack.

Despite all my hard work, all my diligence at running from it, at keeping it as far from me as I can, my past caught up to me anyway. I'm turning out to be just like her.

"Winter." He gives my hand a quick tug, bringing my focus back to him. "He said it was because you were a few minutes late?"

I pull my hand out of his grasp and turn away from him, suddenly wishing I hadn't come here. I should've just gone home, started thinking up a plan. I should've just handled it instead of unloading my problems on him.

Cade follows me around, standing in front of me, and when he tips my face up to his, he must see something written in my expression, because his jaw ticks, his shoulders going rigid. "There's something else, isn't there? Tell me why he fired you. And don't bullshit me."

When my silence is the only thing that greets him, he curses harshly under his breath. "*Why*, Winter. Tell me or I'll go down there and ask him myself."

My eyes snap to his as I jab a finger in his chest. "Don't you dare. Don't you *dare* shove your way into this. You cannot go down there, do you understand? Promise me you won't interfere. This is my life, Cade. *Mine*. I've handled it, and I don't want to talk about it."

"You don't want to . . ." He trails off and turns in a tight circle, scrubbing his hand over his hair, his jaw clenched. "You don't want to talk about it? What the hell else should we talk about?"

"How about the fact that I can't make rent now? I'm not focusing on what happened, because I can't. I'm too busy worrying about what's *going* to happen. Like me being on the streets because I don't have a fucking job."

He stares at me for a minute, his eyes searching mine, and I can almost see the wheels spinning, trying to come up with a solution to my problems. Trying to fix it. When he finally opens his mouth and speaks, it's nothing I was expecting, and with his words he tips my whole world on its side. "Move in with me."

All the breath leaves my lungs, panic and anxiety rushing in, followed closely by a sliver of excitement . . . of happiness. Before it can grow to something more, my trepidation boils over, extinguishing that tiny sliver that tried to sneak through.

Fears I've had my entire life come rushing forward, radiating from those four little words. And I can't do this. I can't depend on him, can't build my whole life around him. If I do, I'm not just toeing the line of my past, I'm falling headfirst into the history I'm running so hard from.

Swallowing down the lump in my throat, I say, "I can't do that."

"Why not? You're talking about losing your apartment, Winter. Are you really that hardheaded that you'd rather live on the streets than accept my help? Why can't you stay with me?"

"Why? God, Cade, have you listened to a word I've said the entire time we've been together? I don't want or need your goddamn help! I want to do things on my own. I *need* to."

"But you *don't* need to! That's what I'm trying to tell you. If you'd stop being so fucking stubborn all the time and open your eyes, you'd see I'm not trying to rescue you or control your whole life. I'm trying to *help* you," he says, his voice rising with every word. "Why can't you just let me?"

"You've known from the first night we met this is who I am. Stop trying to change me! I want to do things on my own. And you need to back the fuck off. All you do is get into everyone else's business and try to fix things that aren't your concern in the first place. Whether you admit it or not, you have a hero complex and you *like* being the one there to rescue the people in your life. Tessa and Haley and me. Have you ever even stopped to ask if Tessa really *wants* your help?"

"Don't bring Tess into something that's between us. This is about you and me, Winter, not anyone else. And this doesn't have anything to do with me wanting to help and everything to do with the walls you've built to keep people out. I've been fighting every fucking day since the beginning to get in, and I'm starting to wonder why."

His harsh words crash into me, penetrating the very walls he spoke of, and I stare at him for a minute, dumbfounded. They're only words, a handful of mean-spirited words that mean nothing when stacked up against everything else he's ever said to me, all the words of love he's showered on me, but that doesn't matter. Not when I'm teetering on the edge anyway. Not when it's the same thought that's haunted me the entire time we've been together. Him giving it life solidifies my fears that we were doomed from the start.

"That's what I've wondered every day since the first, Cade. Why did you even bother?"

# TWENTY-TWO

*cade*

Winter turns and storms out, and I stand there, watching her go. With my hands clasped behind my head, I clench my eyes shut, my muscles coiled and ready to run after her, but I'm rooted in place. "Fuck!"

I'm furious with her and her refusal to let me help in even the smallest way. Her refusal to see my offer for what it is instead of everything it isn't. I'm furious with myself for what I said in the heat of the moment. Something I never meant.

But above all, I'm furious with her boss, who put us in this position in the first place. My anger is building, my temper pushing at me, needing an outlet. Before I can think over what I'm about to do or stop myself, I grab my keys and head out into the night with only one destination in mind. Even though I know I shouldn't, that she forbade me from going, I can't help myself. Something's not right with the scenario, and all the little details of the past few weeks come at me, one after another. The looks her boss has given her, the way he was always watching . . . My gut churns with the possibilities, and I need to find out the truth behind her getting fired.

Speeding the whole way, I get there before my temper's abated at all. I push through the front door, scanning the pub for the guy I've focused all my anger on. When I don't see him, I head straight to the bar, spotting Annette mixing drinks. Her eyes go wide when she notices me, then flit over my shoulder and to the back of the restaurant.

Her voice is tentative, nervous almost, her eyes continually flicking toward the back and where I know his office is. "Hey, honey . . . What can I get ya tonight?"

"I'm not here for a drink, Annette. What happened tonight with Winter?"

She glances over my shoulder again, and when she looks back at me, there's something sparked in her eyes. With a lowered voice, she says, "She was . . . forced to leave."

"Yeah, I got that. What I want to know is why."

"Look, honey, maybe you should ask her—"

"Annette." I lean forward, gripping the edge of the bar. "Why?"

Her voice drops even lower, the words spilling out of her in a rush. "She was late but he didn't say anything about it when she first got here, and then at around ten, Randy called her back to his office." Regret fills her eyes, her head shaking slightly. "If I'd known what he was going to do, I swear, I never would have let her go—"

"Did he touch her?" My entire body is rigid, my muscles aching from tension, and I don't even recognize my voice as it rumbles out of me, low and dark and an angry calm.

"I don't know all the details—she didn't tell me exactly what happened—but from what I gathered, he gave her a sort of . . . ultimatum. To be able to keep her job. Nothing happened, though. She left before . . . well, before."

Everything makes sense now. How rigid she got when I asked her about it, her vehemence that I not come here, that she'd already handled it. But why did she think she couldn't tell me? Was she embarrassed about what that fucker did to her? A thousand possibilities fly through my mind, and I need to take a few deep breaths or I will break his fucking face without a second thought. "Where is he?"

Once again, she looks over his shoulder, and I know when she spots him, because her eyes grow just a bit wider, and she tips her chin in that direction. When I turn around, some creepy asshole is talking to another waitress, his eyes focused on the front of her top. Besides an outline and a vague image of him at the back door of the pub, I've never seen him face-to-face. But from the second my eyes land on him, on his slicked-over hair and his crooked teeth as he offers a predatory smile, I know this is the fucker who's made Winter's life hell, and I see red. I ignore Annette's voice behind me, ignore the looks I get as I stalk across the floor to him.

He doesn't even glance up until I'm in his space. He's too busy ogling the girl in front of him, and I want nothing more than to land my fist in his face. Feel the satisfying crunch of his nose under my hand, see the devastation I could do to him. I *would* do to him.

Instead I steel myself, taking a deep breath and reminding myself why I can't do this kind of thing. Why I don't get into trouble, why it'd be a mistake, all the consequences that would come of it if I beat him to a bloody fucking pulp like I want to.

When I feel like I've got control of myself, I interrupt him, my voice deadly calm. "Are you the piece of shit who owns this place?"

"Who the fuck—" he starts, turning a glare to me, and then his eyes widen, his words cut off, and I know without a doubt he recognizes me. Glancing over at the waitress still standing next to us, he takes a small step back. Pussy. "Get the hell out of my restaurant. You're not welcome here."

"You think I give two fucks if I'm welcome here? Now I asked you a question."

His attempt to stand his ground, to rise to his full height, is lessened by the way he visibly swallows and the slight waver in his voice when he speaks. "Don't make me call the cops on you."

I laugh, crossing my arms against my chest. With a jerk of my chin, I gesture to the door in the middle of the dark hallway behind him. "How about we go in your office. We have some things to talk about."

"You're not coming in my office."

Dropping my arms to my side, my hands tighten into fists, and I lean toward him, my voice low. "Okay, let me put it this way. Either we're walking into your office together, calmly, or I am beating your ass out here in front of all your customers and employees. Your choice."

He stares at me for a moment, sizing me up to see how serious I am. I'm not sure what does it—if it's the tattoos, the metal through my eyebrow, or the fact that I loom over him, but he relents. Finally, he gives a stilted nod and turns to go. I follow behind him quickly, and even before his door shuts behind me, he starts running his mouth.

"I don't know what the fuck your little girlfriend told you, but she's a goddamn *liar*."

I fold my arms across my chest and lean back against the door. My gaze is cool but unrelenting. I've dealt with guys like him before. Slimy fuckers who will try to get away with anything until someone bigger than them, stronger than them, comes along and puts a stop to it. Men who think they own the world. Who push their weight around with women, because they're too chickenshit to do it with other men. And strong women—strong, capable women like Winter and Tessa—get caught in the trap.

"Look, man, I didn't even ask her to. She was the one who said it in the first place, so if you want to get pissed at anyone for talking about sucking my dick, it should be her. I was never—"

I'm on him in a second, his shirt bunched in my fist, his back thrown against the wall, the tips of his cheap shoes barely brushing the ground. "You don't get to talk anymore, do you understand me? You're going to shut your fucking mouth and listen."

His eyes are wide with fear, his hands gripping my wrists, trying to get purchase, and the sight just fuels me more.

"You are a piece of shit. A slimy, disgusting, worthless piece of shit excuse for a man. You think it makes you bigger, better, smarter to force your disease-covered dick onto an uninterested woman? What did you tell her when you dragged her in here?" I slam him once against the wall. "And don't you fucking lie to me."

He swallows again, his panicked eyes darting between mine. "I . . . I told her I didn't want to have to fire her. But I would. If she . . . if she didn't . . ."

"Well, don't stop now. If she didn't what?"

"If . . . if she didn't offer an incentive."

"And by incentive, you mean . . ."

He swallows, his entire body shaking. His voice is low, but the words still cut through me. "Sucking me off."

And I swear to Christ, it takes everything in me not to put him on the floor and swing until he's a motionless pile on his dirty carpet. I pull myself back from the edge of fury, barely. I know this asshole would press charges in a heartbeat if I left him a bloody mess, and I can't take that chance.

Faking a calm I don't feel, I lean close to him, until all he can see is my face. "You don't get to even fucking *think* of her like that. *Ever.* When you have your little fantasies about some girl on her knees in front of you, you think about some other faceless girl, not *my* girl, am I making myself clear?"

He gives a jerky nod.

"Tell me, what'd she do when you told her that? Did she spit in your face? Knee you in the balls? Punch you in the jaw?"

When he doesn't respond, I slam him against the wall again, his eyes growing panicked. "N-Nothing. She didn't do any of that. She just told me to fuck off and left, and that was it."

"She was a lot nicer than I'm going to be." I don't give him a minute to contemplate that before I pull my right arm back and thrust it straight into his chest, aiming for his solar plexus. He doubles over, gasping for air that's not there, and it would be so easy. So fucking easy to snap my knee up and catch him in the face, send him to the ground, but I stop myself. I lean over, my mouth by his ear. "You're going to forget I was here, do you understand? This talk we had? Never happened." I shove him to the side, and he stumbles to his desk, leaning against it as he tries to catch his breath.

Fury curls around my shoulders, my body tense and primed, ready for a fight I can't give it. I walk out of the pub, past the inquiring eyes of everyone, especially Annette, and don't stop until I'm on my bike, rumbling through the city.

Where I want to feel relief and justification, satisfaction at giving that asshole everything he deserves, all I feel is regret. He had it coming, without a fucking doubt, but I didn't stop to think before I went there, didn't stop to contemplate what would happen after I did this. What Winter will think if she finds out. How absolutely *furious* she'll be with me. I didn't think about any of that, only the fact that someone hurt her, and I needed to do something about it.

As I speed through the city, the streetlights only a blur, I can't help but wonder what this will do to our already shaky foundation.

## winter

Cade's words echo through my mind as I step into my apartment. My greatest fears spilled from his lips, and I knew it was going to come to this. From the very beginning, I knew it'd come to this. It was only a matter of time before he asked himself why he ever bothered with me.

I shut the door behind me, the sound jarring in the quiet of the room. The silence has always been a comfort for me, but now I see it for what it is—a completely bare and lonely life—and why did I always think it would be so different? I thought once I got out of California, when I was on my own, everything would be different.

Getting notification of my partial scholarship here was the best day of my life. For once, I was happy. I'd really and truly be on my own, with no one else to worry about, no one else to depend on. But I didn't count on how exhausting it is, how utterly taxing it is to be the only one you can rely on. I'm so *tired* of being on my own. But even with this bone-deep weariness, I couldn't take Cade up on his offer. He blindsided me, and after having just drawn a parallel from my life to what my mother's surely was, I couldn't bear to have another part of me stripped away. Another part of the façade I so carefully built brushed aside because I couldn't stand on my own two feet. My independence is the only thing I have left, and I'm going to cling to it with everything I have.

I drop my bag just inside the door, look over to my fridge and the calendar hanging on it. It's been five weeks since I've marked off a date. I'm not even sure how many days are left until graduation, until I can move on from this place, finally start the life I was supposed to have. Somehow, in the midst of my relationship with Cade, I allowed even the most trivial things to fall by the wayside.

When my apartment is dark and I'm lying on my shitty futon alone, I wonder if I've already started living the life I'm supposed to have. That maybe it started when a too big man forced his way into my life without asking permission. He's everything I never thought I wanted, but I'm not sure I can imagine my life without him. That makes my heart race, makes my palms sweat, makes my stomach clench up in nerves and anxiety and fear.

Love has only ever ended in ruins for me.

I didn't want this. I never asked for this. I didn't want this ache in my chest, this constant flutter in my stomach, this perpetual breath holding while I wait for the other shoe to drop. I didn't want to have to worry about someone else, take someone else into consideration. But I do.

Cade's my first thought in the morning, my last thought at night. He's in every corner of this shitty apartment, taking up too much space in my mind and my body and my heart. And while he's been filling up my life with his light, I've allowed myself to lose sight of what's important, focused too much on someone else, gotten lost. I let someone get in the way of everything I've worked for. I've lost myself and it's exactly what I promised myself I'd never do.

# TWENTY-THREE

*cade*

After a shitty night's sleep, I'm in the kitchen, doing test runs on an entrée for my final exams. My mind is elsewhere, not on the dish in front of me, and it shows. I curse as I look at the less than stellar meal I'm practicing, the balance of flavors wrong, the meat overcooked, the plating clumsy at best. Even with the talk Mark had with me mere days ago, I cannot get my shit together. Not when Winter's been the only thing on my mind.

With a growl of frustration, I dump the entire plate in the sink, the food going down the disposal.

"What the hell, Cade? I would've eaten that. I'm starving," Tessa says as she walks into the kitchen.

The stress of exams and the unknown future with Winter has me snapping at her. "If you want something, make it yourself."

When I turn around, Tessa's eyebrows are raised, her eyes wide with surprise.

"Fuck." I scrub my hand over my face, shoulders slumping. "I'm sorry. Had a bad night."

"Uh, yeah, I heard." She cringes, and I try not to think of how much of the fight she was able to make out through the too-thin walls of the house. She pulls out one of the stools at the island and sits down. "What's going on?"

Bracing my arms on the counter, I drop my head between my shoulders. "I fucked up, Tess."

"I'm sure it's not that bad."

I huff out a laugh, shaking my head. "It's worse."

"What'd you do?"

I take a deep breath, letting it out slowly. "Winter got fired last night." At Tess's sharp gasp, I nod. "Yep, that fucker fired her. She came over to tell me about it, and . . ." I shake my head. "I was stupid. She was being secretive, and I was on edge and not thinking. She was freaking out about making rent and losing her apartment, and I . . . I asked her to move in."

When I look up at Tessa, her mouth is hanging open, her eyes even wider than before.

"I know. I was a fucking idiot. I've known from the beginning I need to take it slow with her, and I just threw that all out the window and dove right in. I spooked her, and when she freaked out, I said shit I shouldn't have . . . shit I didn't mean."

"Everyone says things in the heat of the moment they wish they could take back. I'm sure she'll understand after she's had a couple days—"

"That's not all."

Her lips press into a tight line. "Well, hell, Cade. What else?"

I clench my eyes shut, pressing my thumb and forefinger there before dropping my hand to the counter once again. "Our whole fight started because she was keeping something from me. She said she got fired because she was late, but something didn't add up, and she refused to tell me the reason why. I *knew* it was that asshole boss of hers. She made me promise not to go to the pub, said she handled it, but after she left, I was so pissed off I couldn't stop myself. And what I found out? What that fucker tried to do . . ." I shake my head, my knuckles going white as I grip the counter. "I'm lucky I stopped at a single punch."

"You *hit* him?"

"Fuck, yes, I hit him, and I'm not sorry I did. That piece of shit deserved it. But if Winter finds out . . . if she knew I went there after she specifically told me not to . . . I don't know that she'd forgive me. Not again."

"I'm sure you're making it out to be worse than it is. Call her. Talk to her. You guys can work this out. She'll forgive you, Cade. She will."

She sounds so sure, so earnest, and I want to believe her. But she doesn't know Winter like I do. Tessa doesn't understand Winter's unwavering need to be in control of her life, to stand on her own two feet.

And I know, without a doubt, if my words from the night before didn't push her away, this certainly will.

*winter*

My mind isn't any clearer in the morning, after having tossed and turned most of the night, Cade's words playing on a loop even in my dreams. Even recalling the venom in them, I'm still drawn to him. Even after confirming my worst fear, I want him.

I want to curl up in his lap, fold myself into his arms, have him tell me everything is going to be okay, but I can't.

The jarring realization of how parallel I've let my life run to my mother's is enough to make me second-guess everything, including him. His words only forced me to face it head on instead of tiptoeing around it as I have been from the beginning. I've allowed myself to get lost in him, to be *consumed* by him, and I've forgotten my priorities.

The lessons I learned fifteen years ago are still with me, settled deep in my heart as my truths. The one constant, the only thing I was sure of during that time, was what I saw with my own eyes, over and over again: a man could make you lose yourself completely. And Cade has proven that.

My mother gave herself with abandon, sought out the oblivion, the companionship men could provide, found her worth in too many guys to count, and I sat back and watched. As she bounced from man to man, bounced us from house to house, town to town. Jerry and Ted and Rick and a hundred other names I can't remember. I never knew what was going on, why we had to leave just when we got settled. I only knew the cycles. The beginnings, middles, and ends of her relationships. The roller coasters of my childhood.

I don't want to ride on roller coasters anymore.

My phone rings, the sound shrill in the otherwise quiet room. Cade's name flashes across the screen, and my heart jumps into my throat as I press ignore and let him go to voice mail. I'm not ready to talk to him. I'm too raw, too exposed, too vulnerable because of the realization I've just come to.

Regardless of attempting to run from everything I hated about my childhood, I've unintentionally sought it out through Cade.

He's stoic and proud, bigger than life. Sharp jaw, intense eyes, armor made up of metal and ink. He is intensity and want and desire. He's happiness and frustration and comfort and hope and fear.

He is my roller coaster.

# TWENTY-FOUR

*cade*

"Hey, it's me. Again." I sigh, rubbing a hand over my head. For the last three days, we've done nothing but play phone tag, and I have a sinking feeling it's intentional on Winter's part. "Call me back." Hanging up, I toss the phone on the table in front of me, muttering a few curses as I do so.

"What's got your panties in a twist, pretty boy?" Jason asks as he strolls in from the kitchen.

I glance over at him, the epitome of *I don't give a shit*, and I'm so not in the mood for him tonight. "Fuck off. When the hell did you get here?"

"I love you, too." He plops into the chair across from me, propping his feet up on the dining room table and crossing them at the ankles.

Narrowing my eyes, I stare at what he has in his hand. "Is that one of my cookies?"

"Well, I sure as fuck didn't make them." He bites into one,

crumbs going all over his shirt. I swear to Christ, he's like a tod-
dler. "These are damn good, though. Can I take some home?"

I slap his feet off the table, forcing them down on the ground
with a thud.

He stops mid-chew, his eyebrows climbing up his forehead.
"Okay, seriously, what's your deal?"

Groaning, I scrub a hand over my face. "Fuck. I don't know.
Everything's just catching up with me. I've got finals in all my
classes, my portfolio is due, Mark's been breathing down my
neck, and . . ." I mutter a curse. "Winter and I haven't talked in
a few days."

He studies me for a minute, then says, "Mhmm, just what I
thought. It's like I diagnosed last time. A severe case of whipping
of the pussy variety."

"Get out." I point to the back door. "I'm serious. Get the
fuck out."

"Goddamn. You are *touchy*. Fine, I won't give you any more
shit about it. So you haven't talked in a while. What's the big
deal?"

"She's avoiding me."

"How do you know?"

"Because she never answers my calls, and anytime she returns
them, it's always when she knows I'm working or in class."

"Why's she avoiding your calls, do you think?"

And I don't *think*, I know exactly why. I take a deep breath
and exhale, saying, "We had a fight."

"'Bout what?"

"I, ah . . ." I mutter a curse, rubbing my thumb and forefinger
over my closed eyes. I know exactly what his reaction is going to
be, and I'm not in the mood for it. Not when I'm already pissy
about what's going on. "I told her she should move in with me."

He chokes on the bite of cookie he just ate, coughing and sputtering, his eyes wide and watering. "Fucking hell, man, are you kidding me?"

I answer with a sharp shake of my head, my glare daring him to push this.

He ignores my unspoken threat, sitting up and leaning forward with his elbows propped on his knees. "Okay. Let me get this straight. You've been seeing her for, what, a couple months? And you asked her to *move in with you*?"

"There were extenuating circumstances."

"The fuck kind of extenuating circumstances would call for such a stupid-ass move? Jesus Christ, Cade, that girl is more skittish than a wild animal. Even *I* know that, and I'm not the one fucking her."

"You think I don't know it, too? I know better than anyone exactly how volatile she is, but what the hell was I supposed to do when she told me she got fired and was worried about not having a place to live? It just . . . slipped out. It made sense at the time."

"Well, shit."

"Yeah." I clear my throat and take a swig of the beer I brought out earlier. Placing it back on the table, I spin the bottle slowly between my fingers, staring intently at it. "And I sorta . . . fucked up."

"More than that?" His voice is incredulous. I don't blame him. Our roles have always been reversed—me trying to help him out of whatever fuckup he's gotten himself into.

"Unfortunately." And then I tell him everything that happened that night, from when I left here after Winter stormed out to leaving the pub after confronting her boss.

"Well, shit," he says again. "I mean, I'm glad you hit the fucker, but still. Shit." He takes another bite of the cookie. "You gonna tell her?"

My shoulders slump as I exhale harshly. "I have no fucking idea."

"If you do, let me know. I'll come with and she can cry on my shoulder."

I stare at him for a moment, somehow shocked at his lack of tact, though I shouldn't be after so many years. "You are a worthless best friend, you know that?"

He grins, completely unaffected. "I try."

The back door slams shut and I turn around, watching Tessa come in, her head down as she rifles through her purse. "Cade, can you—" She lifts her head and stops abruptly when she sees Jason. "Oh, hey. I didn't know you were here."

"Hey, Tess. Looking hot as always. Come here and take a load off." He pats his knee and gives her the smile I've seen him give a hundred girls at a hundred different bars.

"Goddammit, Jase, I swear to God you are about to get my foot up your ass. I can't handle your shit tonight."

He laughs, dodging when I halfheartedly try to kick him. "Aww, come on. This is how we are. She loves it, don't you, Tess?"

She doesn't answer, just waves a dismissive hand and turns to go down the hall to her bedroom. Before her door shuts, she pops her head out. "Oh, Cade. What I was going to ask when I came in—can you pick up Haley tomorrow from after-school care? I have a date."

"A date, huh?" Jason calls out. "Where'd you meet him?"

"Probably from that online dating site," I grumble.

Jason's head snaps in my direction. "She's signed up on a fucking dating site? Why'd you let her do that?"

I snort. "When have I ever *let* her do anything?"

Not hearing us, or not caring, Tessa breaks in, "He's a single dad of one of Haley's friends. Older. Established. *Mature.* And he loves kids."

"*I'm* mature." Jason's voice rings with irritation, and the only response from Tess is a disbelieving huff. "And how old is 'older'? Are we talking cradle robber, or what?"

"Well, *Dad*, I'm not exactly sure, but there aren't any gray hairs, so I think we're okay."

"Whatever. Sounds like a loser to me. Why don't you bring him by so we can meet him and make sure?"

I roll my eyes and get ready to tell her I can pick Haley up when Tess speaks up, her voice carrying down the hall. "If you can tell me the last time you were on a date, Mr. Mature, I'll bring him by and you can give me your stamp of approval."

"That's easy. Last Friday." Jason sits back, his hands folded behind his head, feet up on the table again, smug grin on his face.

"I didn't say pick up a girl in a bar and bring her home to sleep with her. I said a date. You know, what adults do. Where you ask for her number, call her a few times, take her to coffee or dinner or a movie. Actually pick her up and then drop her off at her doorstep at the end of the night with nothing more than a kiss."

His whole body sags, his arms dropping to his sides as his mouth opens then closes with a snap, and I don't even try to stop the laugh that slips out.

When he doesn't respond, Tessa says, "That's what I thought. Cade?"

"Yeah, I can. No problem."

"Thanks. I'm gonna change and then go pick her up. Are you making dinner tonight?"

"Aren't I always?"

With my back to her, I can't see her face, but the tone of her voice tells me she's smiling. "Well, I'd be happy to help, but you never let me. *Someone* has a control problem."

Her door shuts with a snick, and I look back at Jason. "What was that all about? Since when do you care who she goes out with or how she finds her dates?"

"I don't. Whatever." He stands up, slaps me on the shoulder as he walks past. "Let me know when you get out of the doghouse with Winter or when I can swoop in. I gotta run. I'm taking some of these cookies, though."

I shake my head at his retreating form, listening to him rummage around in the kitchen before he yells out, "Later," and the front door slams shut.

Looking at the dining room table, my notes, books, and recipe cards scattered over the whole thing, I sag in my chair. The work I still need to finish before next week is staggering, and I should be concentrating on it. Instead, thoughts of Winter consume my mind. I don't know how to fix this, and my gut churns with the fact that I only managed to make it worse by going against her wishes and doing something behind her back. With a groan, I drop my forehead to the table and close my eyes.

"What's wrong, big brother?" Tessa scrubs her hand over the back of my head before she takes the chair Jason vacated. "Still haven't heard from Winter?"

"Nope," I mumble to the floor. "She returns my calls, but always when she knows I can't answer. Her messages are short, and I can't get a read on her."

"Maybe she's just really that busy." She gestures to the

never-ending pile of schoolwork spread out in front of me. "She has finals to worry about, too. I'm sure things will settle down next week."

I grunt and shrug, tired of discussing this and needing something else to focus on. "What was with you and Jase?" I ask.

"What do you mean?"

"I mean, why was he so interested in your date?"

She shrugs and stands. "Don't ask me. I never know what's up with him." Once she has her purse and keys in hand, she heads to the door. "We'll be back in an hour. Make it count," she says as she points to the homework spread all over the table. "Haley's gonna want teatime when we get back. She talked about it all the way to school this morning." With a smile and a wink, she's out the door, and I'm looking down at the work I don't want to do, waiting on a phone I know won't ring.

*winter*

I listen to the voice mail Cade left when I ignored his call earlier. His messages are getting shorter and shorter, and I can tell his frustration is growing with each one he has to leave. I don't blame him, but I can't talk to him. Not yet. Not when all my fears of becoming the one person I've struggled my whole life to avoid becoming have come to fruition. If I have any hope of keeping my head on straight for my finals, not to mention finding a new fucking job on top of that and worrying about getting kicked out on the street, I can't deal with it right now. I can't deal with *him* right now.

Everything is so chaotic, my mind a maelstrom, and I can't get clarity. I can't focus on what I need to. What was so clear in the past, so black and white, has become muddled with things I wasn't prepared for.

Hope. Love.

And where has it gotten me? Stripped of my only source of income, floundering to find something else, soon to be evicted from my apartment . . .

It's gotten me completely and utterly fucked.

Taking a deep breath, I try to push those thoughts to the back of my mind, instead focusing on the list of available positions in the area I have pulled up on my laptop. Why couldn't that jackass have fired me a month ago? If he had, maybe I'd have a chance of finding something. But now, so close to summer, every place around that pays well enough for me to scrape by is bloated with fellow students getting jobs for the next three months.

Even though graduation is around the corner and my goal will be finding something in my field, I know positions are few and far between in the professional world, especially in an industry as saturated as mine. If I don't have something to fall back on, something that will pay the bills in the interim, while I wait for possibly months to find something, what will I do?

I take out the napkin I've carried around every day since leaving The Brewery, the one Annette gave me, telling myself I wouldn't use it. But every day, it gets a little harder to resist. While asking her for help gives me anxiety, it doesn't push me into the blind panic, into the all-gripping fear that moving in with Cade does. The difference between a friend wanting to help me out of a rough spot and a boyfriend wanting forever. And I know Cade . . . he wouldn't settle for less.

The clock is ticking down, the time I have left before I'm forcefully removed from my home, and I don't know what to do.

Having a roof over my head and enough money to pay for food are the last things I need to worry about, especially with finals looming days away and my website still woefully incomplete.

With a sigh, I shove the napkin back in my pocket and focus once again on the list of job possibilities. I'm giving myself two days. If I can't find something on my own in two days, it doesn't matter if I'm ready to ask someone for help. I'm not going to have a choice.

# TWENTY-FIVE

*cade*

"Great work today, Cade."

The kitchen is still bustling around us, my fellow classmates cleaning up their stations from the busy dinner service. I pack my knives away and turn to my mentor, not quite keeping the smile off my face. Even with everything going on outside the kitchen, with all the questions I have regarding Winter and what's going on with us, I can't help the rush I get when thinking about how seamless the service went tonight.

"Thank you, Chef."

"How'd it feel to lead the kitchen?"

I shake my head, looking down at the floor. "Honestly? Fucking amazing."

He grins, claps a hand on my shoulder. "Exactly what I would've said. You have a second to talk?"

"Of course."

We head to the back corner, far enough away that the noise

from the kitchen fades into the background. The open space doesn't afford us much privacy, so he lowers his voice, keeping the conversation from carrying. "What are your plans after graduation?"

"I'll start looking for a job right away. I know I'll probably have to work my way up, but I'm just excited to be in a kitchen, getting paid to do what I love."

"You're hoping to find something close to home?"

"Yes, sir."

He hums, studying me with serious eyes. "I might have an opportunity for you. As a sous chef at a restaurant specializing in traditional Italian cuisine."

I straighten, my eyes widening slightly. "Are you serious?"

"Yes." He crosses his arms, leans back against the wall. "I believe in you, Cade. Barring that brief slip a couple weeks ago, you've shown astounding potential. You are, by far, my most promising student this year. And I know you wouldn't let me down if I recommended you to the owner."

"No, I wouldn't. Never."

"Just what I like to hear. There may be a slight problem, though."

"Whatever it is, I'm willing to work through it. Long hours, early or late shifts, shitty pay, whatever."

"What about moving?"

I still, my excitement fizzling. "Moving?"

"This restaurant is in Chicago."

My heart stops, all my dreams colliding with my responsibilities. The one thing I simultaneously don't want to do and want to do more than anything offered up on a silver platter, but I can't take one without the other. Get my dream job straight out of school, but leave everyone I love behind.

I never once thought about leaving Michigan, moving anywhere. My dreams of traveling to Italy are just that: dreams. I
can't abandon Tessa and Haley. And then there's Winter . . . The
idea of leaving them cuts through me.

"Look, I know it's a big decision for you. But it wouldn't
necessarily be permanent. The owner is looking at opening more
restaurants. One of the locations he's looking at is here, so that's
a possibility. There's also the possibility if you put in your time
as a sous chef, show him what you're made of, you could lead
one of the new restaurants, here or elsewhere."

"I . . . I don't know. I hadn't even thought of this as a possibility. I didn't even consider restaurants that weren't within thirty
miles."

He nods. "I figured as much. And I know why. But, Cade . . ."
He lowers his voice even more, leaning toward me, his hand
curled over my shoulder. "It's time to start living your life for
*you*. You've more than covered your responsibilities here. Tessa
isn't in high school anymore. She's grown and you don't need to
keep looking after her. She has the house, and she and Haley will
do fine. Your parents—your mom especially—wouldn't hold it
against you for pursuing this. Just . . . think about it, okay?
Before you say no, take a few days and think about it. Talk it
over with Tessa and whoever it is who's been messing with your
concentration these last few weeks. This is an amazing opportunity for you. I don't want you to miss out on it because of responsibilities you don't need to shoulder anymore."

I nod and swallow, my throat tight, my chest tighter. A month
ago, I would've answered immediately. No fucking way. I have
a life here, responsibilities and people who need me. But after
meeting Winter . . . seeing how strong and brave she is, hearing
her encourage me to follow my dreams . . . Now, I don't know.

Seems like a cruel twist of fate that I'd meet the one person who could push me into accepting something like this when she can't come with me.

I have to talk this over with her, and calling her isn't going to cut it. I've given her five days, allowed her the space she needs, but I can't wait any longer. I need to see her.

*winter*

With days left until my project is due, I'm furiously working on my final website, putting the finishing touches on it, testing it, fixing broken code. Trying not to think about everything stacked against me right now . . . all the uncertainty I'm facing. Trying to get by enough to focus on graduating. Just as my eyes are starting to blur from staring at my computer, my phone jolts me out of my trance. Expecting to see Cade's name and warring with myself on whether or not I'll answer, I'm surprised when a number I don't recognize shows up. Knowing it could be one of the places I've submitted applications in a vain hope of landing a position, I answer.

"Winter? Hi, sugar, it's Annette." Her voice is so calm, so comforting, and I don't realize I needed to hear it until I do.

"Hey, Annette."

"How are you doing? Everything going okay?"

"Things are . . ." I take a deep breath. What can I say to her? That I'm struggling to get through my classes before I think about what is inevitable? That I've lost my way and I'm not sure how to find my path again? That, though I don't want to, I fear I'll have no choice but to ask for help?

"That bad, huh? You remember what I said. My place is always open to you."

"I . . . don't know if I could do that, Annette."

"That's a bunch of bull, and you know it. You *can*. If you need to, you can. There's no shame in taking a hand to help you up once in a while, sugar."

If only it were that easy. If only I could look at it in terms of just a helping hand, not buckling into everything I've worked my whole life to stay away from. "Thank you for the offer."

She's quiet for a minute, like she wants to say more on the matter. Instead of pressing the issue, she asks, "How's Cade doing after the other night? Can't say I wasn't glad for what he did."

My entire body stills, my mind racing to figure out what she means. I swallow, my throat suddenly dry. "The other night?"

"When he came in to talk to Randy. I wish that asshole had left with a couple black eyes, but ten minutes alone in a room with Cade probably scared him enough even without the physical scars."

A thousand possibilities bombard my mind—everything Cade promised me he wouldn't do—and all I can manage is a short, "Yeah . . ."

"Well, I have to run. You remember what I said."

The line disconnects, and I'm left staring at the phone, trying to process what she told me. Could I have misunderstood her? Was she talking about something that happened before I got fired? Before I explicitly told Cade not to go there? If she's not . . . if he actually went there after everything I said . . .

I'm pulled out of my thoughts by a loud knock at the door. Without even looking, I know who's there. The only person who's ever come here for me, who's ever been invited into this part of my life. The only person I thought I could trust. And if what Annette said is true . . . if Cade went there . . . I can't even trust him with my simple wishes, let alone my heart.

With hands shaky from uncertainty, I unhook the chain, turn the deadbolt, and open the door. He stands there, the bulk of his shoulders taking up nearly the width of the door frame. His hazel eyes are open and alive, a hesitant smile touching the corners of his mouth, and how did I forget how beautiful he is in just a few short days?

"I was wondering if you'd avoid even answering the door." He leans forward, pauses for only a moment, then sweeps his lips across mine. I close my eyes and turn away. If he notices my brush-off, he doesn't mention it, instead walking into my apartment. "Figured showing up would be the only way to get you to talk to me. Why've you been avoiding my calls?"

I swallow, not able to answer him, to open up about my confusion over everything that's been going on—not when all I can think about is what Annette told me. "Annette called me tonight."

There's no confusion on his face, no questioning in his eyes, and my heart sinks. Instead, his entire body goes taut, as if bracing for a fight, and everything I need to know is right in front of me. With restrained anger, I say, "What did you do?"

Instead of denying it, instead of tiptoeing around the subject, pretending he doesn't know what I'm talking about, he shrugs, arms crossed against his chest. "He didn't leave there in an ambulance, so I'd say I held back."

The last ounce of hope I held on to vanishes knowing he went against my explicit wishes and did everything I asked him not to. His promises to me . . . my wishes, my wants . . . mean nothing to him. And everything culminates to a point I can't back away from. Being forced out of my job, having to work there in the first place.

Making rent.

Finals.

Graduation.

Cade.

My anger explodes out of me as I walk over and shove him against the chest. "God*dammit*," I spit. "I told you I didn't need a knight in shining armor! You think I couldn't handle it on my own? Did you think I slunk away like some scared little girl? I can take care of myself, and I don't need you fighting my fucking battles for me!"

"Did you think *I* was just going to slink away after I found out what that motherfucker said to you, sit back and do *nothing*? That when I found out he told you to suck his dick, told *my girlfriend* to get on her goddamn knees, that I wasn't going to do anything? That I'd just walk away and forget about it? Well, fuck. That. I'm not that man, Winter. I've *never* been that man."

"I asked you to be that man. For me. You weren't supposed to go there in the first place! You *promised* me you'd leave it be. I told you I didn't need you to rescue me. I don't need anyone to rescue me. I can do it all on my own. I learned a long time ago that in the end, no one is going to be there but me."

"*I'm* here. I'm right fucking here!" he shouts, his arms outstretched.

"But you won't be!" I swallow, blowing out a breath as I grip my hair in my hands, clenching my eyes closed. Dropping my hands to my sides, I look back at him. "This isn't permanent, Cade, what we have. This isn't forever. You already proved that. Why bother, right?"

The fight drains out of him, his eyes full of regret. "I didn't mean that, Winter. They were just words. I was pissed off, and I shouldn't have said it. I'm sorry."

I shake my head. "Maybe they were just words. But someday they're not going to be. Someday, you're going to get sick of me, sick of my bullshit, and you're going to leave. And that's fine. I've accepted it. But you have to let me keep my goddamn identity in the meantime. Because when you're gone, it's just me. Only me."

He walks a tight circle, his hands folded behind his head, his elbows bent and biceps bulging, his muscles tight. Spinning around to face me again, he asks, "Where the hell is this coming from?"

"Where isn't it coming from? This is me, Cade." I stretch my arms out wide. "This is who I've always been. It's who I've been for as long as I can remember."

He walks to me, takes my face in his hands, and God, I've missed him. I've missed the scent of him, his body eclipsing everything in my sight except for his eyes and his mouth and his perfect words. "It doesn't have to be. I'm here, baby," he says, his thumbs rubbing over my jaw. "Why can't you let me be here for you?"

Because I can't. Because I sabotage anything good that comes into my life. Because I can't settle into being happy, can never get comfortable. Because I'm too used to anxiety and pain and barely scraping by and he is everything, *everything*, and I can't.

I step out of his arms, and I watch as they drop to his sides. Piece by piece, I stack the bricks up again, erecting the wall he somehow crumbled in the short time we knew each other. I don't want this to be about me and how broken I am, so I turn the tables, moving the focus to him. "You've got this tough armor you've painted on you, the tattoos covering your arms, the piercing, every single bit of you screams back off, Cade. Why is that? You're just as scared as I am of letting people in. We just wear our armors differently."

"No. *No.* You don't get to push this back on me. I let you in from day fucking one. I never lied to you. I never pretended to be something I wasn't."

"I didn't either! You knew from the beginning who I was, and it was *your* choice to pursue this."

"So this is my fault now? I pursued you because I knew there was something there. I felt it. I know you feel it, too, even if you don't say it."

I bite my lip hard, choking on my words, refusing to let any escape, because he's right. I feel it. And feeling that is the exact reason I'm in this spot in the first place.

"Fine, you want to know why I have these?" He holds his arms out to me. "You want to know what they mean? What kind of armor they are for me? They're a hundred reminders of what I lost. What was taken from me too early. What *could* be taken from me. Of everyone I've ever loved or lost. Every day I think about who was taken from my life, and everyone I have left to lose. I'm not going to let you be one of them."

I swallow, crossing my arms over my chest, holding myself together. My voice is flat, controlled. "You don't have a choice."

"Don't say that. Don't walk away. *I love you.* Did you hear me when I said that? I wasn't bullshitting my way into your pants. I wasn't trying to get something out of you. I love *you.* Just how you are. Every bit of you."

"You don't know every bit of me."

"Well, how the hell can I when you keep everything bottled up so fucking tightly? I love you in spite of the fact I know nothing about your past. *Nothing.*"

"Exactly. You know nothing about it. You don't know all the shit I've gone through in my life to get me here. Why I am the way I am, why I only depend on myself—why I *have* to depend only on myself. And why I don't need some Prince Charming to swoop in and save me."

"Tell me then! I'm standing here right now waiting for you to tell me. I've been here for two months waiting for you to catch up. I've been patient; I've never once pushed you. Well, you want me to push? Fine, I'll fucking push. You're the one who's keeping a lid on it, Winter. You're the one with the key to your own cage. You're the one keeping yourself locked up tight."

His face, his rigid stance, the red pooling in his cheeks, the pain in his eyes . . . it all crashes over me, crushing my restraint, and everything I never wanted him to know comes pouring out of me. "What is it you want to hear, Cade? You want me to tell you all about my childhood? About what life was like before I came here, before I was scraping to get by? Whether my life was better or worse than a shitty studio apartment and ramen noodles every night and men grabbing me just so I could pay my goddamn rent? Well, guess what? This has been a fucking cakewalk. You want to hear about how I got bounced around from house to house in a state system that didn't want me any more than my own fucking mother? Or maybe you'd rather hear about how she left me. That's a great story. How when I was seven, she brought me to the grocery store, told me I could get whatever kind of ice cream I wanted. I thought it was a treat. A special occasion. I *never* got ice cream. Hell, I barely got bread, so I was ecstatic for this. She held my hand, pulled me into the aisle, set me in front of the rows of freezers, and told me to pick whatever I wanted. Anything at all that I wanted. And then she told me she had to run to the bathroom and she'd be right back.

"Yeah, that look in your eyes right there is exactly why I didn't tell you. You've already figured out the end of the story, haven't you? But me? Seven-year-old me? Do you know how long I walked that aisle picking out the perfect flavor of ice cream? Not the one I wanted, but the one I thought she'd like, too? Do you know how long I stood there, waiting for her to come back? The back lights went off. The manager was doing the nightly sweep of the store and came across me. Four fucking hours later." I swallow, staring into his eyes so full of sorrow and pity and helplessness, and I hate that look.

"The worst part was I thought it was a mistake. When I was at the police station waiting, I thought she'd show up any minute. Even after I got tossed in a temporary group home with half a dozen other kids, I thought she was coming for me. And I wanted her to, because even though she was the kind of mother I wouldn't wish on anyone, the kind who forgot to feed me most days, who dragged me with her while she bounced from boyfriend to boyfriend, crashing wherever we could, she was all I knew and I wanted her back. Even after all that, I wanted her back."

I shake my head, dropping my hands to my sides, all the fight in me falling away. "But she wasn't coming back. After so long of not being able to contact her, I was finally declared property of the state. That has a real ring to it, doesn't it? Winter Jacobson, property of the state of California."

His jaw is clenched, his eyes haunted from the stories I just shared. Except they're not stories. They're *me*. My life. My history. And they'll always be a part of what makes me who I am, no matter what I do. No matter where I go or how far I run, I can't escape them. This baggage will be saddled on my back for the rest of my life.

"So that's it. That's why I am the way I am. That's my whole sob story. That's why I'm broken, Cade. And that's why I can't do this with you."

I turn and walk to the door, twisting the handle and holding it open for him. I ignore the rawness of my throat, the burning behind my eyes, the ache of my heart. "I think it's time for you to leave."

"No, Winter, wait. I don't care about that. I love you, just how you are, regardless of what happened fifteen years ago. It doesn't matter to me." His hands are on my face again, holding me so I have no choice but to stare straight at him. His voice is so sure, his eyes so beseeching, that I almost give in to him, almost fall into his arms, let them come around me and comfort me how I know they would.

Almost.

I close my eyes, step away from his touch. "It matters to *me*."

# TWENTY-SIX

*cade*

The muffled sounds of Jason's grunts register, but I'm too far gone to stop. I land another blow to the punching bag as he steadies it, my arms burning, sweat dripping from my temples and down my back, but I can't stop. I can't because Winter's still consuming my thoughts. When I wake up, she's there. When I try to sleep, the fresh summer scent of her still on my fucking pillow, she's there. She's in my head and my heart and I can't fucking stop.

When I land a roundhouse kick to the bag, Jason groans. "Jesus, Cade, *I* didn't break up with you. Quit taking this shit out on me."

"You're the one who wanted to come over." I slam my fists into the bag again. "If you're too big of a pussy to handle holding the bag for me, get the fuck out."

He's quiet, the kind of quiet that's weighted, and after a couple more halfhearted punches, I sigh and turn away. With quick movements I unwrap the tape protecting my hands. I grab the towel I brought downstairs and drag it roughly over my face and hair before I straddle the weight bench, elbows resting on my knees. Jason ignores me, moving over to the free weights, and begins lifting.

"Sorry I'm being a dick."

He shrugs, his attention focused on his task. "After thirteen years, I'm used to it."

"Still. Sorry. I'm just . . . *Fuck*." I groan, closing my eyes and falling back to lie on the bench. "She's not answering my calls. Again."

"Look, man, I'm the last person who should be giving you relationship advice, but maybe you should give her some breathing room, you know? You can come on a little strong." I snort at his oversimplification, and he finally cracks a smile. "I'm just saying, from what I know of her, from what you've told me, this probably isn't the way to go about winning her back. You breathing fire down her neck probably isn't helping the situation any."

And the thing is, I know he's right. But how can I just . . . stop? Just turn it off and step back? Voicing my questions, I ask, "How can I walk away? How am I supposed to back off? I'm in love with her. I don't give a shit about her past—none of it matters to me."

He grunts as he continues with his reps. Once he completes his set, he asks, "Have you tried the grand gesture?"

My eyebrows shoot up to my hairline. "The fuck do you know about grand gestures?"

"Don't you remember in seventh grade when Tess made us watch *10 Things I Hate About You* over and over again just for that fucking serenade?"

I smile, thinking back to what life was like then. My dad had been gone for a few years, and we were finally settling into the swing of things. We were okay. Happy. Before fate threw us another curveball with my mom's cancer and fucked everything up. "Yeah, but I don't think Winter would go for serenading."

"Sorry, bro, I'm out of ideas then. Unless you think you can fuck her into forgiveness. In that case, I have lots of ideas."

"Of course you do."

He laughs. "But seriously. Just give her a little time. Maybe she'll come around."

Or maybe she won't. Maybe more time away will only solidify the crazy idea she has that she has to do everything on her own. That I can't be there for her . . . to help her or support her. That we're destined for failure, destined for heartbreak. I can hear the doubt in my voice when I answer. "Yeah."

"Okay," he says as he sets the weights down. "We need to get you drunk."

I snort. "Yeah, because I'm not already going to fuck up everything tomorrow with my final."

"Fine, not shit-faced. You make me something to eat, I'll make a beer run. We don't even have to go out."

Before I can decline, he heads toward the stairs and runs up them two at a time. Over his shoulder, he yells, "And you better shower before I get back. You smell like ass."


MAYBE JASON WAS onto something with getting me drunk. No matter what I do, what I preoccupy myself with, I can't stop thinking about the decisions I need to make. About the offer Mark made me. Whether or not I could do it . . . could up and leave everything—*everyone*—here.

Top that off with the decision Winter already made for the

both of us that's always present, hovering in the background, and I'm a complete fucking wreck.

"How come you so sad, Uncle Cade?"

I glance up from julienning some carrots to see Haley leaning forward on the breakfast bar, perched on her knees in the chair. Her eyes are so curious, so free of judgment . . . how can I ever leave her?

"Not sad, short stuff, just concentrating."

"What's that mean?"

"Concentrating?" She nods. "It means I'm thinking really hard."

"'Bout what?"

"Well, lots of things. I'm almost done with school, and that means a lot of work."

"You want me to color you a picture? Mama got me a new princesses color book."

For the first time in what feels like days, I smile. "I would *love* a princess picture."

"'Kay!" She climbs down off the stool and tears off to her room, returning not even thirty seconds later, her coloring book flopping as she runs, crayons flying out of the open jar she keeps them in.

"Slow down, I'll still want it in twenty minutes." I laugh as she scrambles to pick everything up, then starts the serious task of choosing the perfect picture to color for me.

The back door opens and Tessa strolls in, arms full of magazines and hair books or whatever they are. "Hey," she says to me, dropping the load at the dining room table. She walks over, tips Haley's face back, and peppers it with a dozen kisses. "Hey, baby."

"Hi, Mama. I'm coloring a picture for Uncle Cade."

"I see that. It's very pretty. You know how much he loves pink and purple."

She nods her head as I snort, her eyes focused again on her coloring book, back to ignoring the grown-ups.

"What's all that?" I ask, gesturing to the pile she dumped on the table.

"Paige is coming over later. I have some techniques I want to try." She grabs one of the grapes I set out earlier for Haley and pops it into her mouth, leaning her hip against the counter as she studies me. "What about you? What've you got going on tonight?"

This is her delicate way of asking me if anything new is happening with Winter. After I snapped at her the last time she asked outright, she stopped. It doesn't do much to alleviate my irritation, though, when I know exactly what she's trying to ask.

"Jason invited himself over. He's bringing beer."

"Well, if there's anything he's good for, it's cheering you up." She hovers, picking at the grapes, and I know she has something heavy to say. I don't prod, partially because I'm not even sure I want to hear it. I continue my knife cuts, not looking up at her as she finds the words. When she does, it's exactly what I knew she was going to ask. "Have you decided yet? About the job in Chicago?"

I pause, knife mid-stroke, before I pick back up again, slicing through the carrots, my cuts getting less and less accurate. When I give a sharp shake of my head, she heaves a sigh.

"Cade . . ."

Before she can say anything else, I ask, "You really think this is the best time for this conversation?" With a pointed stare, I look at Haley. Of course, I should've known that wasn't going to dissuade her.

"Baby, why don't you go into your room and finish it? That way it'll be a special surprise for Uncle Cade."

"Good idea, Mama!"

When Haley is out of the room, only one lone crayon left behind in her wake, Tessa stares at me, arms crossed against her chest. "Well."

I set down the knife and rest my hands against the counter, my shoulders bunched, head dropped. "I don't know, Tess."

"What's there to know? For as long as I can remember, this is what you've talked about. Why aren't you running to Mark and telling him fuck yes, you want this?"

"Of course I want it, but I want it *here*. Yes, it might be temporary, but what if it's not? What if the owner decides against opening something back here?"

"Then you're living in Chicago, being this badass sous chef, still working your way up to executive chef. It's not like this job is the end of the line for you. It's just a stop. *One* stop."

"It'd be easier if that stop wasn't away from you guys."

She moves around the island, standing next to me as she puts her arm around my waist, her hip bumping mine. "I know. And it'll be hard and will suck, but it's not like it's the other side of the world. It's five hours away. We can even meet halfway sometimes."

"Yeah."

"You're still not convinced."

Looking down at the counter, I shake my head.

She blows out a breath and steps away, going into the dining room and gathering her stuff. "Well, I can't make the decision for you. I can only be here to support whatever you decide. But, Cade? For what it's worth, I think you should take it. In fact, I think you'd be stupid *not* to take it. Haley and I . . . we'll be okay."

"You keep saying that, but how are you going to be able to do all this on your own? Like tomorrow when I'm taking her in the morning because of your class or some night when you have to stay late because of a client or you want to go on a date. How are you going to work that?"

She rolls her eyes and huffs. "Just like every other single parent does. Before- and after-school care. Babysitters. Friends." She shifts everything to one arm and points at me while narrowing her eyes. "Also, can I say how shitty it is that you're putting this all on us? I don't want to live with the guilt that *my* choices kept you from following your dream. That's not fair."

My entire body deflates, the rigid stance I'm in melting away at her words. "You know that's not my intent."

"It doesn't matter if it is or not. It's how it feels to me." Her eyes soften and turn pleading as she stares at me. "At least just go to the interview. You don't have to make a decision then. If you get offered the job, we can talk about it more. What do you have to lose?"

What do I have to lose? What *don't* I have to lose? True, I'd be gaining knowledge in my chosen field and it'd be an amazing opportunity. But I'd also be leaving behind everyone who means anything to me.

*winter*

The minutes have turned into hours. The hours turning into days, and I've run out of time. Where before, the days couldn't come fast enough, now all I want is a pause button to freeze time so I can get things together. Get *myself* together. I have to make a decision, and I'm not ready. I wanted to do this all on my own, to get by without anyone's help, and all this past week has shown me is that I've been fooling myself all along. For the second time in my life, I'm not going to have a choice in the matter, in the fact that I'm going to be a parasite, living off someone else. And I *hate* that I let this happen.

I hate myself for falling in love, and I hate Cade for being so perfect, for making me want things I can't have. Things I should never have.

I wonder how much I can take before I finally break. How many battles I can fight before I feel completely and utterly useless. In the span of one week, I've lost my job, the ability to pay my own way, and the only man I've ever loved.

Though the term *lost* isn't entirely accurate. No, I didn't lose him. I pushed him away with both hands, shoving as hard as I could. Because I was scared. Scared of what it'd mean to let him in, to let him help.

And now I'm no better off. I'm still in the same shitty position, in need of help, and now I'm without Cade. And it's my own damn fault. The only thing allowing me to reach out to Annette, to ask, is the knowledge that it's not permanent. It's a helping hand, like she said, instead of my perpetual savior swooping in once again, wanting to save me at every turn.

My apartment is empty around me, the handful of belongings I had sold off for quick cash to fellow students looking to furnish new places. Sitting on the floor, I'm holding on to the napkin Annette gave me. I run my fingers over the indentation of her pen strokes, trying to work up the courage to just pick up the phone and call. Knowing I don't have a choice.

I've exhausted all my options. After nearly four years, I almost made it, but I can't quite cross the finish line. Not on my own. Though I wanted to, though I had every intention to, I just can't do it on my own anymore.

I look around at my shitty apartment, at the place I've fought tooth and nail for, the place I've called home for years, having to work full-time while juggling a full course load, and the fight drains out of me. Dialing Annette's number, I take a deep breath, close my eyes, and let go of my pride.

*cade*

By the time Jason shows up, my mind isn't any clearer, even after talking with Tessa. She makes it sound so easy, that I should just be able to up and leave. After everything we've lost, we're all we have left. She and Haley . . . they mean everything to me. How can I just walk away, whatever the reason?

I wish I could talk to Winter about it. I want her input, her no-bullshit advice, even though I know what she'd tell me. She'd tell me the same thing she already did when we were talking about our dreams. She'd tell me to go, even if that meant leaving her behind.

I'm already tense when Jason waltzes into the living room, and hearing him running his mouth into the phone he's carrying doesn't help my mood.

". . . still being a whiny asshole about it." He looks up and gives me a grin before dropping onto the couch next to me. "Fuck if I know. I already told him to do the grand gesture thing, but he's not too fond of serenading her apparently." He waits, listening to whoever is on the other line, though from the content of his call, I'd bet money it's Adam. They always were like a couple of gossiping old women. "Hey, if you think you can do better, by all means . . ." He tosses the phone into my lap, then stands. On the way to the kitchen, he calls over his shoulder, "You ate without me, didn't you, fucker? Whatever, I'll forage."

I try my best to ignore him and put the phone up to my ear. "Yeah."

"Jase tells me you're crying over a girl, and I need confirmation on that, because we both know what a liar he is. And I think we also both know how improbable it is for you to be pussy-whipped."

With a falsely cheerful tone, I say, "Hi, Adam. How lovely to hear from you."

"Cut the shit. Is it true?"

I drop my head to the back of the couch and close my eyes, my voice muffled as I run a hand over my face. "Yep."

"Shit, man. I was just there over spring break. What the fuck happened between then and now?"

A girl with light in her eyes and sparks under her skin swept her way into my life, and I'm not the same. "*She* happened. Winter happened."

"Well, what the hell's going on now? Why are you moping like a little girl?"

"I am not moping like a little girl." I glare at Jason when he comes back in with a plate full of leftovers, rebutting my words with an emphatic nod as he sits down. "Fuck you," I say to them both.

"Put him on speaker," Jason says around a mouthful of food. He grabs the phone from me and drops it on the cushion between us, the speaker activated. "You need an intervention."

Before I can say anything, he continues, "Hey, Adam, did you know Mark also gave him the opportunity to interview to be a sous chef?"

"No shit? That's amazing, Cade. When's the interview?"

"That's just it. He hasn't decided if he even wants to."

I don't even know why I'm here for this fucking intervention if they're just going to have a conversation with each other.

After a few moments of silence from the other end of the line, Adam speaks up, his voice serious. "What's going on, man?"

With a deep sigh, I say, "The restaurant is in Chicago."

"Okay . . ." The question in his tone is undeniable.

"Why doesn't anyone else see the issues with this?"

"Is this about Tess and Haley? Jesus, Cade, you have to quit babying her. She's an adult with a *child* for fuck's sake. I think she can get along without her big brother watching her every move."

"It's not about that—"

"It *is*. It is, and you know it. It's been four years, man. It's okay to move on."

I cringe at the casual reference to my mom's death. They were both there through the whole thing, helping me out whenever they could, but they weren't *here*. They didn't live it the way I did. The way Tess and I did. And they sure as fuck didn't hear the last conversation I had with my mother, when I promised to watch out for Tessa. And that was before Haley came along. So yeah, I took it seriously. How could I not?

Without waiting for my response, he adds, "Have you talked to Tess about this? How's she feel?"

Jason stares at me while he waits for me to respond, and I clench my jaw. He doesn't even say anything, just raises his eyebrows like he already has his answer.

"She wants me to go."

"So what's the problem? *Go.* Look, I know things are fucked up right now. You've got Tessa and Haley to worry about, plus whatever shit is going on with Winter. But you will *hate* yourself for letting this go if you don't at least try. Just go to the damn interview. Figure out the rest when the time comes."

"Yeah, what he said." Jason points at the phone with a nod. I huff out a laugh, rolling my eyes.

"Plus, I'll be here to look after her for you."

"That's supposed to make me feel *better*?"

"Hey," Jason says, for once sounding actually offended. "I'd never do anything to hurt Tess or Haley."

I look over at him, seeing complete sincerity, and if I'm not mistaken, underlying frustration at my dismissal of him and his promise.

"I hate to break up this slumber party, girls, but I gotta roll," Adam says. "Do it, Cade. I mean it. I'll talk to you fuckers later."

We say our good-byes and I throw the phone at Jason, hitting him square in the chest.

He fumbles with the plate in his hands, trying not to drop everything. "What the fuck?"

"You are a dick for springing an Adam lecture on me, you know that?"

He shrugs, unconcerned, as he rights the plate, then shovels more food in his mouth. "Yeah, well, don't act like you lost your damn puppy anymore and I won't need to resort to such drastic measures. And I was serious before. About Tess. You don't need to worry about her being on her own while you're gone."

I stare at him, his normal carefree façade showing something completely serious. With a nod of acknowledgment, I close my eyes and rest my head back against the couch, thinking over what they said. It's all true, every bit of it. I know Tessa's responsible enough and doesn't need me around, but that doesn't make the pressure I feel to protect her lessen. Even with Jason's assurances.

But in the end, what Adam says is what seals it. I will hate myself if I don't at least try.

# TWENTY-SEVEN

*winter*

It's amazing how even after four years, the feeling of being a
burden can come on again so suddenly. That overwhelming,
sinking sensation that you don't belong, that you're a bigger
hassle than you're worth. The need to shrink as much as you can,
to leave no trace of yourself, like you were never there in the first
place.

If they can't tell you're even there, they won't want you to
leave.

Even though I've been at Annette's for a few days, I still keep
my stuff in my single duffel bag, hidden away in a closet. She had
the couch made up for me when I arrived, and every day I make
sure to clean it up, fold the sheets and blanket, and hide them
away. I'm out the door before she even gets up in the morning.
Like I'm a ghost.

She leaves me little notes. Telling me I don't need to leave so early. Telling me to help myself to whatever is in the fridge. Telling me I can stay for however long I need.

Telling me what a failure I am.

How I fucked this up, fucked up my life, and I just sat there and allowed it to happen. I knew it was happening, saw it as it did, and I sat back, too blissed out on, what? Love?

Love is a fairy tale, and my life is anything but a fucking fairy tale.

A key turns in the lock, and Annette pushes her way inside. "Hey, sugar."

"Hi," I mumble, not taking my eyes off my laptop. "How was work at the shithole?"

"Shitty."

I crack a smile as she moves about, doing her nightly routine. When she comes out of her bedroom, having changed out of her jeans and work T-shirt, she grabs her trashy magazines and a glass of water and settles in on the opposite end of the couch. She spends this time winding down from the night until she's relaxed enough for sleep. It's quiet and peaceful, and the only other time I've ever known this sense of calm was with Cade. I wonder if that's because I just get along so well with these two people, or if this is how it could be, if only I gave others a chance. If I let others in, maybe I'd feel that comfort around them as well.

After a while, she gestures to my computer and asks, "What are you working on tonight?"

"I'm finishing up a site someone commissioned. I agreed to do it really cheap, so it won't be much money, but it'll be something, at least."

She looks at me over the rim of her glass as she takes a sip. "You're sure a lot happier behind your computer than I ever saw you working the tables. You positive you can't just find something doing programming or whatever it is you do?"

"Designing, and I wish I could. I mean, I've got a few jobs like this here and there, but there's no way it's enough to live on. I've been looking at some larger firms, but with most of those places, you have to start as an intern, and then get hired on if you're a good fit, if they like your work. And I just can't afford to start out as an intern. I need to get paid *now*."

She hums. "Well, I think you should look closer at starting something on your own. I've told you a dozen times you can stay here as long as you need, so you don't have to worry about making money right away."

I glance up at her, my doubts written all over my face.

"No, don't give me that look. It's true. I know you want to make it on your own, and we can work out a payment for rent once you start getting paid. But I understand that takes time. And I love having you here. It's so lonely being by myself. Plus, you're like a free maid."

Cracking a smile, I shake my head. "Why are you doing this, Annette? I'm not your responsibility."

"Sugar, you've gotta stop thinking of yourself as a burden. You're my friend, and friends help each other out. That's what they're there for. And . . ." She trails off, the curve of her lips fading slightly as she glances down at her lap. "Let's just say I've had a lot of years to catalog all the ways I screwed up with my own kids. I don't know what happened with your parents, and I don't need to know. But it's obvious they're not helping you out. Let me. It makes me happy to be able to do it when you need it. I wish I would've paid attention when my own kids needed it."

Her words, so honest and open, so beseeching, take root under the wall I've erected, a fissure spreading along the bricks surrounding my heart. I feel my eyes fill with tears, and thank-fully she looks away, moving her attention down to the gossip rag opened in her lap.

"Well, now that that's settled . . ."

I like to think I would've accepted her offer, would've said the words and swallowed my pride, again, told her I want to stay, but I love her a little more that she didn't make me. One step at a time is about all I can handle.

## cade

"Cade Maxwell? It's nice to meet you. I'm John Stevens. Chef Foster has a lot of impressive things to say about you." The owner of the restaurant extends his hand to mine for a shake. He's younger than I imagined—maybe mid-thirties—and this rush of excitement crashes into me. He's maybe ten years older than me, and already he's accomplished so much. Two successful restau-rants with plans to open more.

And I want that so fucking bad.

I grip the hand he offers, giving it a firm shake. "Thanks for allowing me to cook for you. Hopefully I live up to everything he's been saying."

He smiles. "I'm sure you will. If you want to follow me, I'll give you a quick tour . . ."

As he takes me through the space, empty now save for a few employees prepping for their dinner service, I already know I want to work here. Even on the drive here, I was unsure, my worries still present in my mind. But now, seeing the possibilities, I know without a doubt, I want this.

The kitchen is spotless, all white tile and stainless steel. It reminds me a lot of the kitchen at the bistro, but it's a different level completely. There are a handful of fresh ingredients sitting out on one of the prep stations, and he gestures to them. "Rather than ask you to make a specific dish, I want to see some of the creativity Chef Foster went on and on about. I'd like you to make a main dish using mussels or scallops or both. Shawna will be back here if you have questions regarding where anything is." He points to an older woman currently prepping agnolotti on the other side of the kitchen. Slapping a hand on my shoulder, he says, "I'll be back in ninety minutes. Wow me."

Once he's out of the kitchen, I flip through my mental recipe cards. A dozen possibilities pop up in my mind, but ultimately I settle on cioppino, an Italian-American fish stew that's rich and multidimensional. It's deceiving in its simplicity because there's a certain finesse in developing the ingredients to bring out the intense, hardy flavor. And I have to do it in about half the time as I'd prefer to let the flavors marinate. I haven't made it in a few months, but I know I can nail it. And I know if any dish is going to lock this position for me, it's this one.

I block out everything else and focus completely on my task as I dice and sauté. I don't think about what's waiting for me three hundred miles away. I don't think about what nailing this interview will ultimately mean. I immerse myself completely in the food I'm creating and think about what it would be like to do this every day. To be here, working in this professional kitchen, straight out of culinary school. It's more than I ever thought was possible, and now that I'm here, now that the option is staring me in the face, I want it.

As I put the last crouton atop the bowl, John pushes through the swinging door, a smile on his face. "Smells good, Cade. What'd you make for me?"

"I've prepared cioppino, and topped it with some freshly made French bread croutons. I hope you enjoy."

"Ambitious."

"Yes, sir."

Hands locked behind my back, I hold my breath as he takes a bite, watching as he gets his first taste of my food. His face creases, his eyes locked on mine.

My stomach drops and soars at once. And I know my fate before he even says a word.

# TWENTY-EIGHT

*winter*

When am I going to start feeling normal again? Normal and flat and stale. Because it's been a week and I still feel this horrible, hollow pit where my heart used to be. Regrets and uncertainty weigh me down, and I just want to be free.

Instead I'm trapped. Inside my head and inside memories I'm not sure I want and inside this apartment that isn't mine. Trapped and I don't know how to get out. I want to call Cade back, to just pick up the fucking phone and return one of the dozens of messages he's left me, just to say hi. Just to tell him I miss him and I maybe made a mistake and I don't know what I'm doing and I love him. I should've told him I loved him.

Instead I'm floundering. And I want nothing more than his arms to fall into, to clutch to keep me from drowning.

Somehow, even in the midst of all this turmoil, I made it through finals, submitted my website, and I finished. For all intents and purposes, though we haven't yet had the ceremony for the design students, I am a college graduate. I wasn't sure I'd ever get here. I wasn't sure I'd survive long enough to make it through to the end. But I'm here. And while I thought I'd have this sense of completion, this sense of satisfaction, I don't.

Because the only thing that's ever made me feel complete isn't a thing, but a man. A man who stood by me, who supported me, tried to help me, and I let him go.

I forcefully stop that train of thought, making myself focus on the details in front of me. The list of things I've researched for starting my own business. Which I can't even believe I'm contemplating. And maybe that's why I'm actually going through with this. I don't have *time* to contemplate anything. Not all the ways this could fail, all the ways I could fall flat on my face. I'm jumping off a cliff without a harness, and I don't have time to give it a second thought.

The small bit of money I have is running out quickly, and even though Annette assured me—again—that I can stay, rent free, for as long as I want, I'm not going to leech off her any more than I have to. I *will* pay my way, as soon as I can. As such, I need to get up and running immediately. All the small jobs I've done over the years have been on the side and nothing of monetary significance, but they've allowed me to build an extensive portfolio.

A portfolio I'll be showcasing on my own site. I've started designing it, building the code. I sort through hundreds of font choices and color palettes, focus on coding the basic site and adding what I want to it. This is how I keep my brain busy. Too busy to think about a tall man with dark hair and arms of steel and the sweetest lips I've ever tasted.

But I know my diversion won't last. I know tonight, when I'm lying here in the dark, nothing but my memories to keep me company, he'll meet me there, in the place where my mind fades into my dreams. And I'll be happy again.


*cade*

I tape up the bottom of a box, flipping it over and filling it with books. It's hard to know what to take and what to leave. I'll be gone at least a year, but after that, if I can show John what I'm made of, I hope to be back here eventually. Back home and the head chef of a restaurant.

It's hard to believe it's been only a few days since I returned from Chicago. Hard to believe how much my life can change in seventy-two hours.

Before I went, I was still torn. Part of me wanting to stay behind, to stay in the house I grew up in, to support Tessa, to be there for Haley. But another part of me, a selfish part I never listened to before, thought about what it would mean if I got the position. Once I got in that kitchen, though, I was done. I wanted it. Bad.

I was on my way back home when John called and left me a message, and I'd already made up my mind before I listened to the voice mail, before I called him back and was offered the job as sous chef.

In that moment, I wanted nothing more than to call Winter, to share it with her. And I tried. A dozen times, I've tried. And a dozen times I've left voice mails, hoping after each it will be when she finally calls me back.

"When do you have to leave?"

I glance up, seeing Tessa leaning against the door frame. She's been nothing but supportive since I told her. Excited, even. And while I thought staying behind was being selfless, I know now I was being selfish by forcing that burden on her. I wasn't staying for her as much as I was staying for *me*. I realize we're both old enough to make our own choices . . . our own mistakes, and she doesn't need me here to protect her anymore.

"He wants me out there right away. My first day's a week from Monday."

"Have you found a place to stay yet?"

Shaking my head, I add a few more things to the box, then tape it shut. "Not yet, but he gave me a list of some areas to check out. I'll probably be staying in a hotel for a while, though."

"I wish I could come with, help get you settled."

"You'd just boss me and Jason around, telling us where to put everything."

She laughs. "You're probably right."

"And you guys can come down this summer. I'm counting on it, actually. I don't know how much time I'll be able to get off right away."

"We'll be there." She moves over to sit on my bed, resting back on her hands. "It's gonna be weird not having you here anymore. I'm so glad you're doing this, but I'm going to miss you."

"You'll miss my amazing dinners every night. My socks on the living room floor? Not so much."

She cracks a smile, moves to stand. Coming over, she wraps her arms around me, squeezing tight. "I'll miss it all."

I return her hug, my chin settled on top of her head. Think about everything—*everyone*—I'm leaving behind. "I know. Me, too."

# TWENTY-NINE

*winter*

I shouldn't be here. I should've just waited, gotten my diploma in the mail, and spent the afternoon in Annette's too-dark apartment, working on a site, instead of here, surrounded by nameless people. At least there, I'm alone because I choose to be. Out here, in front of all these smiling families and friends of my fellow classmates, I feel more isolated than ever.

Even in the midst of hundreds of people, I feel completely and utterly alone.

After years of this, it shouldn't be difficult. I should be used to it, used to the solitude. Every school function, every assembly or graduation or ceremony, was completed on my own. No one was there for National Honor Society induction or year-end award ceremonies. No one watching me, cheering for me as I graduated high school in the top ten percent of my class. No one celebrated my scholarship, my answer to a better life.

And now, as I put a period on the last four years, as I celebrate my accomplishment—all the times I scraped by, the weeks and months when I wanted to give up but didn't—there's no one here but me. No one will clap when they call my name, no one will take my picture when I walk across the stage, accept my diploma, and officially become a college graduate.

No one is here.

As I sit among fellow design graduates, surrounded by the buzz of happy voices, of excitement and cheer, a startling realization hits me. No one is here because I *chose* that. All my life, even before my mother actually left, I felt abandoned. I was on my own, from day one. And somewhere along the way, I decided it was better that way. That rather than get left behind again, it was better not to get involved at all, not to open myself up, not to be vulnerable with anyone. Ever. It's been my choice all along to keep people out. To keep my head down and power on, and to do so all by myself.

And after twenty-two years, I'm so *lonely*.

I just want someone there to lean on. Someone to cheer me on when I need it, someone to help me up when I fall, someone to comfort me when I'm having a shitty day.

But not just *someone* . . .

An image of Cade flits through my mind. The same image that's been haunting my dreams. The sight of him in my apartment the last night we spoke. The look in his eyes, the heavy emotion settled there. At the time, I assumed it was pity. For the first time, I consider the possibility that I was reading him wrong. Maybe what I saw shadowed there wasn't pity, but empathy.

Cade lost not only one but both parents, and that was after they'd been there to love and support him, after they'd given him an amazing life. He's been abandoned and left behind, and even though neither was done willingly, it doesn't change the fact that he's alone. And he still picked me. He still wanted to take the chance on me, on what we had together.

And instead of returning the favor, instead of accepting him into my life, into my heart, I spit in his face.

If anyone has proven they'll be there for the long haul, that they'll stick around, it's Cade. Willing to give up his dreams just so he can stay and protect his sister and niece, so he can be there for them. To prove he'd never turn his back on them. I couldn't see it—didn't *want* to see what kind of man he was because I was too scared.

God, I ruined the best thing that's ever happened to me because I was *scared*.

I don't want to be scared anymore.

I want to be the kind of person Cade sees in me. The kind of person who's fearless, who spreads her wings instead of staying frozen on the ground.

I want to fly for him.

If living with Annette has taught me anything, it's that it doesn't always have to be all or nothing. Sometimes things are going to go wrong, things aren't going to be perfect, but that doesn't have to mean decimation, either. It means picking yourself up and apologizing and moving on. It means swallowing your pride and asking for help. It means offering more of yourself than you want to keep hidden away.

I want to give so much of myself to him. I want to give *everything* to him.

And, finally, I'm ready.

*cade*

I shouldn't be here.

I don't even know if Winter would want me here, but I can't *not* be. Not when I know I'm the only one, the only one in the audience cheering her on, and even if she doesn't know it, I want her to have *someone*. I want someone to see her accomplish this. Even with all the odds stacked against her, she made it, and she deserves to have someone who loves her witness it.

From where I'm standing toward the back, I can just see the profile of her face, that indent of her cheek a glaring sign of her nerves. The closer they get to her name, the more she fidgets. She's restless, shifting constantly in her seat. I want to walk over to her, to pull her into my lap and comfort her, tell her how proud of her I am.

These last couple of weeks without her have been unbelievably shitty, but I didn't realize just how much until I saw her. When I caught that first glimpse of her, it took all of my willpower to stay back here, out of sight.

I miss her. And after tomorrow, it's only going to get worse.

I wish I could talk to her, just to tell her everything that's happened. To tell her everything that *will* happen. She was such an intricate part of my decision, the final push I needed to do this for myself, to stop thinking of everyone else's needs, to let go of some of the responsibilities I carried without needing to. I want to thank her for everything she said that encouraged me to pursue this, but I don't know that I'll get the chance.

I watch as they call her row. She stands, moving with confidence, her head held high as she shuffles behind her classmates, and she's so fucking beautiful. The line of people in front of her gets fewer and fewer until her name is finally called. She climbs the steps, walks across the stage, and accepts her diploma, shaking the hand offered.

And even though I should stay silent, should slink out of here without letting on to my presence, I can't. Seeing her up there, against all odds, sets off a wave of pride in me. Putting my fingers in my mouth, I whistle loudly as she releases the hand she was shaking. At the sound, her head snaps toward the crowd, her eyes darting around as she scans the faces that make up the audience. Part of me wants to stay standing right here, wait and see if she notices me. Watch her face as she does. Will it light up at the sight of me? Or will it fall?

That final thought has me moving before she can spot me, not giving her the chance to do either. I slip out of the crowd and into the parking lot, my mind churning with all the things I want to say to her. All the things I want her to know, that I wanted to tell her in person. All the things that won't happen. Not now.

I rev my motorcycle, speeding out of the parking lot. As I go the long way home, I imagine Winter seated behind me, how she felt there the first time she rode with me. How she wrapped her arms around me, pressed her head to my shoulder, her legs on the outside of mine. I'd give almost anything to feel that again.

Haley's in the front yard when I pull up at home, already dressed for her recital. She waves when she spots me, twirling and pointing at her outfit, making sure I notice it. "Do you like it, Uncle Cade? Isn't it the most prettiest?"

I step off my bike, setting my helmet on the seat, and walk over to her, picking her up and tossing her in the air how she likes. She giggles, her laughter washing over me, and I wonder how long I'll be able to do that. How many visits before suddenly she's too big. Will I be here when that happens, or will I be hundreds of miles away and surprised by this once-little girl who grew six inches since I last saw her?

"It is the *most* prettiest. You look just like a princess."

"That's what Mama said. She did my hair. It's pretty, too, huh?" Her long, dark hair is curled and pinned in some sort of fancy style Tessa probably spent an hour on.

"Very."

"You comin' to the 'cital?"

"I wouldn't miss it."

She squirms from my grasp, and I set her down as Tessa pokes her head out the front door. "Hey, we have to leave in ten. Are you coming with us or are you going to come later?"

"I'll come with you guys now, but I'll ride my bike over."

"You sure? The recital doesn't start for a while. There'll probably be just a lot of standing around for us."

Shrugging my shoulders, I follow Haley into the house, shutting the door behind us. "Doesn't matter. I'm still coming."

On my last day home, I'm spending as much time with them as possible.


FIFTEEN MINUTES LATER, I pull into the parking lot behind Tess, getting off my bike and heading over to the car. I go around to the back and open Haley's door, getting her unbuckled from her booster seat.

"Mama, where's my sparkly thing?"

"What sparkly thing, baby?"

"For my head."

Tessa whips her head around, her eyes wide. "Oh, crap! Your tiara! I *knew* I forgot something. Cade, can you—"

Holding up a hand to stop her, I say, "Just tell me where it is."

"It's on my nightstand. Oh, no, wait . . . I used it when I did her hair. My bathroom then."

"No, s'not," Haley says. "I played with it after."

"Well, where'd you leave it?"

"Dunno." Haley shrugs.

"Okay, how about *I* take her in, and you go back to look for it," I say. "I don't even know what a tiara is . . ." I grab Haley's hand and help her out of the car. "I'll see you shortly."

"I'll be back as soon as I can."

I nod and shut the car door, squeezing Haley's hand as Tess drives away. "Ready, short stuff?"

"Ready." She tugs me along behind her, looking back at me with a full-toothed smile. And my heart aches. God, I'm going to miss her.

# THIRTY

*winter*

I run.

In my gown, my cap clutched in my hand, I run. I've never much minded not having a car. I've managed to get around for four years without one, but now, as I'm trying to catch Cade, I wish I had one. I don't even know if it was him, if it was his sharp whistle that rang out while I received my diploma. I searched the crowd, but with hundreds of faces staring back at me, it was futile.

But still. I hoped.

I get to the bus stop just as one is pulling up to the curb, and for once thank my luck. Grabbing a seat, I stare out the window, thinking about what it would mean if it was Cade who was there. If he came to watch me.

But even if it wasn't him, I already made my decision. I have to go to him, tell him how sorry I am, how stupid I was. How scared and hurt and broken and *stupid* I was to have let him walk away. To have *made* him walk away.

All along I thought I'd lost myself when I was with him. That I didn't even know myself anymore, that I forgot about what was important. What I didn't realize was I *found* myself with him. I'm not supposed to go through life angry and lonely and pissed off at the world. I can be happy. I deserve to be happy.

I get off at the stop closest to his house and run down the street, my shoes pounding the pavement as I round the corner. My heart speeds up the closer I get, my stomach doing somersaults. When I'm on his front porch, I take a few deep breaths, steeling myself to ring the doorbell. Before I can, someone pulls up along the curb, and I turn back to see Cade's car.

Except it's not Cade who steps out.

Tessa slips from the driver's side, regarding me wearily as she walks up the front path. "Winter."

"Hi, Tessa."

"Productive day?" she asks, gesturing to the front of me.

With a furrowed brow, I glance down, noticing the black gown I'm still wearing. A slightly hysterical laugh breaks from my throat as I think of how true that statement is. In more ways than one. "Um, yeah, you could say that. I was just about to knock."

"Ah, well, no one would've answered. I just came back to get Haley's tiara. She forgot it on the way to her recital. Cade's with her there."

"Oh." My shoulders sag as I realize that wasn't him at the graduation. Even so, it doesn't matter. I already knew, even before, I wanted to do everything I could to get him back. "Do you . . . do you know when he'll be back? Or if he'll be around tomorrow?" After the day I've had, I don't want to wait, but I will if I don't have a choice.

"I'm not sure what time we'll be done. And tomorrow . . . um, no, he won't be around much."

I can tell by the way she studies me, by the flat line of her lips that she's keeping something from me. "Tessa, please, I just . . . I really need to see him. There are some things I need to say."

She leans against the front door, crossing her arms against her chest. "Things that are going to break his heart again? Because I gotta tell ya . . . living with him for the last couple of weeks hasn't exactly been fun."

The thought of Cade hurting, of him hurting over *me*, is just another thorn in my side, and I hate that I did this. I hate that I'm the cause of his pain, of *our* pain, and if I could go back, I would.

But going back isn't possible. I can't go back in time, change what I said to Cade, the things I did, any more than I can go back and change my childhood. I just have to accept it for what it is. Accept it and move on, move forward.

Shaking my head, I say, "No, nothing like that. I hope."

She studies me, her eyes intense as she regards me. "He will give you everything he has, Winter. Every ounce. Until there's nothing left for himself. Give something back to him."

I swallow my nerves. If she can help me get to Cade, she deserves to know this. My voice just above a whisper, I say, "I want to give him everything."

It seems like forever as she stares at me, reading my intentions. Finally, she gives a nod. "Haley's recital is at Christine's Dance Studio, over on Washington. It goes until six."

"Okay." I nod, stepping back as she opens the door. "Okay,

thank you." I turn to jog down the steps, but Tessa's voice stops me.

"Winter? Don't wait till tomorrow, okay?"

There's something in the tone of her voice that gives me pause. When I offer her a nod of agreement, she turns and enters her house, closing the door behind her.

I've got enough time to run back to Annette's and change out of my gown and get to the dance studio. I don't know what tomorrow is going to bring, but I'm not going to wait to find out.

## *cade*

Backstage is a complete clusterfuck, too many squealing kids, and I need to step away for a bit. Even while I was watching Haley twirl and prance around on stage, doing the routine she practiced for months, I wasn't entirely focused. My mind's been elsewhere all day.

The clock is ticking faster, the minutes I have left here speeding past, and I can't leave without trying one more time. If there is a chance Winter will talk to me, a chance she'll answer the phone, and I don't take it, I'll kick myself for the rest of my life.

I find Tess in the crowd, squeezing my way through throngs of parents. I grab her arm, pulling her close so she can hear me over the commotion. "Hey, I'm going to head outside for a bit."

She raises both eyebrows in question, glancing behind me, then returning her eyes to mine. "What's outside?"

"Nothing, I just need to make a phone call."

"Okay, I'm not sure how long we'll be back here. Are you going to follow us home?"

"Probably. I'll wait outside, but text me if it's gonna go on forever."

She nods, allowing Haley to pull her farther into the chaos as I weave my way through the hallways and slip out the front door. Families have spilled out onto the front lawn, and I walk as far away from the commotion as I can, the too-loud squeals of children fading in the background as I round a corner. My back pressed against the exterior of the building, I palm my phone, staring at Winter's name highlighted, finger hovering over the send button. Without second-guessing myself, I press it and wait as the line rings. My heart sinks when her voice mail picks up, then beeps, waiting for my message.

I take a deep breath, blowing it out slowly. "Hey, it's me. I was hoping I wouldn't get your voice mail, that I could talk to you. I don't even know if you'll listen to this . . . I don't know if you've listened to any of them. But I had to try one last time." With my head down, hand in my pocket, I kick at a stray rock, trying to find the words to tell her everything. "I . . . I'm leaving, Winter. Tomorrow. I got a job offer as a sous chef for a restaurant in Chicago, and I took it." I close my eyes, press my thumb and forefinger to them. "I just . . . I wanted to tell you why. Why I decided to take it. It's because of you. You're the reason I decided to even try for this. That day in your apartment, when we were talking about what we wanted after graduation, what you said . . . it stuck with me. You were right. I want you to know I listened to everything you said. All of it. Even the shit I didn't want to. I never meant to swoop in and rescue you. And I can't tell you how sorry I am for stepping in even after you asked me not to. I just . . . I protect the people I love. That's who I am. It's what I've always done, even before my mom died. And I love you. Still.

Even after everything you told me. I don't ca—" The beep of the voice mail cuts me off. With a frustrated groan, I end the call and scrub my hand over the top of my head, eyes clenched. "Shit. *Fuck*."

"You should probably watch your language. There are children around."

I whip my head toward the voice. *Her* voice. Winter stands a few feet from me, hands fidgeting at her side. Her cheeks are red, her eyes bright, and *Christ*, the distance I saw her at today didn't do her justice. She's breathtaking.

I'm momentarily speechless, and when my mouth finally works, the only thing I can think to ask is, "What are you doing here?"

She smiles, just the slightest curve of her lips, and it's the best thing I've seen in days. "I ran into someone earlier who told me where I could find you."

Tilting my head to the side, brow furrowed, I ask, "You asked where you could find me?"

She nods, stepping closer to me, and I want to pull her to my chest, feel her curves under my hands after so long, sink my fingers into her hair, bury my face against her neck and inhale. Instead, I stay rooted in place, waiting.

"I, um, I graduated today."

I try to get a read on her. Did she see me? Is that why she's here, to tell me once and for all to stay out of her life? Nodding, I say, "I know. I saw. I'm proud of you, Winter."

"You . . ." Her eyes widen, a glossy sheen filling them before she looks to the ground, shaking her head. "I didn't know for sure if it was you, but I hoped."

"You did?"

She nods, meeting my gaze again. "I ran straight off the stage, searched for you in the parking lot, and when I didn't find you, I went to your house."

"I wasn't there."

"Nope."

My mind is finally catching up, filling in the blanks, matching the time she would've been at the house with the time my sister had to run back home. "Tessa was."

"Yeah."

"She told you?"

"Just where you were going to be tonight, and that I shouldn't wait until tomorrow."

The thought of what tomorrow will bring means something completely different now that she's standing in front of me. Before, tomorrow would've just been another day I didn't get to hear her voice or see her face. But now . . . tomorrow is full of possibilities. Possibilities I won't be around for.

"What'd you come here for? What couldn't wait?" I try not to get my hopes up. For all I know, she's going to tell me to fuck off one last time. But something about her stance, about the set of her shoulders and the emotions in her eyes, lights hope inside me.

She steps closer to me, a storm of worry in her eyes. "I needed to apologize to you. I'm sorry for so much, Cade, but mostly for hurting you. I was so focused on staying away from what could hurt *me* I didn't pay attention to what I was doing to you. You were so patient with me. Even after I told you about my childhood and my mother . . . even then, you were ready to stand by me."

Reaching out, she grabs my hand, staring down as she fidgets with my fingers. "I was the one who wasn't ready yet. I wanted to be, but I just couldn't see it. After being on my own for so long and not having anyone care, it was surreal to have someone standing there telling me everything that's been keeping me locked in a cage, all the baggage I've been suffocating under, just . . . didn't matter."

"It doesn't matter. Not to me."

She looks up, her eyes glassy, and gives a subtle nod. "I know. I think I knew it then, too, but everything just sort of piled up on me and I felt strangled, and I projected that onto you. I'm sorry. You didn't deserve that. You *don't* deserve that. You're incredible, Cade. And you're more than I deserve." She squeezes my hand as I try to interrupt, and I snap my mouth shut to let her continue. "You showed me so much. Everything I experienced with you was new. New and amazing and scary as hell. I was just scared," she whispers and shrugs, tears spilling down her cheeks. "I've never been in love before."

It takes a few moments for what she says to register, but when it does, I close the distance between us, her face gripped in my hands. I search her eyes, looking for a hint of apprehension, but they're clear. Brushing away the tears with my thumbs, I ask, "Did you just say what I think you said?"

Settling her hands on my hips, she nods, more tears trailing down her face.

A breathless laugh leaves me, and I can't keep my mouth from hers any longer. I tilt her face up to mine and lower my lips, meeting her in the middle. When my mouth settles against hers, she sighs, her eyes fluttering closed, and if that's the only sound I hear for the rest of my life, I'll die happy.

I've missed this. So fucking much. Her sounds, her smells, the feel of her skin against my fingers, the pull of her teeth on my lips, and I want this *always*. Against her lips, I say, "I think this is where you're supposed to say something like, 'Aw, fuck, I didn't mean to say that.'"

Laughing, she shakes her head. "Nope. I meant every word. I'm sorry I didn't say it before. I've felt it for a long time. I just couldn't admit it. I couldn't admit a lot of things. I'm so sorry."

"Stop saying that. Just . . . next time you freak out, promise me you won't push me away. Whatever it is, whatever comes up, I can handle it. I'm not going to bail."

She nods, but her eyes show her worry, the corner of her mouth dented in. I reach up, coaxing it from her teeth. "Hey, I'm serious. Trust me, Winter. Trust *us*."

"I do. I trust you, Cade. More than I've ever trusted anyone."

"Good. I only want you to be happy. I know I can make you so happy."

"You do."

"I know I'll probably piss you off sometimes, too." She snorts and I crack a smile. "I can be a little overpowering, but I never want to hold you back or swoop in to rescue you. I just . . . I want to help you when you need it. I just want to be there for you, no matter what. Will you let me?"

Her eyes are clear and bright, sparking with that light that I first fell in love with. And I fall a little more in love with her as she whispers, "For you? Yes."

# THIRTY-ONE

*winter*

I missed this. This connection, this feeling of completion. The overwhelming sense that I can't get enough, that I want to swallow him whole. I want to do nothing but float around in this feeling, bask in its euphoria.

The house is quiet around us, Tessa and Haley still at the recital, and I can't stop myself from touching him. Cade's lips coax mine open as his hands peel my clothes from my body. We stumble back to his bed, our hands and mouths clumsy and hungry and greedy.

"I missed you," he says against my breast, his tongue teasing the tip. "I've missed you so fucking much."

I grip his head in my hand, clutching him to me, my legs cradling his hips. He's hard for me, the length of him brushing over where I'm aching, bumping my clit as he rocks against me. The moan rips from my throat, and I press my fingers into his ass and lift my hips, hoping he'll give us what we both want.

Instead, he pulls back, lifts his whole body until he's hovering over me, the muscles in his arms rippling. His eyes are intense, focused on mine. He drops down, presses his lips to mine, and says against them, "Tell me."

"Please, Cade, please . . . now. I want you."

His mouth brushes mine as he shakes his head. "Not what I mean."

I stare at him, his eyes imploring me, and I know. Reaching up, I run my hands over the short crop of his hair, trailing them along the back of his head until they rest on his neck. He's so close, his breath mixing with mine in the mere inch between us, and I want to inhale him, keep him inside me forever so I never have to let him go. And what I was so scared about, what I feared the most, comes so easily now. I say the three little words that have never left my lips, knowing with absolute certainty I was just waiting for him to come along.

"I love you."

His mouth lifts on one side, the subtlest of smiles, and he rewards my words with a shift of his hips. The head of his cock presses into me, just enough to drive me crazy with want.

"More . . ."

"Again," he counters.

"I love you."

He rewards me with another slow, delicious thrust, though he isn't close to filling me.

"Cade," I groan, digging my heels into his ass, begging him without words to go farther, deeper. When he doesn't relent, I shift my hips up, whispering, "I love you, I love you, I love you, Cade, please . . ."

He mirrors my groan, finally giving me all of him as he drops his head, his forehead nestled against my neck. "Always."

I start to repeat what he said, but my words are lost on a moan when he starts moving, slow and deep inside me. How did I ever think I could live without this, without him? How did I ever think my life would be better without the happiness he brings to my heart, the weightlessness I feel when I'm around him?

He rolls us, settling me astride his hips, and the way he looks up at me as I ride him, the way his eyelids droop, his mouth parted in pleasure, the love burning bright in his eyes, wraps itself around me like a blanket, cocooning me in comfort. I smooth my hands over the wide expanse of his chest and up to his shoulders. With my fingers, I trail along his tattoos, tracing the straight lines and curves, the intricate designs and bold lettering, his past laid out for the world to see.

When I reach his hands, he clasps our fingers together and moves them back to settle on either side of his head, pulling me toward him. He lifts his head, capturing my mouth as I shift and rock against him, chasing my pleasure.

"Take it, baby. Take whatever you need. Take all of it. It's yours."

And I know he's talking about so much more than what my body is craving from his. He's talking about everything, every bit of himself, and for once I'm not scared.

I'm not scared of the failure at the end of the road. I'm not scared of the fall.

I take him, everything he gives me, and I give it all back to him, all I have, every ounce of myself as I burst into a million pieces and fly free.

*cade*

The sight of Winter when she comes has always brought me to my knees. The sight of her when she comes, words of love falling from her lips as she gives herself to me completely, is better than anything I could've dreamed. Combined with the way she pulses around me, squeezing me and coaxing me to go with her, I'm a goner. I reach down, gripping her hips and holding her tight to me as I let go, groaning her name.

She collapses forward against my chest, our bodies damp with sweat. While we both catch our breath, I trace a line along the indentation of her spine, smiling smugly when I feel a wave of goose bumps spread over her skin.

"Wow," she mumbles into my skin. "That was definitely as good as I remember. Better, even. Been practicing?"

I chuckle, press my lips to her forehead. "Yeah, you've got a lot of competition with my right hand. Better watch out."

I feel her mouth curve against my chest, and then she shifts, rolling off me to lie at my side. Propping her head in her hand, she looks down at me. "So what do we do now?"

Raising my eyebrows, I say, "Well, right *now* we don't do anything, but give me a few minutes and I'll be ready again."

She smiles, but it's short-lived, her cheek pulled into the cage of her teeth. "I mean tomorrow, and every day after. I heard what you said outside the dance studio . . . You leave in the morning for Chicago?"

I nod, reaching up and brushing her hair over her shoulder, trailing a finger over it and down her arm. When I get to her hand, I pull it over and set it on top of my chest. In the back of my mind, from the minute I saw her standing there outside the building, I've been working out a way for this to happen, a way we can be together. There's only one way. And a part of me is terrified to suggest it, considering what happened the last time. But I want her with me, and she's finally admitted to wanting the same. Brushing my thumb back and forth against the back of her hand, I say, "Come with me."

Where only mere weeks ago I would've seen panic and fear, now her eyes are clear. Clear and full of sadness I never want to see, and I know her answer.

"I want to, Cade. I do. More than anything." She takes a deep breath, looks down at our hands against my chest, then lifts her eyes to mine again. "When you left me that voice mail, you mentioned that day at my apartment when we were talking about what we wanted to do. Do you remember what I said?"

"Of course. You wanted to get in a car and just drive, see what was out there."

She nods. "I made you a deal that day that I would go follow my dream if you followed yours. I know you're not going to Italy, but you're taking one step toward it, you're finally putting what you want first. I promised you I would chase my dream if you did that."

I swallow, excitement and sadness colliding within me. I want her to experience that. I want to give her her dreams. But I also want her by my side. "What are you going to do?"

"I'm staying with Annette for a while, just until I can save some money. I haven't been able to find anything in my field around here, so I've been doing some freelance designs, and I . . . I love it. And I can do it anywhere. When I have enough money saved up, I'm going to just go. I want to see what else the country has to offer besides the place I grew up or the place I escaped to. I *need* to, so I'll know when I pick a place to settle down it's for more than just the distance from my past. I'm not running from it anymore. You showed me it doesn't matter, that my past doesn't define me. It's only one piece of my puzzle. And I'm so grateful for that. You set me free, Cade."

I curl up to her, catching her lips in a kiss, and pull her toward me until she's lying half on top of me, our legs tangled together. And I can't believe I have to let her go when I just got her back. But I know, as fervently as I know how much I love her, she needs to do this. And she'll find her home with me, wherever that may be. "You do whatever you have to do. And then you come back to me."

# EPILOGUE

*winter*

Fifty-four minutes.

My estimated arrival time hasn't changed since the last time I looked at my GPS, approximately thirty seconds ago. My fingers gripping the steering wheel, I roll my neck, then flip through the radio stations until I find something else to listen to. It doesn't help, my mind still consumed with how many minutes I have left. If I thought the time leading up to graduation dragged by at an excruciatingly slow pace, it has nothing on the time standing between me and Cade. I count down the minutes as I pass through suburbs, the road nothing more than a blur under the tires. The cities along my route have started to blend together, nothing standing out anymore, and I'm so done with this trip.

I just want to be home.

It took me two months to realize *home* is a relative term. It's not a place, not a city or a house. Not an address you can write down, not somewhere you can plant a garden or paint the walls.

It's a feeling—when you're complete, accepted, and loved unconditionally.

My home is not a place. My home is in whispered words and quiet phone calls. In Skype dates and postcards sent from the road. My home is in the heart of a boy who swept his way into my life uninvited, tore down my walls without regard for himself, for what it might cost him, for how much it might hurt when I inevitably put the brakes on.

My home is thirty-six miles away, living out his dream and waiting, patiently, for me to live mine. Except it's not my dream anymore.

It took me two months to realize my dream, my *real* dream— the one I never admitted to myself, the one I never thought was possible—is the safe haven he provides. The unconditional love, the comfort and support and security he gives me without question.

And it took me two months to realize belonging to someone doesn't chain you down. The shackles I had on myself were my own doing, residual effects of a shitty childhood and shitty life. No, belonging to Cade doesn't feel like I'm locked in a cage, trying to break out.

Belonging to him, I've never felt freer.

*cade*

I glance down at my watch, cursing when I see how late I'm running. Several people called in sick at the restaurant, so we all pitched in, staying later or coming in earlier than our scheduled shifts. I got out two hours after I was supposed to, and I have my nightly Skype date with Winter in twelve minutes. I don't know if I'm going to be home in time. I tried texting her, letting her know I might be late, but I haven't heard anything back.

In the two months since she's been gone, there have been a few instances of nothing but silence coming from her end for hours at a time—not a lot, but enough that I've had to learn to deal with the worry that comes from having your girlfriend thousands of miles away, by herself. While I thought this trip had been solely for her, it's been an exercise in restraint on my behalf, as well. Being away from Winter, Tessa, and Haley—the three most important girls in my life—has been a lesson in letting go. In realizing I can't always be there to make sure they're okay. That I don't have to be.

When I get off the 'L', I hurry home, climbing the steps two at a time until I'm on the fourth floor, my legs eating up the distance to my door. As I pull my keys from my pocket, I try Winter one more time, dialing her number. An echo sounds as I unlock and push open my door, the ringing coming from the phone held up to my ear and somewhere around me, as well. It takes me a moment to realize it's because a phone is ringing in the apartment, and I whip my head toward the living room.

And she's there, standing next to the couch. Her hair's down and longer than I remember. Her skin, once a creamy white, is tanned now, courtesy of all the places she's been over the summer. We've talked on Skype every night, but it hasn't been the same. Through a computer monitor, I can't see the freckles on her nose or her collarbone, the paint-splatter birthmark on her hip. I can't feel her lips on mine or her curves under my hands.

"Hi." Her voice is quiet, the corners of her mouth tipped up. "I went to the apartment manager, like you told me to. Got the key you left for me." She holds it up, waves the single key hanging off one finger.

I don't wait another second before dropping my shit next to the door and getting to her in three long strides. She gives a breathless laugh when I put my arms around her, crushing her to my chest as I lift her feet off the ground. Her arms are tight around me, the scent of her everywhere as I bury my nose in the crook of her neck. "Hi," I mumble into her skin.

She laughs harder and squeezes me closer to her. After a moment, I lower her until her feet touch the floor, and I pull away only far enough to grip her face in my hands. My fingers are around the nape of her neck, my thumbs rubbing idly against the smooth, soft skin of her jaw. Her bee-stung lips smile at me, and I can't wait any longer to taste them. I steal a kiss, starting soft and slow, but when the first brush of her tongue swipes against my mouth, I'm gone. Groaning, I pull her against me, putting everything I've felt over the last two months into the kiss. How much I've missed her, how hard it's been for me to let her go, even though I needed to.

With a few soft kisses, I pull back. Her eyes are bright, shining, and I want to see that look on her face every day for the rest of my life. I hope her being here means I will.

"You came back to me."

Her lips lift at the corners, her hands clutching my forearms. "I told you I would. I'll always come back to you, Cade. You're the only place I've ever felt like I belonged."

"That's because you belong with me."

She smiles and makes my world spin with soft words whispered from her lips. "I do."

Turn the page for a preview of
Brighton Walsh's next book . . .

# TESSA EVER AFTER

Coming soon from The Berkley Publishing Group!

# ONE

*tessa*

Some days I feel like I'm running forever on a treadmill that won't get me anywhere. Constantly behind, yet always moving.

I glance at my phone, noting the time, and try to rush my client out the door without being obvious about the fact that I'm doing it. It's not that I don't love her, because I do. She's a regular, someone who took a chance on a girl barely out of cosmetology school, and has stuck with me for the last three years, referring dozens upon dozens of friends my way while she was at it. But tonight, when I'm already running late getting Haley from daycare, I just want her to stop talking and *leave*. I stayed late as a favor to her, and I'm paying for it now. I should've known I could never squeeze her in, not when she likes to stick around after her appointment to chat.

Once I've finally ushered her out the door and I've cleaned up my station, I wave good-bye to the other girls working tonight and head out into the bitter fall air. I stuff my hands in my pockets and rush to the car, not waiting for it to warm up before I'm speeding down the streets, hoping to get to Haley before her daycare officially closes for the day. But as the clock creeps toward six and then slowly ticks past, I know that's futile.

I pull in the driveway at quarter after and jog up the front walk, opening the handle to the door and pushing through the threshold.

"Mama!" Haley runs at me full force, her smile as bright as the sun, and I squat to catch her in my arms.

"Hey, baby. How was your day?"

"Good! Miss Melinda had us make our own turkeys for crafts today. Lookit! Mine has all kinds of colored feathers and one of those gobbley things."

I laugh at her description. "I love it! We'll have to put him on the fridge when we get home. Why don't you go grab your coat so we can go."

She spins and runs off without a second glance, and I stand to my full height and see Melinda leaning against the wall next to the door Haley just disappeared behind. "Hi, Tessa."

"Hey. I'm sorry I'm late again, but I ran behind with a client."

"Tessa . . ." And from the look on her face and the soft tone of her words, I know what's coming. "You know how much I love Haley, and I realize what an adjustment period this has been since your brother moved away. These last few months can't have been easy for you. But I have a family, too, and six o'clock is the start of their time."

"I know. God, I'm so sorry, Melinda." I glance to the door Haley is hidden behind and lower my voice so she doesn't over-hear. "It's taking me longer to get into the swing of things than I thought it would since Cade left. I can't apologize enough."

"I know you don't do it on purpose, honey, but the fact

remains that it keeps happening. I think I've been more than understanding, considering how long it's been. I wanted to give you some leeway since Cade helped so much with pick-ups. I haven't implemented the tardy fees, but going forward, I'm going to have to."

I nod my head, my lips pressed in a thin line. It's not the fees—while they're exorbitant to dissuade parents from being late, I could swing it if I needed to—it's the fact that she even has to have this conversation with me. I feel like a kid in the principal's office, and whether or not I'm barely twenty-two, I haven't been a child in a long, long time.

"I understand."

She pauses and shifts her weight from foot to foot. "I hate to even suggest this, but maybe you can find something closer to your work? Make it a bit easier to get there before closing? I could give you some referrals . . ."

I'm shaking my head before she can even finish, knowing I will do anything—*anything*—to keep Haley here. It's the only daycare she's been in since she started going when she was only a baby. And after all the upheaval—her uncle leaving in the summer, and then starting pre-K this year—I don't want to force any other changes on her.

"I'm not going to do that. I'll make it work."

Just then, Haley comes running out of the walk-in coat closet where all the kids' cubbies and coat hooks are, her long, dark hair flying behind her, her eyes sparkling as she smiles. She's . . . remarkable. The best thing I've ever done in my entire life, and ever since Cade left, ever since I've been truly on my own, I feel like I'm failing her.

I always thought I had a good grip on the majority of things in her life, shouldered the bulk of it, but since my brother moved away, I've become blatantly aware of exactly how much he was helping, how much slack he was picking up. It sent me into a tailspin.

And I'm still trying to find my way out.

## *jason*

It's nights like these that make me want to shoot myself in the face.

Smells from the kitchen waft into the formal dining room where my mother, father, and I sit, our conversation stilted as it is every Tuesday evening. The clank of silverware on dishes is the only sound in this too-big room, filled with knickknacks you can't touch, paintings that cost more than some people make in a year, and furniture you feel like you shouldn't even sit on. My childhood home. If you can call a museum a home.

As if my mother has a bell under the table signaling when we're finished with the first course, the maid comes sweeping into the room to clear our soup bowls, only to return moments later with salad plates. I hate Tuesday nights. Having to come back here and listen to the two people who view me as merely a means to an end . . . well, I think I'd rather get kicked in the balls repeatedly than be forced to suffer through this week after week.

Alas, they pay the bills . . .

"I saw Sheila at the club yesterday," my mother says, her voice dripping with disdain.

Dad hums, briefly looking up from the *Wall Street Journal* spread out in front of him. Bastard can't even spare twenty minutes without his attention focused elsewhere. No wonder my mom had a fling with the gardener.

My father doesn't say anything, but Mom takes it as a cue to continue. "It's obvious she got Botox. And, if I'm not mistaken, she got those saline lip injections, too. Honestly, if you're going to have work done, at least be a little more discreet about it. She could—"

And just like that, I zone out, filling my mind with a hundred different things, just so I can get through the next half hour with my sanity intact.

It's not until the main dish is in front of me—duck confit, I'm told—that I register my father clearing his throat, the room otherwise silent. I glance up, finding both my parents staring at me.

"What?"

My mom tsks, shaking her head. "Hardly the way to speak to your parents, Jason."

I roll my eyes, because they've been a lot of things to me in my twenty-four years, but parents haven't been one of them.

"Your mother's right. You'd think you've forgotten just who pays your bills."

"Oh, believe me, I haven't forgotten. How can I when you remind me every week?"

My father's eyes don't leave mine as he takes a sip of his bourbon before placing the glass back on the table. That stare has been known to make both men and women weep. Having been on the receiving end of it more times than I can fathom, I simply stare back.

"I think we've been very lenient and understanding about your . . . *education.*" The way he says it, the way the word almost seems to get stuck in his throat, like he has to spit it out, makes my shoulders tense. He doesn't believe an art school—despite it being one of the top art schools in the country—could ever provide me with the kind of education I walked away from when I

left his alma mater, a well-regarded business school I had absolutely no desire to attend. Unaware, or just uncaring, of my stiff-
ened posture, he continues, "We allowed you to take a year off
after high school to do God knows what while living off our
money. And since that little break, we've given you five years to
complete your degree, which is laughable, quite frankly, especially for someone who ranked in the top five percent of their
graduating class. We've allowed you to switch schools from a
prominent and distinguished university to something . . . better
suited to your tastes. And in doing so, we've been on the receiving end of judgmental whispers at the club."

"Oh, Jesus. Not *the club*. How ever did you survive?"

"Jason Daniel, that's enough," my mother snaps.

As if I never spoke, my father continues, "We're done, Jason.
You've screwed around long enough."

I wait for a moment for him to say something more, to clue
me in on what he's threatening this time. We've been here before,
too many times to count, and I'm not in the mood to play games.
"You're going to have to spell it out for me, Dad, because I'm not
sure what, exactly, you mean."

"What I mean is we will allow you this semester. I had our
lawyer check your records at school, and you have more than
enough credits to graduate, if you'd just select a program." He
sits back, dropping his napkin on the table before he folds his
hands over his stomach. He's like an older version of me—dark
hair with only a hint of gray at the temples, dark eyes that can
turn cold in an instant, and enough height to feel prominent when
walking into a room. I can only hope our similarities end at our
appearance.

I try to see him through the eyes of someone else, someone
who might look up to him, might even fear him, but no matter

what I do, he's still the same guy I've known my whole life. The same guy who's paid more attention to the newspaper or his phone or his computer than he did to his only son. The same guy who was always too busy to attend even one of his son's little league games. The same guy who pushed for only the best out of his child—not for his child's happiness, but for how it would be perceived by others.

When he's sure I'm not going to say anything, he puts it bluntly, "Tuition will be paid through this quarter. Your allowance for rent and necessities will continue to be deposited into your account for one month succeeding that, during which time I expect you to be working beside me at Montgomery Financial, learning the ropes. You'll be added to the payroll so that once your allowance ceases, there won't be any lapse. I'm not getting any younger, and I'd like to retire sometime in the next decade. God knows it'll take that long just for you to figure out what the hell you're doing and not fuck everything up."

"Lawrence . . ."

With a careless hand, my father waves off my mother's rebuke, not sparing her a glance. "Two months, Jason. Not a day longer. I'm tired of waiting for you to come around and stop this bullshit of playing computer games or whatever the hell it is they have you do at that arts and crafts school. It's time you stopped acting like a spoiled child and stepped up to take your place at the company."

# TWO

*jason*

I stalk out the front door of my parents' house, letting it slam shut behind me, muttering every swear word I can think of as I head straight to my car. Really, their ultimatum doesn't come as a shock. In fact, I'm surprised it's taken them this long to institute some sort of deadline. After all, it doesn't look good in their circles to have a twenty-four-year-old son still in college—not unless he's getting his MBA or doctorate.

I'm getting neither.

While I know I've got it good—parents paying for my degree, as well as all my bills—it's not what I want. Growing up, I'd have given anything to be part of either of my best friends' families. Both Cade's and Adam's parents made it a point to be involved in the lives of their kids. Made it a point to talk about more than getting straight A's, college-prep courses, what the stock of the company was doing. I can't even remember the last time either one of my parents asked me a question that actually gave them insight into my life. Or asked a question and waited for an honest reply.

I peel out of my parents' long, circular drive, uncaring of the tire marks I no doubt left, and I don't even realize where I'm heading until I see the familiar streets. For as long as I can remember, this place has always felt like home, much more than mine ever did. It's different now that Cade's gone, but this sense of peace still settles over me whenever I walk through the door.

It's not too late—the clock on my dash showing just before eight—and I hope I'm early enough to catch Haley before she goes to bed. If anyone can make me smile, it's that little girl. While it's a bit jarring to realize just how much I've grown attached to her in the months since Cade left, I can't argue with the truth.

Tessa's car is out front, and I head for the back door, twisting the knob like always, only to find it's locked. Since Cade's been gone, she's been more diligent about locking up—something her brother probably beat into her head before he went. I knock softly in case Haley is sleeping, but after a few minutes with no answer, I dig out my keys, using the spare I've had for years to let myself in.

The scent of fried foods greets me, and a glance in the kitchen shows leftover chicken nuggets and a few fries on a small princess plate. Definitely a change of pace from the days Cade was living here. He'd have a coronary if he knew what Tess has been feeding his niece.

I walk through the dark hallway to get to the living room, stopping short at what I see. Haley's in front of the TV, markers spread out around her as she draws some pictures. When she turns around to look at me, I jolt in surprise at the state of her face, but don't have time to say anything before she rushes me.

"Jay!" She hops up from the floor and runs at me full force.

I catch her and scoop her into my arms, careful to not get whatever the hell she has all over her face on my clothes.

"Hey, shorty. What's, uh, what's all this?" I ask, gesturing to her eyelids and cheeks and lips painted in too many colors to count.

Instead of answering, she looks down, avoiding my eyes.

"Haley . . ."

She leans in and whispers in my ear, "I found Mama's makeup."

Oh, shit. If there's one thing I've learned in the many years I've known Tessa, it's that her makeup and whatever hair product shit she brings home are off-limits. And anyone who touches them is taking their lives into their own hands. She's been like that since she was a teenager, and it's only gotten worse since she went to cosmetology school. Haley clearly did this without permission.

"Okay," I say calmly. "And where is your mom?"

She twists in my arms and points to the couch. I walk over and peer over the back, finding a passed-out Tessa lying there, still in her all-black clothes from the salon, one arm covering her eyes, the other hanging off the side of the couch.

"How long's your mom been asleep for?"

"Since Doc McStuffins started." Her eyes well up as she looks at me, her bottom lip quivering. Her voice is shaky as she asks, "You're not gonna tell her, are ya?"

I probably should. Grown-up solidarity and all that, but I have a soft spot for Haley. And I'm not much for being a grown-up. "Nah, it can be our little secret. Let's get you cleaned up and to bed. It's late and you have school tomorrow."

If Tessa fell asleep and managed to stay that way through the blare of some of the most obnoxious cartoons known to man, as

well as Haley's and my conversation, she must be tired. I'll let
her sleep while I get the munchkin ready for bed. I carry Haley
down the hall, grabbing a washcloth out of the linen closet before
heading into the bathroom. When she's perched on the counter,
I turn on the water to warm it up, then start the daunting task
of getting this shit off her face. She looks like a goddamn clown,
her cheeks bright pink, her lips covered in red lipstick spread
down to her chin, green crap all around her eyes.

I shake my head. "How long did this take you?"

"I dunno."

"You know you're not supposed to get into your mom's stuff,
right?"

Head hanging, she pouts. "Yeah."

"Have you ever done this before?"

"Just once."

"I bet you got in trouble, too, didn't you?"

"Please don't tell her, Jay." And this time, the tears roll, fat
and plentiful, down her rosy cheeks. One look into those dark
brown eyes and I'm a goner. I'd always thought she was a cool
kid, but that was about it—a cool kid I saw every once in a while.
Ever since Cade left, though, she's clung to me, and in the process
gotten me wrapped around her little finger.

"I won't, but only if you promise me something."

"I promise."

I laugh, wiping at the mess over her eyes. "I haven't even told
you what it is yet."

"I still promise."

"Are you sure? Because I was going to make you promise to
play Transformers with me every day for a week instead of your
tea parties."

Her mouth drops open, her eyes comically wide.

"Just kidding. But you can't do this again."

"Okay."

"I mean it, shorty. Not again."

"Promise." She holds out her pinky for me to shake—some girly thing that apparently means it's serious business—and I hook mine in hers.

"All right. Now, let's get you changed and then I'll read a story."

"*Two* stories."

"One, but nice try."

She looks off to the side, clearly thinking about how she can get something extra out of me. "'Kay, one, but with funny voices."

"Deal."


ONCE HALEY IS in her pajamas and I've read a story and tucked into her bed, I head back into the living room, finding a still-sleeping Tessa curled up on the couch. Her mouth is parted, her lower lip pouty and full and taunting the hell out of me. Her breaths are even and deep, and though I try to stop it, though I try to tell myself not to look, the movement draws my eyes right to her chest. I glance away quickly, though not before getting an eyeful, frustrated and irritated with myself that I can't seem to get past this sudden, overwhelming attraction to her. Though *sudden* isn't entirely accurate. It's been building for longer than I'd care to admit, even before Cade left, and in the months since he's been gone, it's only grown.

Feeling guilt that this is Cade's little sister—the same girl I've known since I was nine years old . . . the same girl Cade asked me to look after like she was *my* sister—I force myself to turn around and then start cleaning up the small mess Haley left, capping her markers and putting her drawing station where it belongs. Once that's done, I go into the kitchen and put the leftovers away. I see only Haley's plate and wonder if Tessa got anything to eat. Knowing her, she didn't, too focused on getting her daughter taken care of.

When everything's put away, I make my way over to the couch to try to rouse Tessa. She sleeps like the dead—always has. I should be ashamed of some of the shit Cade, Adam, and I did to her when we were younger. Basically every practical joke you could play on a sleeping person was in our weekend repertoires for too many years to count. I don't think she's ever forgiven us for making her wet the bed when she was fourteen. And thinking that only reiterates how much more like a sister she *should* be to me than a girl I fantasize about when I jack off. The whole thing is completely fucked up, and I'm right at the center of it, wishing I was doing the fucking.

I squat beside the couch so I'm eye-level with her. Once I'm close enough, I notice the faint bruises under her eyes, the exhaustion cloaking her face, even in sleep. Her short, dark hair is falling over one of her eyes, and I have to physically restrain myself from reaching out and pushing it behind her ear. What in the hell is wrong with me?

Shaking that thought away, I grab her hand and give it a little squeeze. She doesn't move, her eyelids not even fluttering. Knowing I won't be able to wake her, short of me tossing ice water on her face, I bend and lift her easily from the couch. As I walk down the hallway toward her bedroom, I force myself to think of a thousand different things other than how her body feels pressed against mine. How her legs feel under my arm, under my hand. How sweet the scent of her shampoo is and how she presses her face into my chest, trying to get closer.

Though it's not *me* she's trying to get closer to. She's subconsciously reaching for something—or someone—and it's definitely not me.

Once I get her on the bed, I turn on her bedside lamp, then take her shoes off and toss them to the side. Even that simple act has me thinking of all the other items I'd like to remove from her body, and just like that I'm hard as a rock. Closing my eyes, I hiss out a curse and shake my head, pissed at myself for thinking this shit and pissed at my dick for being happy about it.

Once I've talked my cock down and have myself under control, I try to shift her so I can get the covers out from underneath her. She finally rouses and turns toward me, her eyes fluttering once before she bolts upright, her forehead knocking me right in the chin.

"Jesusfuck!"

"Ow!" she groans as she presses her fingers to her forehead. "Jason? God, you scared the shit out of me! What are you doing in here?" She glances around the room, then down at her clothes before she checks the time. "It's almost nine? Shit, I have to get Haley ready for bed. I must've fallen asleep." She moves to get up, but I stop her, dropping on the end of her bed as I rub my chin where she whacked me.

"It's all right. I took care of it."

She snaps her head toward me, her eyebrows raised. "You did?" At my nod, she asks, "How long have you been here?"

"About an hour."

Her mouth drops open. "An *hour*? Why didn't you wake me up?"

"*Could* I have woken you up? Besides, I figured there was a reason you were passed out on the couch, so I thought I'd let you sleep. It wasn't a big deal."

"God, I am failing left and right today," she says as she falls back on the bed, her head on her pillow. The defeat bleeding into her voice is unmistakable.

"What do you mean you're failing left and right today?"

"It's nothing."

I raise an eyebrow, staying silent as I stare her down. We've played this game before, and I always win.

With a huff, she says, "I was late getting Haley from day-care . . . *again*. Melinda says if it happens anymore, she's going to start charging me the tardy fees. And it's not even the money, you know? It's that I can't even get there to pick Haley up in the first place." She shakes her head, her arm going over her eyes. "I just feel like such a failure since Cade left. And I love that he went—hell, I *pushed* him to go. I didn't want him here anymore, not when he had that amazing opportunity. But . . . it's hard. I mean, I fed Haley frozen chicken nuggets for dinner tonight because I didn't have time to cook anything decent. Last night was boxed mac and cheese. The night before, Spaghettios. Mean-while, Cade always had dinner worthy of a five-star restaurant ready for us every night."

"Cade's a chef, Tess."

She drops her arm to the bed as she looks at me again. "Doesn't matter. Every day, I feel a little worse about how I've been handling—or not handling—everything since he left. One of these days I'm going to wake up with a World's Shittiest Mom trophy next to my bed."

"Oh, Jesus."

"Don't 'oh, Jesus' me." She shoves her foot into my thigh,

kicking me lightly. "I'm telling you how I feel. You don't get to poke and prod and push me to open up and then roll your eyes when I finally do. You wanted it, so you get the full brunt of it now."

I concede with a nod. "Fine. What else?"

She blows out a deep breath, her eyes on the ceiling. "I was just blind to everything he did for us, I guess. Which makes me a shitty sister on top of everything else. I feel like such an ass."

I roll my eyes—can't help it. She always was one for dramatics. "You're not an ass, Tess, or a shitty sister. And you're sure as hell not a shitty mom. Yeah, Cade did a lot when he was here, but you had one-hundred percent of the responsibility heaped on you in a week when he was suddenly gone. Give yourself some time to acclimate."

"I maybe could've bought that back in June or even July, but it's been five months, Jason. Five *months*. I should have my shit together by now."

"Don't be so hard on yourself. You do a hell of a lot more than I ever could. It took me forty-five damn minutes just to get Haley in her pajamas and get her teeth brushed."

"Yeah, she needs a lot of direction at bedtime," she says with a laugh. "Thanks, by the way. She didn't give you any trouble, did she?"

"Nah, she's a good kid, Tess."

She smiles, the kind that lights up her whole face, and once again I'm struck by how fucking *gorgeous* she is. I don't know when she went from being annoying Tess, younger sister to my best friend, to being this . . . hot, amazing woman who I'd rather not be related to any of my friends. It would sure make these near constant and almost always inappropriate thoughts easier to handle.

"Thanks, I think so, too." She yawns, stretching out as she tucks her feet between my thigh and the bed, and the easy physical affection between us is just another reminder of why I need to get my shit together and stop thinking about her in my bed. "Why'd you come over, anyway?"

The reminder of what happened before I came over is like a bucket of ice water over my head. Closing my eyes, I groan and scrub a hand over my face.

"Uh oh . . . only one thing gets the always unshakable Jason that frustrated. Dinner at your parents', huh?"

"Yep."

"What happened now?"

I lie back on the bed and prop myself up on my elbows, turning my head to her. "They gave me an ultimatum. I have 'til the end of the semester and then they're cutting me off."

Her mouth pops open as she stares at me. "Seriously?"

I nod. "They found out I've got enough credits to graduate if I'd just declare a major, so they're not buying my bullshit anymore. No more stipends, but of course I'll get a paycheck just as soon as I take my place next to dear old Dad."

She's quiet long enough for me to raise my eyebrow at her in question. When she still doesn't say anything, I ask, "What's with the silence?"

"I don't know . . ." she says, hesitancy in her voice, then waves her hand while shaking her head. "Nothing, never mind."

"Jesus, Tess, just spit it out."

"I just . . . I don't get you. I mean, you've got this amazing job waiting for you after graduation, one most people fresh out of college would kill for, where you'll probably make three times what I could ever even *hope* to make, and you're moping around like a petulant child. What gives?"

"Look, I know how good I have it, okay? And I feel like a selfish asshole for not being grateful for it. But how would you like it if your whole future had already been mapped out for you from before you could even walk? It's a lot of pressure. And not only that . . . What they want me to do? Being the vice president of a financial investment company? It's not me. I hate that shit, you know that."

"I do . . . But it's not *so* bad. Have you talked to your dad about maybe doing a different job within the company?"

I shake my head. "Nope. No way he'd go for it. It's all or nothing with him. He doesn't know the meaning of the word compromise."

"So you're total opposites, then, huh?"

"When you start comparing me to my father, that's my cue to leave." I move to get up, but Tessa laughs, pressing both her feet on top of my thigh to get me to stay put.

"You're nothing like him, not really. But you *are* stubborn. Which is why I'm so surprised you're taking this lying down. Just try it. What have you got to lose? He might surprise you."

Or he might prove every thought I've ever had of him right, and I'd be back at square one.